Sweet Asylum

Tracy L. Ward

Willow Hill House
Ontario, Canada

First Edition
ISBN-978-0-9881334-8-8

Edited by Lourdes Venard
@ Comma Sense Editing

Chapter Headings are linear excerpts from the poem
"Approaching Night"
by John Clare (1793-1864)
Full text poem appears following epilogue

Tracy L. Ward tracywardauthor@gmail.com

For Jennifer,
my sister, my best friend

Chapter 1

O take this world away from me;
Its strife I cannot bear to see,

Kent County, 1868— Forceps in hand, Dr. Ainsley squinted at the body in front of him, ensuring it was dead before proceeding with his work. The surgeon positioned his magnifying glass in such a way that would allow him to see the finer details of the specimen. The head was the most delicate part, as he understood it, and he must proceed with caution if he were to keep the butterfly intact and undamaged.

"*Papillon...papillon.*" He repeated the words as he worked to spread the butterfly's wings on the board. He varied his enunciation while trying to recall the manner in which their French tutor from years prior preferred it to be said. So much knowledge, previously held in similar regard to other subjects, had been lost after years of intense medical studies. It was an unfortunate circumstance that Ainsley was determined to rectify. Revisiting his interest in insects seemed a natural place to start.

Beside him he had a small cache of pins and a pile of thin paper with which to work. He had to be careful to ensure symmetry. Already that day he had dislodged an antennae and an assortment of legs from other insects he had hoped to include in his permanent collection, but the mounting frustration he felt remained harnessed inside. He wasn't about to allow anything to disrupt the peace he so desperately craved.

Entomology was proving to be far less taxing on him than surgery ever was. Here in his claimed laboratory, which used to serve as the library at his family's country home, Dr. Peter Ainsley could live as Peter Marshall, second heir to a wealthy peer of England and nothing more. Unlike St. Thomas Hospital, there was no rush to move on to the next questionable death, no pressure to find a culprit, natural or otherwise. Here, in the sanctity of his childhood home, Ainsley could forget that the seedy and base city of London even existed. Instead, he could hide away with his moths, beetles, and butterflies, pushing down deeds of his past, both vile and incomprehensible, which threatened daily to overwhelm him.

He heard someone enter the room but he dared not look up. His work required him to move quickly before the butterfly hardened. He needed to position at least twenty-five pins around the wings to keep them from shifting, and he was not about to turn away. He suspected it was his sister, Margaret, whom he hadn't spoken more than a handful of words with since they arrived. He kept mainly to his room and the library, while Margaret walked the grounds restlessly revisiting old haunts and no doubt mourning a childhood that was unmistakably dead.

All that they had gone through—the murder of their mother, the continued absence of their father, and a steady stream of scandal and gossip nipping their heels as they fled the city—ushered them firmly into adulthood. For this brother-sister pair, there was no going back. Innocence had evaporated.

When on his own, Ainsley had come to enjoy his solitude at The Briar immensely and had succeeded in convincing himself that a world beyond his little country lane didn't exist. Margaret's presence, though innocent enough, shattered this illusion, bringing all the hysteria and madness to the forefront of his mind.

He could sense her pacing the room, and he could feel her eyes dashing between him and his new hobby. She said nothing at first, preferring to survey the scene as she often did before making any statements or enquiries.

Finally able to look up from his *papillon,* he saw that Margaret had traced the outer edges of the room and now her eyes were transfixed by an upper corner of the wall where water damage had seeped in from the outside. The wallpaper, stripped blue and gold, sagged at the top and threatened to buckle from the moisture, mold, and mildew that weighed it down.

"I had heard it was bad," Margaret said at last, not bothering to turn around and look at him. "Though I never believed it could be this bad. I haven't the faintest idea where to start."

Ainsley chuckled to himself. "Plan to save us, do you?"

The state of The Briar was a testament to their parents' ill-conceived marriage. Denying funds to complete necessary repairs had been a way for their father to wield power over his wayward wife, who preferred the quiet of the country over his exceedingly gloomy company.

"The house, yes," Margaret said, at last turning to face him. "I'm certain you can fend for yourself."

Ainsley noticed the thickly bunched lace scarf at Margaret's throat, tucked neatly into the upper seams of her bodice to cover the pale skin of her collar and shoulders. Ainsley knew what she hid under it, but could not guess at the severity of the wound. Like their mother before her, Margaret was a beautiful woman with copious brown curls and striking blue eyes, an ideal picture of grace and elegance befitting her place as the daughter of an earl. Ainsley, however, knew that beneath her satin and taffeta gown lay a ferocious strength Margaret had yet to realize. It was only a matter of time, he mused, before her punctuated questions and relentless challenges morphed into unflinching commands and daring ultimatums. The little injury at her neck would not only strengthen her skin but her resolve as well.

Margaret must have spotted his lingering gaze and turned, waving a dismissive hand. "I won't show you, if that is what you are hoping."

"Why not?" he asked.

"It's nearly healed," she said with a shrug. "There's little you can do for it." Margaret walked to the far windows, which overlooked the expansive grounds to the back of the property.

The Briar was unlike any other country manor house they had ever visited. More like a well-appointed cottage, the house was plain and unassuming on top of a hill that overlooked dales and meadows as far as the eye could see. Toward the back lay a thick cluster of trees, the woods where they romped as children, climbing trees, building forts from sticks and other found objects. Margaret played alongside her older brothers, Peter and Daniel, never giving a thought or care to acting as a lady should. Their late mother cared little for propriety, so she was never the voice of reason. They were pretty much left to do as they liked until their father realized what was happening to his final political bargaining chip and put an abrupt end to the country antics of the Marshall children.

Whether Margaret pined for days gone by Ainsley did not know. If the last six months had taught them anything it was that nothing would ever be the same.

Ainsley had not looked out the windows much since he arrived. Rain had been pelting the landscape relentlessly for weeks, turning the laneways to mud and the gentle flowing creeks to swiftly moving rivers that cut wider paths through the fields.

Even if the weather had been fine, Ainsley doubted he would have ventured far. Afraid of frightening the staff or some unsuspecting visitor with the sight of his grotesque facial wounds, he remained in his own world, revisiting his French studies and concentrating on his newfound art form. His eye had gone from the deepest purple to black and now yellow while his swollen cheek had flattened considerably, though sometimes he still caught the inside when he spoke or ate. He had pulled his own stitches a week ago but a few slim, red lines marred his features. He wasn't sure if they would ever heal entirely.

The scars he suffered internally, however, were a different matter entirely.

"I'm sorry, Margaret. I had to get out of the city," Ainsley said from behind his table. He had thought to get up and go to her but stopped himself. He wondered if she worried about Jonas, their mutual friend and his colleague at the hospital. They had so little time to inform him of their departure or where they would be staying. Ainsley knew Jonas's absence weighed on her.

Margaret nodded, slowly, with her gaze trained out the window. Evening approached quickly judging by the long shadows cast through the tall, slender panes. "I know why we left," she said stoically.

Ainsley's gaze shot up from his work. He wondered how much Jonas had told her. They never had an agreement of silence but if they hoped to stay on the good side of Newgate prison, silence was precisely what they needed.

"The case had been all-consuming," she said. "Your man was caught and you needed some respite." She chuckled slightly as she turned to face him. "You forget, Peter, I understand you better than anyone."

Ainsley did not doubt that, but there were some things he never intended to ever tell her. He could not confess the real reason why he fled so suddenly or why he felt it necessary to abandon his post in the morgue at St. Thomas Hospital. These reasons shamed him beyond measure and any resentment cast on him from his sister would be too much to bear.

"Margaret, I—"

Margaret suddenly jerked her head to the window. "What is that?" She leaned closer to the glass and peered out into the dusk. "There's someone in the trees."

"Probably one of the children from the village," he said.

"Certainly not," Margaret answered. "Not this far into the country. Besides, it's a girl, a young woman, and she's soaked to the bone."

Ainsley pushed back his chair and stood. Within four steps he was at the window and looking over Margaret's shoulders. He did not see anything but the stables, and beyond that the line of trees that signaled the boundary of the Everlasting Woods, dubbed so by two precocious children who scarcely spent as much time inside of doors as they did outside of them.

Ainsley frowned. "I don't see anything," he said. The sky darkened, transforming the grey, soggy landscape to black as the sun disappeared entirely. Ainsley left the window and went to light the oil lamp on the table. Margaret, however, remained steadfast. She watched the landscape viciously before suddenly crying out.

"There, I see her again," she said with a pointed fingered pressed against the glass. "She's hidden by the trees."

Ainsley returned to the window.

A flash of white fabric appeared amongst the density of the trees, revealing a small, slender form scampering through the underbrush. Ainsley looked on, doubtful of what he was witnessing. So often he had been deceived into seeing and hearing imaginary things. The hem of a dress here, the whisper of a voice there. The most disturbing of his experience had been when the cold hands of a dead child groped his. He did not doubt that the dead had been haunting him for many months, their intensity so marked that even finding the bottom of a liquor bottle barely helped free him from the torture of it.

"Do you recognize her?" Ainsley asked, wondering if it could be a child of one of the staff. Margaret shook her head but her expression was doubtful.

"It's too far to tell," she said.

Droplets of rain began to patter on the window as the weather worsened.

While the strange girl walked, the fabric of her skirt caught a branch, which appeared to confuse her, sending her into a panic. After a short struggle, she fell into the brambles.

"We have to go to her," Margaret said.

Ainsley swallowed back the instinct to run to her aid. This nagging sense of chivalry, evident in him from an early age, had only served to get him into staggering amounts of trouble.

"Peter!"

Ainsley avoided his sister's gaze, knowing what she expected him to do. How shocked she would be when she found out how little he wanted to care for the plight of others. How that piece of his soul had died back in London.

Margaret pressed her lips together and made for the door, watching her brother intensely to show her displeasure. Ainsley stood behind the heavy, wooden desk, a match in his hand, ready to light the lamp. He returned his sister's gaze defiantly, willing himself not to be shamed into assisting. He heard her frantic call for Jamieson, the country house butler, and the other staff to assist her.

With a short exhale of breath, Ainsley relented and went for the door, chasing Margaret down the hall. She was already halfway through the kitchen garden when Ainsley's long stride overtook her. He couldn't risk Margaret getting to the girl first, not that he felt terribly threatened by this mysterious woman traipsing through their back forest, but experience had taught him caution should never be in short supply.

Once through the covered gate and past the stone wall that surrounded the garden, he took off at a sprint, rounding the corner of the stables. He stopped at the top of the hill, nearly tumbling down in the grass from the abruptness of it. Dotting the meadow were hundreds of ghostly images, each a few feet apart from the others and all with their backs to Ainsley, who stood over them taking in the incredible and terrifying sight. Grey in colour and not quite sharp in form, they seemed to turn their heads toward him and then their bodies followed abruptly without the need to turn in place.

The spectres, men, women, and the occasional child, looked

similar to the girl they had spotted from the window—but she had been real. Ainsley had been sure of it. But now the degree of his certainty was slipping away with each passing moment.

He turned to Margaret, a few paces behind him, who looked perplexed.

"What is it?" she asked. With a few more steps she was at his side, surveying the meadow and the line of darkening trees. The look on her face bore no resemblance to the panic that must have been evident on his.

A high-pitched scream pierced the relative quiet of the countryside, shattering any doubt that the girl did not exist. When Ainsley turned his eyes back to the meadow he saw the figures had parted, creating an unobstructed path to the woods where the girl was last seen. This gesture did nothing to squelch the rising feeling of terror that struck at him from the pit of his stomach.

Margaret, however, seemed wholly unaffected and charged forward, unaware that anything stood between her and the girl suffering in the woods. Ainsley followed suit, willing himself to ignore the innumerable eyes that bore down on them as they ran to find the girl.

By the time they reached the trees the figures had gone, vanished into nothing. They found the girl collapsed in a wallow of knee-deep mud, her skirt and bodice soiled and ruined by the brambles. Night was falling over them quickly as the rain intensified. Their only light was a thinning strip of dusk that was quickly turning everything and everyone into shadows.

The girl screamed horrifically as they approached, before beginning to mumble incoherently as she frantically tried to free herself from the branches she had become caught on. As Ainsley drew closer, he realized she was reciting *The Lord's Prayer*.

"It's all right," Ainsley found himself saying as he approached, cooing to her as if she were a fussy baby. With no other choice, Ainsley slipped into the mud alongside her, feeling the liquid folding in over his shoes and touching the skin beneath his trousers.

Panic propelled her movements. She raised her hands as if meaning to strike him but he easily caught hold of her wrists.

"We are here to help!" Margaret pronounced over the chaos.

"No!" the girl screamed. She attempted to pull her wrists

free and Ainsley could feel her skin twist beneath his tight grasp. "No, no, no!"

Ainsley waited for her to calm enough so he could free her but she grew more frantic by the second. A nod from his sister was all the permission he needed to take a firm grasp of the girl and hoist her up over his shoulders. Her hands pounded his back as he led her from the woods.

Chapter 2

Its very praises hurt me more

Jamieson and the other servants met them at the edge of the woods. Julia, Margaret's lady's maid, held a wool blanket which she hugged closer to her chest upon seeing the terrified woman beating at Ainsley as he held her.

"Goodness' sakes, my lord," Jamieson gasped as he approached, his arms outstretched, willing to take over the burden of carrying the girl.

Ainsley shook his head and kept a steady pace for the house, determined to get all of them out of the rain. It had been a feat to get her thus far. It would be far more efficient for Ainsley to keep putting one foot in front of the other no matter how much strength it required of him.

The girl's movements became weaker. By the time he reached the back door of the house she behaved as if she were asleep and Ainsley was able to shift her weight to cradle her in his arms in front of him. He turned sideways to fit through the narrow hall, as Julia ran ahead and opened the door that would lead them into the main part of the house.

Julia stepped back from the door, pressing as far back into the corner as she could, and bowed her head.

"Don't cower, girl. Help me with my bags."

Julia gave an uncertain glance to Ainsley as he slid through the door. The unmistakable shape of Aunt Louisa Banks came into view as he neared the front door.

"Merciful heavens!" The delighted look on her face melted into confusion before morphing into hostility as she took in the scene—a mud-soaked Ainsley carrying a sopping wet girl, who couldn't have been a day older than sixteen.

"What on earth!" she gasped as Ainsley passed, determined to pay no heed to the aunt they scarcely knew.

"Peter! Peter!" She chased after him but was unable to match his determined steps. "Goodness gracious, Margaret, who is that girl clinging to your brother?"

A young man, striding childhood and manhood, stepped to the side rather awkwardly as Ainsley approached the bottom of the stairs. He nearly bumped into two little boys in matching brown knee pants and caps that stood agape at the front door. The eldest was Nathaniel, Aunt Louisa's firstborn. The other two, often mistaken for twins, were Hubert and George, the youngest cousins in the Marshall clan. A year separated their births but nothing else had come close in the eight years that followed—they were that dependent upon each other.

Hubert gasped and raised a hand to cling to his older brother's arm as Ainsley passed by, the girl's muddied dress creating a long trail of filth from the back door as they went. Ainsley nodded in their direction before heading up the stairs. There was enough time for pleasantries later. The girl, soaked to the skin, shivered in his grasp and all he could think to do was get her before the fire and in a warm bath.

He could hear Margaret behind him, trying to explain the abnormal state of chaos that marred Aunt Louisa's and the boys' arrival. "Everything is not as it seems," Margaret said.

On the stairs Julia scurried by Ainsley and dashed down the hall to open one of the guest rooms. She'd had the same thought he did. By the time Ainsley turned into the room Julia had the fire lit and was building the flames higher by adding a generous helping of wood.

"Set her here," the maid indicated, pulling a chair closer to the fire. "I'll order the bath."

Ainsley laid the shivering girl into the chair as Julia ran to the door. Instantly, there was a blanket thrust at him, which was quickly proceeded by another. Together they disrobed her to her shift and then wrapped the girl tightly and adjusted the chair as close to the fire as they could without risking the wool of the blankets catching.

The girl's blue lips quivered uncontrollably, matching the convulsions that sprang up from the rest of her. Hypothermia was a real risk, even in April. The rain was cold and her adornments were soaked before they found her. There was no telling how long the girl had been suffering.

"It's not enough," Ainsley said. He turned to the door just as Jamieson and the footman ushered in the copper bath. A pair of chamber maids and the scullery maid trailed in behind them with their arms burdened with water. The male servants placed the bath just before the fire and instantly the maids began draining their pails into it.

Ainsley tested the water with his hand and found it lukewarm at best. "More," he said, calling loudly to the maids who were nearly at the door. "Summon everyone from the kitchens!" Ainsley turned to the butler, who was ushering his staff to hurry. "Jamieson, tell Margaret we will need dry clothes. Perhaps something from her winter closet."

Jamieson nodded and left the room.

The girl, fair, blonde, and extremely waif-like, shook as her body worked tirelessly to preserve what little body heat remained. Ainsley gestured for Julia to get closer to the girl. "Wrap your arms around her," he instructed. "Use your heat to keep her warm."

Julia nodded and did as instructed. She slipped into the chair beside the girl and hugged her close. Social conventions were easily abandoned in such situations, but not enough so that Ainsley himself could have done the same. He was a doctor—but even doctors had to observe a certain degree of decorum, especially with their female patients.

Another troop of marching maids came into the room, each depositing her heated water into the bath. Finally, Ainsley gave the signal that he and Julia should place the girl in it. Together, Ainsley lifting her upper body and Julia grasping the girl's knees, they pulled her from the blankets and slipped her into the bathwater, muddy shift and all. The girl flailed slightly, clearly unsure around water, and Ainsley was forced to hold her to keep her from leaving the bath.

"Peter, I found my warmest nightclothes," Margaret said, rushing into the room.

Ainsley pointed to the bed from his crouched position beside the bath.

"And—" Margaret hesitated as she placed the clothing on the bed. "Aunt Louisa wishes to speak with you…"

"What?" he snapped. "What is it?"

Margaret swallowed. "She intends to stay."

At first, Ainsley did not see the harm in it. So often they had played host to friends and family, never once shirking their duty. But Margaret's tone, combined with her clear need to inform him at that inopportune moment, told him there was more to this decision to stay. Aunt Louisa had no intention of staying for just the fortnight. She was informing them she would be staying much longer than that.

"Lord help us," Ainsley muttered. He pressed his lips together and turned from his sister's apologetic stare. "I haven't the luxury of time at present," he said through gritted teeth. "She will have to wait."

Margaret nodded and approached the bath. The girl's chattering slowed substantially and her entire demeanor became calm. Ainsley's attention turned from keeping her warm to keeping her head above water as she drifted toward sleep.

"No, no," he said, struggling to keep her upright.

Her eyes shot open then, staring at him unblinkingly. "You saw them," she charged.

Ainsley looked at her uneasily.

"You saw them, as I did," she said again, this time sitting upright in the water. Her thin shift clung to her form, forcing Ainsley to look away out of pure decency. "Don't deny it," she said, brushing away his and Julia's hands. She grasped the side of the tub and drew closer to Ainsley. "You can't hide from them. You can't. They found me and they will find you."

Ainsley felt a tremor begin in his hands, and then realized his heart was quickening as well.

"Say it!" she yelled. "Goddamn it, don't deny it!" She reached for him then as if to strike him or pull him into the water with her.

Ainsley stumbled back, putting himself out of her reach and then some. Julia tried to hold back the girl, who now screamed at him to confess what he had seen on the lawn. What did she expect him to say? That he was haunted, day and night, by similar apparitions. Such a confession would never leave his lips.

The girl pushed against Julia's arms, clawing and biting at the maid's exposed flesh. A growl escaped her lips. Julia sprung back, pulling her arm away, but she was too late. Three deep welts began to form on her arm where the girl had grasped her.

"Margaret, fetch my bag," he commanded, a stern look

slipping over his features. He did not take his eyes from the girl, who flailed in the tub. "My doctor's bag."

"Where is it?" Margaret went for the door slowly, waiting for his reply.

"Under my bed!" he called out over the ruckus. He had stored it there almost as soon as he had arrived at The Briar, hoping he'd not have to look at it for some time.

Within seconds, Margaret returned and opened it in front of him. Ainsley hastily prepared a syringe, filling it generously with a sedative, a mixture of morphine and chloroform, which would calm the girl, and hopefully save himself and the staff from further abuse.

"Hold her," he said, shooting a quick glance to Jamieson, who had stood at the door, unsure how to help or proceed, most likely due to the girl's state of dress.

Jamieson came to the side of the tub and grasped the girl's upper arms, holding them to her sides. She struggled against his grasp but the butler held firm.

"I warn you, if you continue to move, it will hurt," Ainsley said.

The girl looked at him defiantly, probably unsure what he meant to do. As the needle drew closer she backed away, pressing against the farthest edge of the tub. Ainsley came in swiftly, piercing the skin of her arm and pressing the plunger. Within seconds, the girl's muscles relaxed and she nearly slipped below the water's surface. The house, and all its occupants, was suddenly enveloped with an unnerving quiet.

"Can we dress her now, my lord?" Jamieson asked as Ainsley restored order to his medicine bag.

Ainsley nodded from his spot on the floor.

Regaining his composure, Ainsley stood as Jamieson and Julia wrestled the unconscious girl from the water and placed her on the bed, wrapping her in the blankets once more.

"Peter, you should clean yourself up," Margaret suggested.

"Not until I see to Julia's wounds," he said. He gathered his medicine bag and gestured for her to follow him.

Given the house's small footprint, Ainsley and the maid reached the door to his room within a few strides. Once Julia was past the doorframe, he stepped aside and allowed her to enter. Julia clutched her forearm weakly and gave a slight shrug.

"I'm quite all right, Mr. Marshall," she said, "'Tis merely a scratch."

Ainsley ignored her dismissive nature and raised her arm so he could see clearly. He carefully lowered his medical bag to the floor. He pressed his lips to her minor wound and began leaving a trail of attentions up her arm until finally finding her lips. She tried to pull away, most likely from embarrassment or fear of discovery. After a moment, she returned his kiss freely, almost excitedly, as he brought her closer to him. She enjoyed his attentions and hadn't turned him away in the weeks that passed since their first encounter.

A slight laugh escaped her lips when Ainsley finally pulled away. She bit hard on her lower lip, as if to stifle the noise, and then they both listened for any movement beyond the door.

"She didn't hurt you?" he asked. Julia gave a quick shake of her head.

"When I saw her go after you I…" He paused as he ran his hand through his hair.

Julia smiled. "I can hold my own."

He knew this to be true. She had proved this time and time again and yet it still did not diminish the overwhelming protectiveness he felt for her. "I should clean it, in any case," he said, pulling his bag up from the floor. "If only to justify us being alone together."

He saw Julia smile as she followed him toward his desk. There he opened his bag and pulled out a large amber bottle and a square of cloth. Holding the cloth beneath her arm, he gingerly poured some of the liquid over her flesh.

"You did not flinch," he said.

"Pain does not bother me," she said softly.

"I was talking about the cold," he said, referring to the liquid's temperature. Placing the bottle on the top of the desk, he repositioned the cloth over her wound and held it there for a long time. "Do you think anyone knows?" he asked suddenly.

Julia licked her lips and shook her head. "No."

Seconds later there was a rap on the outer side of his door and they both turned, startled by the intrusion. Their relationship had not been compromised, but each time they were found together, even innocently, a sense of alarm overtook them.

Margaret appeared a moment later. "She's sleeping," she said as she walked in the room. "How is Julia's arm?"

"All cleaned up, miss," Julia said, pulling her hand from Ainsley and holding the bandage for herself. "I'll go help the others set the room to rights."

As Julia left, Ainsley could feel his anger returning, rising from his feet to the top of his head. "Who is that girl?" he asked gruffly as he replaced the cap on the amber bottle and reset it in his medicine bag.

Margaret shrugged. "I don't recognize her," she said. "I asked the staff already, but no one knows." Margaret paced the room, no doubt taking in the numerous sketches, torn from the pages of his sketchbook and strewn about the room.

"She can't have come too far," Ainsley said. "It's been raining for nearly two days straight."

Margaret nodded. She fingered a scattered assortment of drawings on one of the tables and began shifting pages to view the others. "How come no one has come in to straighten this all out?" she asked. Finally choosing one, she held it up, angling it toward the light so she could get a better view of it.

Ainsley exhaled. He had no care to show anyone his art, Margaret being the only exception until he had met Julia.

Suddenly, Margaret stopped, replaced the paper to the table and turned. "What are we going to do?" she asked. "Send her on her merry way after breakfast?"

Ainsley chuckled at the suggestion and pondered it two seconds too long. "As promising as that sounds, I don't think anyone would thank us for it." Ainsley pulled his bag from the table and returned it safely under his bed, hoping he would not need it again for a very long time. "She is very troubled."

Margaret nodded. "What did she mean, you saw them too?" she asked. "What was she talking about?"

"I don't know," Ainsley answered. "Rantings of a delusional woman, I suppose. Nothing to worry ourselves over. If no one comes forward in the next day or so, we should make arrangements for her to go to St. Andrew's House in Barning Heath, as I doubt the workhouse will accept her."

"The asylum?"
Ainsley nodded. "The very one."

Chapter 3

Than een its coldness did before,

Margaret stood outside the guest room door as one of the kitchen girls waited behind her, a tray of food held in her hands. Margaret gave the girl, Patrice, a quick glance, looking for encouragement, but got none. The entire staff remembered the outbursts from the night before and Patrice was the only soul brave enough to venture inside with Margaret.

"Jamieson said she slept soundly," Margaret said as if to reassure them both.

There wasn't so much as a peep that could be heard on the other side of the door.

"Ready then?" Margaret whispered to herself as she turned the key and pressed on the door.

Inside they found a dishevelled bed but no girl amongst the bed clothes. A panic rose from the pit of Margaret's stomach and she almost fled to notify Ainsley but then she saw her standing iron straight at the tall window. The pale clothes she wore, clothes that Margaret hadn't worn since the death of her mother, blended easily with the morning light shining in the east-facing window.

"Good morning," Margaret said as cheerily as she could muster. Neither Margaret nor Patrice ventured farther into the room.

The girl turned and took a step toward them, a movement that made the kitchen maid flinch. The girl stopped as if suddenly aware of their fear.

Maintaining her composure, Margaret spoke again. "I have brought you some breakfast." Margaret indicated the table where Patrice was to place the tray of food.

The maid set it down and then fled without waiting to be excused. Margaret sized up the room, quickly making mental calculations. Were the woman to rush at her she could easily back away into the hall and turn the key in the lock. Seemed silly to have such an escape plan, but then Margaret's hand went up to the scarf at her neck that hid a permanent reminder to trust her instincts.

"You are kind," the mystery girl said as she stepped toward the table. She plucked a grape from a small china bowl. "Forgive me," she said, raising a hand to hide the fact she was speaking with food in her mouth. "Would you care to join me?"

There was one chair at the table and Margaret intended to refuse but the girl quickly turned and pulled the chair at the writing desk toward the table. She set it opposite the existing chair and gave a pat on the cushion. Margaret only moved forward once the girl had retreated to the other side.

Margaret had no intentions of eating but she thought it rude to expect their guest to eat alone. The only reason why the mystery girl was not expected to join them at breakfast was because she was entirely unpredictable. No one in the room the night before could have anticipated such a civil creature by morning.

"There is but one teacup," the girl said apologetically.

"By all means, this was brought for you," Margaret said. "I am merely here to keep you company."

The girl devoured a handful of grapes without a second glance.

In the silent minutes that passed, Margaret watched as the blonde girl poured a tea with one hand while stuffing grapes into her mouth with the other. Her eggs disappeared as quickly as her first two cups of tea and Margaret could not recall a time when so much marmalade had been used to drown a biscuit. The girl was an anomaly. She possessed a rudimentary understanding of airs and graces, the beginnings of a highborn lady, yet much was tossed aside while she ate, or perhaps it was because she felt comfortable. Or even spectacularly hungry. Margaret could see hints of breeding. However, she was far too old, sixteen or seventeen, to still be behaving as childishly as she was the night before.

"My name is Margaret."

"I know."

"May I ask your name?" Margaret said, eyeing the young woman. "We are very interested in learning from where you originate."

The woman swallowed what had been puffed up in her cheek. "My mother called me Ivy."

"And your family name?"

Ivy shook her head and bent further over her plate of food.

"Ivy, I cannot help you if you do not tell me who is responsible for you," Margaret said.

"They say grandfather is ultimately responsible for me."

"And where may we find him?" Silence followed and Ivy's feasting slowed.

"If I told you, you would take me there and life would be even more wretched than it already has been."

"Wretched in what way?"

Ivy said nothing. She replaced her fork and looked over what little remained of her breakfast.

"We wish to help you." During the entire exchange Margaret remained guarded, watching Ivy uneasily from her side of the table.

Ivy shook her head slightly but still avoided Margaret's gaze. She pressed her lips together and divided her attention between the food in front of her and the shiny finish on the table. "I would like the opportunity to apologize to your brother, Mr. Marshall, in person," Ivy said, fully aware that she was changing the subject, "for my behaviour last night. I was frightened…I … I wasn't myself."

Margaret licked her lips, which had suddenly become dry. "What are you frightened of?"

Finally, Ivy looked up, a pair of pale green eyes revealed as she did so. "Everything."

A gentle rap on the door pulled Margaret from Ivy's mesmerizing stare.

"Breakfast is served, my lady," Jamieson said from the doorframe. "Mr. Marshall and Lady Louisa wait for you."

Aside from the obligatory morning greeting, breakfast began in silence with only the odd clink of silver touching china. Margaret kept her gaze to the food in front of her, unable to shake the look of terror she had seen in Ivy's eyes. It was not surface fear, Margaret realized, but a fear deeply rooted and embedded in the girl. It was rather upsetting to Margaret.

Aunt Louisa sat next to her while Ainsley sat across from them alongside Nathaniel. In the corner of her eye Margaret could sense their aunt eyeing Peter, every so often lifting her gaze as if hoping to catch him looking at her. There had been no time in the previous evening to greet each other properly or speak freely regarding arrangements for them. Even after Ivy fell into a restful sleep, cleanup ensued, which monopolized much of Margaret's and Peter's time.

Margaret herself could not fathom what could have brought their father's sister to their doorstep. Years ago, before Nathaniel had reached the age of his younger brothers, the Banks family left their home in Kent to live in India, where Aunt Louisa's husband, Rodrick Banks, was stationed as colonel. As far as she knew, the Banks family still owned a sizeable estate an hour's carriage ride away, and it seemed much more reasonable for Aunt Louisa to take her boys there.

Aunt Louisa cleared her throat daintily. "I realize this is a terrible imposition," she said. "We've been away a number of years, you understand. The abbey needs preparation and we weren't expecting to return quite yet."

Margaret watched as Ainsley nodded across the table. He seemed willing to accept any explanation if only to end such an awkward meal.

"We didn't expect anyone to be here," Nathaniel offered with an amused smile until he saw the look on his mother's face. "We had heard you were all in London," he continued shakily. "Well, that is"—his eyes switched from his mother to Margaret and back again—"what we heard." He quickly snatched his glass of water.

"A letter came from your father explaining his visit to Barbados. He said you were all well looked after in London. Given the current state of the abbey I thought The Briar was the next best thing." She tried to lighten the mood with a smile.

"Is Uncle Rodrick arriving shortly?" Margaret asked.

"Oh, Rodrick? No. I don't think so. He's been detained a trifle longer in Mumbai."

"You travelled halfway across the world alone?" Margaret asked, deliciously pleased at the prospect.

"I wasn't alone, my dear. I have one son nearing manhood."

Nathaniel puffed out his chest at his mother's remark and Ainsley chuckled into his breakfast plate.

"The younger boys have been instructed to take their breakfast in their rooms," Aunt Louisa said, as if purposefully changing the subject. "I have asked Mrs. Hoffman to see that they are well supervised. I am told there may be an extra staff member who can see to this task."

Ainsley finally looked up.

It was clear Mrs. Hoffman, the housekeeper, hadn't yet realized how much added strain the servants would be under with the arrival of so many unplanned guests. The Briar had already been running on a skeleton crew of servants, namely due to their father's miserly efforts to control spending on the country house. Their town house could only spare two servants, Maxwell, the new butler who could learn much from Jamieson, and Julia, Margaret's lady's maid. Any servant pulled from their duties below stairs would surely crumble the delicate balance of the household.

"May I suggest you place an advertisement for a governess, or au pair," Ainsley offered. "Unless you haven't any intentions of staying long."

Aunt Louisa's composure faltered slightly. "Quite right," she said. "I shall be out of your hair within the fortnight."

Ainsley gave a nod.

With their father out of the country and their older brother, Daniel, occupied with business matters, not to mention his new wife in the city, much of the responsibility of the house fell to Ainsley, who really just wanted The Briar to himself. Yesterday, Margaret hadn't felt the least bit guilty for impressing upon him a need for charity but now, seeing him burdened with so many unintended responsibilities, she saw him haggard and weary. She had thought his need for respite in the country was a jest but now she realized how desperate he was for it. Something weighed upon him, something greater than the weight of a household bursting at the seams.

When Peter looked up from his plate Margaret realized she had been watching him, biting her lower lip ever so slightly. Ainsley gave a slight shake of his head and glanced quickly to Aunt Louisa. Much needed to be said but Margaret knew he did not want their conversation to happen in front of her. Though closely related on their father's side, Aunt Louisa was a stranger in their midst and Margaret knew that whatever her brother's decisions were regarding the girl in the guest room Aunt Louisa would surely expect to be made aware of any developments. Between Ainsley and Margaret there flowed an unwritten rule that seemed to govern much of their recent activities—*keep your playing cards close and your dance card empty.*

"I'm finished," Margaret proclaimed suddenly, pushing herself from the table. "I shall be in the library if you have anything to say to me." Margaret gave Ainsley a marked look before turning to leave.

She was barely out of the room before she heard Ainsley declare the end of his breakfast as well. "We shall speak later, Aunt," he said. "I'm very interested to learn more about your time with the Indians."

Margaret turned at the door, deciding to wait for her brother.

Aunt Louisa snorted her disinterest. "There is so little to tell you," she said, "I shan't bore you with the details."

Ainsley paused with his hands grasping the chair back. "Is everything all right?" he asked.

"Quiet all right," she answered hurriedly. Aunt Louisa gave a quick glance to Margaret at the door but returned her gaze to Ainsley. "Why do you ask?"

Ainsley shrugged and straightened his stance. "If you need anything, ask and I shall see what I can do."

Aunt Louisa gave a smile. "Thank you, dear."

Margaret entered the library ahead of her brother and for some reason went straight for the very window where she had seen Ivy running through the rain. She heard Ainsley close the door tightly before he said anything. "I shall send someone to town to make enquiries."

"I have already made plans for Julia and me to go," Margaret said, leaning on the window ledge slightly.

"Julia?"

Margaret shrugged. "Mrs. Hoffman has a short list of provisions required and I asked if I may go as well. Who would be better to send than someone loyal to you and me in every way?"

Margaret saw Peter turn his head and suppress a smile.

"We won't take long," Margaret added.

"And what line of enquiry do you plan to take? Somehow I cannot see you rapping on the doors of all and sundry asking which house is missing a young lady."

Margaret bristled at this. "Certainly not. But there are other means of broaching the subject, dear brother."

"I am glad you have chosen to go. I simply wouldn't have the patience for it. Not today."

Margaret could see as much. Ainsley could not stand still and his expression looked fierce.

"Have you spoken with the girl today?" Ainsley asked. "Have her senses been restored?" He shook his head slightly, probably wondering how he had gotten himself involved in such drama. He made no effort to hide his contempt for the girl or the predicament they all found themselves in.

"Her name is Ivy," Margaret answered rather forcefully.

Peter raised an eyebrow.

"I accompanied one of the kitchen girls in with a breakfast tray," Margaret said by way of explanation.

"How long ago was that?" Ainsley asked. He leaned into the edge of his desk and rested his arm over his thigh. Judging by his half smile Margaret's forwardness seemed to be amusing him.

"Just before breakfast," Margaret replied.

He gave a long exhale. "The best scenario is one in which Julia and you return with an address in hand so we can send this mad woman on her way in a carriage." He shook his head then and eyed his insect specimens, specifically the one butterfly he was in the midst of positioning when he was called to the window.

Margaret watched as he fingered the hardened wing. His newfound interest in entomology was quite evident; a number of completed frames already existed, scattered throughout the room, and related paraphernalia interspersed throughout.

But it angered Margaret that Peter should be so cold toward a girl who obviously needed their help.

"I think there is more to it than madness," Margaret said, feeling a certain degree of heat rising to her cheeks. "I believe she is disturbed, but not in the way we are led to believe. What do we know of her origins? How can we know she should be returned there?" Margaret took a few steps forward, perceiving her brother's silence as contemplation. "Perhaps we should take some time, think things through."

Ainsley's gaze dropped to the floor before he closed his eyes. "We are not in a position to offer charity to anyone who decides to traipse through our gardens."

"Peter—!"

"It cannot be done!" Peter stood, towering over her by nearly half a foot. He had done such manoeuvers in the past, especially when he wanted to silence an argument or curb a forthcoming one.

"Why can't it be done?" Margaret asked, raising her voice to further prove she would not be silenced so easily.

Peter turned, running his hand through his hair.

"What has happened to you?" Margaret asked following him around the desk. "You used to—"

Ainsley rounded on her angrily, stepping close and leaning in toward her. "What?" he asked. "I used to what? Charge in headfirst without a thought to safety or ramifications? Yes, yes, I did that but no more. I know"—he gave a quick glance to the scarf delicately secured around Margaret's neck—"we both know what happens when we get involved where we don't belong."

Margaret watched as his eyes, at first filled with rage and anger, turned sullen and mournful. "Peter, I don't—" She reached for him, to hug him or force him to look at her, but he brushed her hand away and turned.

He walked the length of the room swiftly, only turning once he reached the bookshelves. For a moment it looked as if he might relent, listen to Margaret and use this opportunity to move beyond their past troubles. But then he spoke, and all hope Margaret had of him agreeing to help Ivy vanished almost instantly.

"No more," he said, refusing to look Margaret in the eye. "As soon as we know where she belongs, she will go there, even if I have to deliver her there personally."

Walking the main road of Tunbridge Wells was an

unearthly experience for Margaret. She hadn't been there in a number of months. Nothing much had changed but she had changed considerably. She was no longer able to clutch to her mother's side and feign disinterest. She was it, the female face of the Marshall family, and everyone who passed by her knew it. The looks of pity were almost too much to bear.

Margaret knew she would do well to ignore them and turned to her maid once they were alone on the street.

"We should be careful not to ask for Ivy by name," Margaret said quietly. She kept a lightness to her face as she regarded the buildings that surrounded them. If anyone saw them they would just think she was giving her maid some final instructions.

During their carriage ride to town they had hatched a plan. Separately, they would seek the name of potential casual help that could be hired locally. They would describe the need for a girl who fit Ivy's description and see who the proprietors recommended. Hopefully, they would recommend Ivy specifically, and reveal where Margaret and Julia could find her family.

"If her situation is as bad as she says it is, then I will not reveal her whereabouts unwittingly," Margaret continued.

Julia nodded. "Knowing who they are first will allow us time to find out more about them."

"Exactly." Margaret smiled slyly and gave Julia a sideways look. "What a devious maid I have."

Julia gave a wink.

A couple passed them then. The gentleman tipped his hat and the lady gave a closed-mouth smile as they slid past. The street seemed to swell almost instantly with people exiting shops and waving to nearby carriages. Others strolled leisurely down the main road, looking into shop windows and waving to others they recognized.

"I'll see to Mrs. Hoffman's list," Julia proclaimed, gesturing to H.C. Bell's Household Goods. "Perhaps you ought to enquire at the clothier."

Margaret followed the direction of Julia's nod and saw a dense consortium of women at the window of the dress shop. She did not recognize anyone at first, which wasn't too extraordinary given the scores of tourists that made their way to Tunbridge

Wells each year.

Margaret smiled and nodded to Julia before turning and making her way toward the shop.

As usual, the bell above the door signalled her entrance and, once shut, Margaret found herself in a deafening quiet with only a distant conversation taking place toward a back part of the store. The shop displayed a number of dress forms, each adorned with a different style and colour of dress. She knew some pieces would be available straightaway, while most would have to be ordered and would not arrive for a week or more.

Drawn to a particular dress in blue, Margaret ran her fingers over the lace that circled the low collar and simultaneously felt a pang of jealousy for the woman who could wear it. Absentmindedly, she touched the lace scarf at her neck that hid her scar but didn't bother to wish it away. Such thoughts so far had proved to be fruitless.

"May I help you?"

Margaret jumped and turned abruptly. A shop girl slid a stack of fabric bolts onto the front counter and smiled at Margaret expectantly.

"I'm looking for some scarves. Lace, if you have them. Nothing too transparent."

The girl nodded and asked Margaret to follow her. She was shown to a sizeable mirror next to a medium-height shelf. Small, oblong boxes were piled within the openings.

"Was there a particular colour you had in mind, ma'am?" the girl asked.

Margaret shook her head, trying to find the right words to broach the subject of Ivy.

Moments passed as Margaret was presented with scarf after scarf, many of them too thin to serve Margaret's purpose. Inattentively, she watched the girl open the box and pull out a light green silk scarf, edged in lace, and her face alighted. It was a gorgeous shade.

When the shop girl reached for the scarf Margaret was already wearing she jumped and snapped her hand over the collar of her bodice.

"Oh, excuse me, ma'am," the girl said, taken aback. "I thought you'd like to try some on."

Margaret shook her head. "I can do it." Margaret took the scarf and looked over her shoulder to a new group of customers who had just entered. "You should go help them. I might be here a while."

The shop girl nodded and left her.

After making sure the customers would be kept at the front of the store, Margaret placed the green scarf around the back of her neck. Only then did she pull the white one she wore out from her bodice. Before tucking the front of the green scarf into the neckline of her bodice, Margaret stole a glance at her scar, running her finger over the deep pink flesh that bubbled up from her lily-white skin. A lump formed in her throat and tears stung her eyes but she could not take her gaze from it.

"Miss Margaret Marshall?"

Margaret hastily tucked the scarf in place before turning toward the person who said her name. "Yes?"

Standing a few paces from her was Lady Isabella Thornton, an old family friend and their closest neighbour in Tunbridge Wells. A young woman, not as old as Margaret, stood beside her with crimson hair and a delicate splashing of freckles.

"I have not seen you in years, my dear," Lady Thornton said. "I had thought your family gave up on The Briar years ago."

Margaret smiled. "Peter and I have returned for a time. For some rest."

Lady Thornton nodded and offered genuine condolences for the loss of her mother. "My heart broke at the news," she said.

Margaret could not think of a proper reply but was saved when Lady Thornton, most likely noticing her distress, turned to her companion. "This is Miss Priscilla Stratton, her father is Sir William Stratton of Essex." The young woman bobbed a slight curtsey and glanced to Lady Thornton as if to ask if she had done it properly.

"How do you do, Miss Stratton," Margaret said.

"Priscilla is promised to my son, Brandon," Lady Thornton explained. "The nuptials won't take place for another year, but Priscilla and her parents are visiting Breaside for a few weeks before heading to the continent."

Margaret remembered Brandon, and his older brother, Blair, fondly. As children, they would meet in the forest that separated their families' properties and spend hours riding their horses, splashing in the creeks or telling stories while resting in the crooks of trees. It was hard to imagine Brandon being promised to marry anyone because, in her mind, he was still a boy of eleven with muddy feet and jam on his cheeks.

"What an interesting shade of green," Priscilla said, breaking Margaret's reverie.

Margaret's hand shot up to the scarf and realized how horrid the colour must look against the rose-coloured dress she chose to wear that day. "I was just trying it on," Margaret answered feebly.

Lady Thornton smiled.

The bell above the door rang out again and Margaret could see Julia stepping into the shop. Instantly, Margaret was reminded of her true purpose for coming to town. "Miss Stratton, do you by chance have any siblings? A sister near the age of sixteen, perhaps?"

Priscilla furrowed her brow and shook her head. "No, why do you ask?"

"For a second I thought I recognized you," Margaret explained. "I see I was mistaken. Do have a good day, ladies."

Margaret bought her green silk scarf and wore it out of the store while tucking her other one into her reticule. Julia fell in line slightly behind Margaret as they walked. "What have you discovered, Julia?"

"Nothing much, I'm afraid. I have a list of names but none of them belong to our young lady."

"I think it's fairly obvious I was no help," Margaret said. "Wherever I go someone recognizes me. I can do nothing without the entirety of good society taking notice. It's so constricting I could just scream."

"Why can't we ask at the constabulary?" Julia asked. "Perhaps someone has reported her missing."

"I imagine that is what my brother will do," Margaret said, "but I am less inclined." Margaret exhaled and glanced to her maid. "There is something about this girl. She's absolutely terrified and I fear returning her home will do more harm than—" Margaret stopped when she spied a man with a top hat and valise not too far in front of her. At first he looked around the street, as if in awe of the quaint buildings and shops that made up the tourist town. When his face turned toward them he smiled broadly.

"Jonas?"

Chapter 4

Its hollow ways torment me now
And start a cold sweat on my brow,

Ainsley found it difficult to concentrate on his sketches in the library while The Briar practically bounced with life thanks to all the unannounced visitors. His sanctuary had been tainted and the respite from the city he sought had been reduced to ash. Less than twenty-four hours prior he had been enjoying the exclusive sound of the rain pelting the window panes with nary a care as to what happened beyond the stone walls. Such reprieve was a distant memory now. He wondered how long it would be before he could claim any space as his own again.

Earlier he had stumbled upon Hubert and George in the cupboard hidden in the wall. It was a small section carved out of the space beneath the stairs. The doorway had been fashioned to match the paper and trim of the rest of the room, creating a seamless door alongside the fireplace. Its original purpose had been long forgotten in the history of The Briar but as children Ainsley and Margaret used it for picnics on rainy days as well as to spy on their parents until such activity became too painful to watch.

Ainsley now heard the boys running the length of the halls upstairs, banging doors and evading their appointed nanny. He rubbed his temples in an effort to relieve a pain in his head. He had not slept well and he needed rest. But there would be no rest, he reasoned, not while he ached for calm in his soul. Margaret hadn't a clue what kind of man he truly was, what he was truly capable of. Prior to that fateful night he wouldn't have thought himself capable either and yet, possessed by a vengeful spirit, he acted, committing a crime that haunted him still.

Ainsley's throat grew dry at the thought of it. He wasn't sorry for what he'd done. He doubted he'd ever feel sorry for ridding the world of such vile filth. But his spirit had been broken by it, jarred and shaken as if caught in a whirlpool of doubt and self-loathing. He reached for the flask tucked away in his inside pocket and downed its entire contents. Even that did little for him anymore.

"Peter!" Aunt Louisa's voice echoed in the foyer. "Peter, come quick. She's crawling to the roof!"

Ainsley charged for the guest bedroom, Aunt Louisa at his heels, where Ivy had been placed. He pushed on the door and found it blocked from the inside. Aunt Louisa went farther down the hall and gestured frantically for him to come to her room. "Down here!" she said.

Sure enough, just outside Louisa's window Ivy stood, clutching the stones that made up the exterior of the cottage while trying not to slip from the narrow sill. She did not see them through the glass and continued inching along. There was one more sill for her to traverse before she could drop herself to the kitchen roof, a later addition to the house that jutted out the back.

Ainsley only guessed she meant to go there, but knew even with a lower roof, it was still a long way down to safety. Ainsley tried the window latch and found it steadfast. The tiny lever pushed deeply into the flesh of his palm as he pressed against it.

"Get the staff outside in the garden with sheets!" he yelled without taking his eyes from the windows.

The sound of his voice so close startled Ivy. Her face turned to the window with a look of panic. Her escape was in jeopardy and she quickened her pace.

Ainsley ran to the next room, startling his two cousins and the bored kitchen maid who appeared to be sleeping in the armchair.

Hubert quickly gathered himself from the floor where he played and positioned himself behind his brother George.

The window latch gave instantly and Ainsley was able to turn the bottom portion of the window. As the window pane swung out, it nearly caught Ivy in the legs, forcing her to stop midstep.

"Ivy, I want you back inside," Ainsley commanded.

Ivy froze and returned his stern gaze. For a moment, Ainsley thought she might do as she was told, but then her head turned and he realized she was surveying her options.

Below, Aunt Louisa and Nathaniel appeared on the gravel garden path, the kitchen staff filing out after them. There was a chorus of yelps and screams once everyone saw what was happening. Ainsley could see Aunt Louisa trying to coordinate everyone on the ground. They all took a portion of the sheet's edges and pulled it taut. There was no telling if the sheet would hold against her weight and the force of a fall but it would be better than letting her hit the gravel.

"Ivy… Ivy!" Ainsley yelled to get the girl's attention. "You are going to fall. Come back inside, now… please." Ainsley stretched out his arm as far as he could but still fell short. He hoisted himself onto the ledge, slipping his upper body through the small opening of the window. He felt two pairs of little hands clinging to his trousers from inside the room.

"Ivy…" he called to her again, wanting her to look at him, to see his face and not be frightened by the distance to the ground.

But when she turned her head she wasn't Ivy anymore, but another girl, a girl he'd met many months ago. The same girl who haunted his nightmares.

"Lillian?"

Confusion set in. Lillian had died after a fall such as this. Not straightaway but after lingering for weeks in her deathbed, most likely in pain and unresponsive to anyone or anything. He had offered to operate, perhaps alleviate her suffering, but her family refused. A few weeks later, he received a short note from her sister saying she had finally passed on.

Lillian looked at him sharply. "I'm cold, Peter," she said. "I'm really, really cold."

Ainsley swallowed. "Take my hand!" he yelled.

Lillian inched closer, stretching out her hand to him, slowly shuffling her feet along the slender stone ledge.

"It's all right," he said, "I can help you."

Their hands were inches from touching when she stopped.

"I loved you, Peter," she said, tears slipping down the crest of her cheeks.

Ainsley struggled to get closer. Her eyes searched his face, a look of pain and heartache within. "I loved you too," he said, swallowing hard to cover up the lie. He inched closer, his fingertips gracing the billow of her dress.

Suddenly, her face hardened and her mouth sneered. "You liar!" she yelled, her voice deep and throaty. "You will rot in Hell for what you did! Do you hear me? I'm waiting for you, Peter. We're *all* waiting for you."

She turned unexpectedly and reached for his hand, but before he could tighten his grip around her cold wrist she fell. Time slowed as he watched her descent. Suddenly, all who had been below with the sheets were gone and Ainsley watched Lillian land with a thud. Twisted and mangled, her body lay motionless as a pool of blood slipped out from beneath her. Then her head turned in an unnatural way to look up at him. "Join me, Peter…" Her singsong voice came to him without her lips moving. She smiled slyly and sent a kiss into the air. "I'll be waiting."

Ainsley closed his eyes.

"Peter, help her!" Aunt Louisa's voice shattered his thoughts. When he looked up he saw his aunt, Nathaniel, and the kitchen staff looking up at him, the sheet stretched out between them and his vision of Lillian gone. He turned his head and saw Ivy trying to climb higher on to the roof.

"Ivy, no!" Shaking the weak grasps of Hubert and George, Ainsley climbed farther out the window. He felt the heavy lead glass window bang back into place. The ledge where he stood was only half as wide as his foot and his fingers struggled to find an easy grip on the stone. He was only a foot away from Ivy and he could see her arms trembling from fatigue.

"I …I don't want to go home," she said. Her eyes searched for a way out but Ainsley blocked her exit to the kitchen roof.

"You can't run forever," he said.

She snorted and looked at him as if disgusted. After a moment of thought she spoke again. "Then my only way out is death." She licked her dry lips and looked to the crowd, which stood transfixed below them.

Ainsley saw her grip lessen and her body eased away from the wall. She closed her eyes and allowed a smile to overtake her lips. Ainsley released his grip from the wall and wrapped his arms around her waist. With a desperate strength he redirected her fall and together they collided with the kitchen roof. They rolled from the ridge pole down the roof tiles. Ainsley tried to grip the roof with one hand but they were already falling, tumbling down the slope and over the edge.

Ivy landed abruptly, partly on the sheet and partly in the arms of Nathaniel and Jamieson. Ainsley missed the crowd altogether and impacted with the stone gravel that made up the walkway.

"Oh my God!" a kitchen girl screamed and a communal gasp erupted.

The hurried shuffling of shoes on gravel was the only sound Ainsley could hear at first. He had fallen on his stomach, raising his hands as if to catch himself. He felt his body groan as they turned him over, and he spied George's and Hubert's little heads poking out of the window from where he originally started.

Jamieson and Nathaniel ferried Ivy to the grass while Aunt Louisa knelt at his side. The sky was a radiant blue, without a single cloud marring the surreal beauty of it. Ainsley waved off her concern, preferring instead to lay back and take it in. The fact that he was still alive to enjoy such a view was marvellous.

"Peter, don't move," Aunt Louisa warned as he raised a hand to pull sweaty strands of hair back from his forehead.

Ainsley closed his eyes and he rested his hand on his head. The pain was dull, encompassing every part of him. With each minor movement below his skin he could feel sharp pains, especially in his left knee and rib cage. His mind tried to shake off the images he had seen from the window, and the incomprehensible memories they brought forth. Adding to that, his previous injuries from a prior brush with death hadn't yet healed. He would have been worried about them were everything, mental and physical, not so damned entertaining.

As he lay on the ground, fully aware of each stone pressing into his sore back, Ainsley smiled. Within seconds his smile broadened and then he started to laugh heartily.

"He's hysterical," a kitchen maid said soberly.

Aunt Louisa pulled away, no doubt put off by Ainsley's nonsensical reaction. "He must have injured his head."

Ainsley's laughs grew louder with each passing moment, attracting the attention of everyone in or near the house. He continued on this vein for some time, unable to stop himself, but not trying too hard either. Eventually, his strength waned, the pain became too much. His fit of laughter ended in a deep sigh.

"Forgive me," he said, "forgive me." He rolled over and pushed himself from the group, very aware of the tiny pebbles that dug into his palms as he did so. As he gathered himself to stand he saw Ivy nestled in Jamieson's arms surrounded by the sheet that saved her. Panic and remorse played equally on her face. A maid appeared then with a basin of water and some rags to treat the small abrasion on Ivy's face.

"The rose bush," Nathaniel qualified. "I think she received some scrapes from the shrubbery."

Ainsley nodded and turned away, happy she was not greatly injured, but angered that she had put both of them in such danger. Without putting his full weight on his injured knee, Ainsley turned and limped toward the house.

Chapter 5

Its noise I cannot bear to hear,

"Peter!"

Ainsley heard Margaret hurry into the house, out of breath and panicked.

"Peter!" She appeared at the library door just as Ainsley began to pour himself some brandy. "What happened? Are you all right?"

His first instinct was to confide in her, tell her everything that he saw and felt as he tried to keep Ivy from falling. But he knew it would only upset her more. Little could be done for it now and though his leg still pained him the worst had passed. He knew he would mend if he could manage to stay off his feet for a while.

Julia appeared at the door behind Margaret, her expression terrified at first before giving way to relief at the sight of him.

"Maxwell told us you'd fallen from the nursery window?" Margaret walked the width of the room and came to his side. She looked him over, using a hand at his chin to search for any marks on his face.

"I am right as rain," he answered, brushing off her concern. He returned his attention to his brandy, drinking the contents of the glass quickly before pouring another.

"I'll fix a tray for tea, ma'am," Julia said.

Margaret looked over her shoulder and nodded. "Thank you, Julia."

It was only when the maid left the doorway that Ainsley saw someone else was with them. Valise firmly in hand, Jonas stepped into the library and removed his hat. "Calamity seems to follow wherever you lead," he remarked, with a half smile and knowing gaze.

Dr. Jonas Davies and Ainsley had attended medical school together, and continued to enjoy some lighthearted competition as far as their medical careers were concerned. For the time being,

Jonas had the upper hand after securing a position within the surgical staff at St. Thomas Hospital, while Ainsley could feel himself rotting away in the morgue.

"Have you come to escape the rigours of city life as well?" Ainsley asked. "I warn you, no respite can be found here." Ainsley could feel himself scowl. Jonas was like another brother to him and he hadn't meant for their greeting to be so cold, but after the events earlier in the day Ainsley was in no mood for jovial speech or baseless conversations. Anyone who dared to enter his vicinity must learn to steel themselves against his newfound embitterment.

"Peter seeks solace amongst dead insects and drink," Margaret explained as Ainsley found another glass for his friend. "Solitude seems in short supply."

"I can stay in town," Jonas suggested, dividing his gaze between Ainsley and Margaret. "There is no trouble in it."

"Certainly not," Ainsley said instantly. He approached his friend with a tumbler of brandy and exchanged it for the valise. "We can manage, as long as you don't mind a pair of ruffians streaming through the halls."

Jonas gave them both a quizzical look.

"Our aunt has returned from India with her three boys," Margaret explained, "and I'm not entirely sure she would approve of them being called *ruffians*." Margaret gave Ainsley a sideways glance.

Maxwell appeared then and took Jonas's bag.

"Maxwell, Dr. Davies can be placed in Daniel's room," Margaret said.

"Pardon me, ma'am, but Mr. Nathaniel has already been situated in that room."

"Oh good heavens." Margaret ran her hand over forehead. "Father's room then."

"I don't wish to be a bother," Jonas said, stopping the butler from leaving. "I come unannounced."

"'Tis no bother," Margaret said. "I'm just not sure when Father plans to return."

"Or even if he plans to return," Ainsley interjected. He turned and made his way to one of the sofas. While taking a seat he was careful to lean more on one hip than the other and then stretched his leg out in front of him. He stopped himself from wincing at the pain for Margaret's sake.

"Lord Marshall hasn't returned from abroad?" Jonas asked. "I was told no one was residing at Marshall House at present, that you had all come here. I assumed Lord Marshall came with you. How long has he been gone?"

"Nearly a month," Margaret said. "There's no reason to expect him anytime soon." She gestured toward the sofa opposite Ainsley, indicating an invitation to sit down. Jonas nodded but waited for her to take a seat first before settling in on the other end. A space remained vacant between them.

"Perhaps you have come to entice me back to work," Ainsley said, eyeing the remaining brandy in his glass. "Perhaps a certain supervising surgeon has sent you."

"Crawford is beside himself." Jonas gave a quick look to Margaret.

"As he should be," Ainsley said unsympathetically.

"I think it's fair to say the hospital needs you, Peter," Jonas continued.

"But I don't need it."

"That may be, but your current state of apathy will be short-lived and then where will you be?" Jonas shifted in his seat and stole another glance at Margaret, who was unusually quiet. "I understand your apprehension," Jonas said, as Ainsley cocked an eyebrow at the word, "but you'll soon need to address this." Jonas reached into an inner pocket and pulled a folded newspaper from his jacket. He handed it to Ainsley, ensuring he saw one article in particular.

Amongst the numerous articles interviewing neighbours and acquaintances of the recently dispatched child killer, one inset titled "NOBLE DISGUISES AS DOCTOR" had been circled, most likely by Jonas's pen. Ainsley pulled the paper closer as if disbelieving what was in ink.

"What is it?" Margaret asked, inching closer to the edge of her seat.

Putting his brandy glass down on the table beside him, Ainsley began to read. "*During the course of this tragedy, it has come to the attention of this journalist that a certain gentleman from a prominent noble house has been leading a double life, masquerading as a surgeon for a particular London hospital."*

Ainsley set the newspaper down and leaned back in his seat.

Margaret lurched forward and plucked the paper from him. *"Whether he is appropriately trained in the art of medicine, this journalist has yet to find out. More information to follow as it becomes available."*

"I am ruined," Ainsley whispered. "Father will have me killed."

"He doesn't mention you by name," Margaret pointed out. She looked to Jonas, who nodded.

"No one has any clue," Jonas added, "at least not that I can tell."

"I should have been more careful," Ainsley said, downing the last of his brandy quickly. Suddenly he turned his attention to Jonas. "Why do you bring this to me? Nothing can be done for it now. I cannot return even if I wanted to." Ainsley stood and began pacing the room, running his hands through his hair. He resisted the urge for another drink.

"If you remain here talk will start, and eventually people will begin to put two and two together," Jonas explained.

Margaret nodded.

"I told administrators your uncle passed away and you have been charged with settling his affairs," Jonas said. "That will buy you some time, a week or two perhaps, but avoid the city for any more than that and you will be sniffed out."

"It doesn't matter," Ainsley said. "I am finished. Father will disinherit me. I made him a promise."

"This"—Margaret glanced to the newspaper—"Theodore Fenton doesn't mention you by name."

"Peter, he was there that night," Jonas said. "He knows what you and I know."

A look of questioning came over Margaret's face.

"If he wanted to reveal everything he could," Jonas continued, "but he didn't."

"What does he know?" Margaret asked. "Peter?"

"Too much," Ainsley said with a distant voice. "Far, far too much."

Chapter 6

Its joy is trouble to my ear,

Margaret peered over her hand of cards to Ivy, who sat across from her. The girl giggled, though Margaret couldn't see beyond the backs of the cards. Ivy's eyebrows alighted and Margaret could tell she was smiling. Margaret placed down the queen of diamonds and Ivy trumped it with a king of diamonds. Ivy giggled again. "I won the trick," she said, sweeping the pair of cards away.

Margaret nodded. She was winning, though barely. Ivy was a quick study at Piquet and if Margaret wasn't careful she'd owe Ivy more chocolate and peppermint pieces than could be possessed.

Ivy placed her last card and laughed, knowing Margaret couldn't trump her king. Without waiting, she snatched the tiny bowl of candies that sat between them. Daintily she plucked out a square of chocolate and ate it, closing her eyes as if the sweet was the most delectable morsel she'd ever had. "Would you like one?" Ivy asked, opening her eyes suddenly, remembering her manners. "I'm fairly certain you let me win."

Margaret chose a peppermint and popped it in her mouth. "No," Margaret corrected her, "you won all on your own."

Ivy beamed. "Where did you learn Piquet?" she asked.

"My brother taught me," Margaret said, gathering the cards from the table between them. "Apparently more than a few men have lost their shirts playing at the clubs. They tend to play for higher stakes than chocolate."

"Is Mr. Marshall a gambler?"

Margaret nodded dismissively. "Most men are, to a certain degree."

"Yes," Ivy answered thoughtfully. Then, after a longer pause, she spoke again. "He is a good man," Ivy declared, slipping a peppermint into her mouth.

Margaret paused momentarily. Ivy wasn't the first person to

say so. Even as a child, Margaret noticed her brother was guided by a strong sense of chivalry. His decision to go into medicine was completely in line with the type of man he desperately wanted to be. It wasn't enough for him to throw money at a cause as their father did. Peter wanted to be more involved than that, to affect change through his own deeds, not just his family's money and title. However, since their mother's death the previous Christmas, Margaret had seen a marked change in him that she couldn't quite put her finger on. He was angry and resentful, almost bitter, and it pained her greatly, especially since he hadn't always been this way. Once obliging and empathic, he grew to be cynical and sour.

"He was once," Margaret said, unable to keep herself from uttering the truth. "He could be again, should he wish."

"I am grateful to him, nonetheless," Ivy said lightheartedly. She smiled and peered into the bowl of sweets.

Margaret watched the girl pick her way through the chocolate. Ivy was nymphlike, unbelievably slender and pale, almost sickly, when Margaret thought about it. "There must be someone who is worried about you," she said.

Ivy shook her head.

"Your mother at least."

"My mother passed when I was a young child."

The words were spoken with indifference. Ivy was neither ashamed nor saddened and was merely repeating the fact, no doubt the same way it had been expressed to her since she was little.

Margaret hesitated. "Your father then?" she asked.

Ivy remained still, acting as if she hadn't heard Margaret.

"Your grandmother? Or aunt? Someone must be at their wits' end looking for you."

Ivy swallowed and gently placed the bowl back on the table that sat between them. "I am a burden," Ivy said, "more so now, and I wish to unburden them."

"Please don't talk so—"

"It is true!" Ivy's eyes glared at Margaret, the easiness in her features gone. "I wish to be rid of this place and any memory of it." Ivy softened suddenly. "If you would just let me go I promise I'll never bother you again."

"You are not a prisoner here," she said. "Our only wish is to keep you safe."

"Then you must let me leave."

"Where will you go?"

Ivy opened her mouth to speak but stopped short.

"I cannot help you unless you are honest with me," Margaret said in a final plea.

"You'd be less likely to help if you knew, Miss Margaret," Ivy said.

What could this slight, unassuming girl have done? Margaret studied her as she tucked a tendril of hair behind her ear while her cheek puffed out slightly from the peppermint. She looked both old and young at the same time, wise yet naïve as well. It was so confusing to Margaret, who couldn't decipher any of the clues normally offered to her when she met someone new. The girl was obviously terrified at the prospect of returning to her home, wherever that may be.

"I'm going to speak with my brother," Margaret said at last. "I'm sure we can help, if you let us."

Ivy gave no answer. She merely pressed her lips together and looked to the lace pattern of the table cloth. Margaret stood slowly and stepped toward the door.

"I'm not going to lock the door," she said, turning to look at Ivy before she left the room. "You may leave if you like," Margaret said, paying close attention so her voice did not quiver. "But I hope that you will choose to stay."

Ivy gave nothing away. Even a slight nod of acknowledgement would have been better than the blank stare that she gave Margaret. As Margaret left she pulled the door closed but left the key alone and said a silent prayer for the shattered girl that so desperately needed them.

Margaret found Ainsley in his room, seated near the window. An open book was laid out on his leg but he wasn't reading it. He propped up his chin on the heel of his palm as he stared out the window, which had a good view of the family's stables and the pastures beyond. He didn't move until Margaret was halfway across the room and then he only shifted his gaze to the floor. He placed a hand on his book but didn't pick it up. When Margaret got close enough she could see their coachman,

Walter, guiding the horses through the meadow to the farthest paddock.

"Peter, I've come about Ivy. We need to help her," Margaret said. She placed herself in front of him and sat down on the windowsill. "She is terrified."

"She should be," Ainsley said, finally looking at her. "We could have both been terribly injured. I have no sympathy or patience for that girl."

Margaret nodded but it didn't temper her resolve. "Wherever she came from, she is desperate not to return there."

Ainsley returned his gaze to the window. "I haven't the inclination to help," he said. "You know what happens when we get involved."

Unconsciously, Margaret's hand went to the scarf at her neck. Ainsley saw it and turned his head.

"I can't let that happen again," he said.

"I can handle myself," Margaret said, forcibly pulling her hand away.

"Margaret, she's a very troubled girl. I don't know what she's told you but I have to wonder if it's true."

"There is no reason for her to invent falsehoods." Margaret could feel herself becoming agitated. It was becoming very difficult to get her brother to see reason.

"Isn't there? We know nothing about this girl. She could have committed a crime and has escaped custody. She may have escaped from the workhouse. You don't know the risk we take keeping her here."

"What do you suggest we do?" Margaret asked harshly.

"That's why I came up here, to think about it." Ainsley folded his book and placed it on the table next to his chair. "I'm going to have to send for a constable."

"When?"

"This evening."

"Peter, you mustn't!"

"I haven't a choice! We cannot keep her here like some sort of pet. Whoever she belongs to, she must be returned to them."

Margaret stood, feeling the vibrations of her anger cascade down her legs to plant her firmly on the floor. "She doesn't belong to anyone. She is practically a grown woman. She should have some say in the matter."

"I wish I could help, Margaret, but I can't."

"Why not?" Margaret inched closer to him, which only seemed to aggravate him more.

Ainsley stood, returning her challenge. "Because I can't!"

A tiny knock on the door ended their standoff.

"A gentleman is here asking for His Lordship," Julia said when they turned to the knock. "I've told him that Lord Marshall is away at present but he insists on speaking with someone. Should I tell him to leave a card?"

Ainsley ran a hand through his hair and took a deep breath. "No, I will meet with him. Show him to the library. I will be down shortly." Julia nodded and left.

Ainsley gave a glance back to Margaret. "You are becoming quite the handful, Margaret," he said, before leaving. Margaret suppressed a growl and followed him out the door. If Ainsley knew that she followed, he made no indication and did nothing to stop her. Jonas was exiting his room at the other end of the hall.

"What's going on?" he asked quietly as he and Margaret met in the hall.

"I don't know," Margaret answered honestly.

When Margaret and Jonas rounded the library door, she saw a man, not much older than Ainsley. He stood next to the desk where Ainsley had laid out his entomology supplies. A newspaper was grasped in the man's hand but upon seeing them he quickly returned it to the desktop.

"I'm Mr. Marshall, Lord Marshall's son. Can I help you?" Ainsley asked cautiously. It was clear her brother didn't recognize the man either.

"Good day," the man said, squaring his shoulders as he spoke. He coughed slightly before continuing. "My name is Garret Owen. I believe you've found my sister, Ivy."

Chapter 7

Its ways I cannot bear to see,

"I hope she hasn't been too much trouble," Garret said from his place on the sofa.

Ainsley saw Margaret glance in his direction but he chose not to divulge anything. The four of them—Garret, Ainsley, Margaret, and Jonas—fell into an awkward silence as Julia brought in the tray for tea. Margaret stepped forward and gave Julia a nod.

"How long has your sister been missing, Mr. Owen?" she asked as she poured.

"Three days, miss, er, ma'am—I mean, Lady Marshall." He stammered and then exhaled as if to calm his nerves.

"Miss Marshall is sufficient," Margaret said as she presented him with a cup of tea.

Ainsley leaned into the arm of his chair and looked over Garret. A slender man, Garret looked to be in his early twenties and well situated, though Ainsley could not guess his profession. His suit, well fitted, was of good quality if a bit dated, Ainsley noted, and his shoes gave off a gleam indicative of regular care.

"How did you know Ivy was here?" Ainsley asked.

Garret swallowed. "My man, Truman, heard your maid speaking with the grocer's wife," he explained. "He waited to speak with her in the street, where they could speak without an audience, but he says he could not find her."

"You had alerted no one that she had disappeared," Margaret said. "I imagine much turmoil could have been avoided."

Garret nodded and switched his gaze between Ainsley and Margaret. "Yes ma'am." He hesitated slightly. He closed his eyes and bowed his head, a gesture of defeat, Ainsley thought. "My father is a very proud man. And given Ivy's history in the village, he would not allow me to raise alarm." Garret spoke slowly enough to pronounce each syllable, allowing the words to flow deliberately. "Ivy is...a special soul. She—" Garret looked up when Jonas shifted his weight in his chair. Suddenly, the man looked nervous and realized the peculiar looks he was generating from his audience. He laughed. "She is unlike any other."

Ainsley huffed. "I'll drink to that." He could feel Margaret's daring gaze as he took a sip of tea. "We found your sister in our back woodlot," Ainsley explained.

"I will pay for any damages—" Garret shuffled forward in his seat, a reassuring hand pressing the air in front of him.

Margaret was quick to shake her head. "There have been no damages."

Ainsley pressed his lips together and chose to avoid an awkward exchange. The woman needed to go. The sooner the better.

"She was hypothermic," Jonas interjected. "Were it not for these kind people she would have died from exposure."

"Yes, we are deeply indebted," Garret answered slowly.

Ainsley shook his head and slipped to the edge of his seat. "Certainly not," he said. "We only care that she is safe." He stood then, ready to hand her off and restore peace.

Garret stood as well, a small smile spreading on his lips. Margaret stepped forward to receive his empty teacup. Garret looked beyond her to Jonas, who was the only one who remained seated. "You are the doctor then who treated her?"

Jonas looked to both Ainsley and Margaret before replying. "Yes," he lied.

Garret smiled a bit wider and reached out a hand to Ainsley. "I only ask because I saw this article here and thought...well, maybe..." His smile widened as he looked over the three of them. "Never mind. Thank you so much for your hospitality, sir. May I see my sister now?"

"Of course," Ainsley said. "Margaret?"

Margaret paused. "You must stay and have dinner with us," she said suddenly. "It would be a shame for you to come so far for such a short visit."

"'Tis not far, Lady Margaret," he said. "We are only a mile or two down the road."

"Are you now?" Margaret kept a steady smile. "You shall stay nonetheless. We insist."

Ainsley's mind raced at the prospect of dining with the girl and her brother. He already had an estranged aunt and a nearly grown nephew to endure.

"Don't you think that's a good idea, Peter?" Margaret asked expectantly.

Ainsley smiled. "A splendid idea."

"This is quite the spread you have here," Garret said, over his plate of Cornish hen and cranberry salad. "I hope you haven't gone to any great trouble on our account."

Ivy sat next to her brother but she barely touched any of her food. To Ainsley, she appeared rigid and ill at ease. She jumped slightly at any sudden noise or movement and endured numerous sideways glances from her brother.

"No trouble at all," Aunt Louisa said reassuringly.

"Tell me, Mr. Owen, where do you and Ivy live exactly?" Margaret asked, looking down the table at him. "Owens is not a familiar name for me and we've owned The Briar for a number of years."

"We live at Summer Hill Farm, ma'am," Garret said. "My father, brother, Samuel, and I breed and train racing horses."

"How interesting," Aunt Louisa said. "You must be busy then."

"Yes ma'am," Garret said. "We supply thoroughbreds to a number of local families, and some others as far as Brighton. We also lease horses for fox hunting and other diversions"—Garret glanced around the table—"should any of you have need of some."

Ainsley nodded, though he was wholly unimpressed by Mr. Owen's attempts to sell them a horse at the dinner table.

"You will also find us at a number of local race courses," Garret said. "You can't go wrong putting money behind our beasts."

"How did your family start in the horse racing business then?" Margaret asked, her tone hinting at interrogation.

"My grandfather learned from the gypsies who used to camp on the farm where he worked as a stable hand. A small inheritance allowed him enough to purchase our property."

"Oh my, a grandfather, father, and two brothers—Miss Ivy must be in desperate need of some female companionship," Aunt Louisa said with a smile. Ivy looked up at this and licked her lips, but a glance to her brother prevented her from saying anything in reply.

"We are a very close family, aren't we, Ivy?" Garret said. "I wouldn't worry on that account, ma'am."

"Even still, it would be nice to have you come visit us periodically," Margaret said, giving Ivy a marked look.

"Ivy?" Garret prodded his sister to reply.

"Yes, ma'am," Ivy said on cue without lifting her eyes from her plate.

Margaret gave Ainsley a calculated look and it took a great effort to ignore it.

Not long after dinner ended, Ivy was installed in her family's open-air carriage, given a seat beside her brother. Margaret held her hand as she stood beside the large wheel. "If you need anything," Margaret began, "even a cup of tea, I should like you to call on me."

Her hands shaking, Ivy patted the top of Margaret's hand and glanced to her brother, who gave no reaction to Margaret's offer of friendship.

"Step away, Margaret," Aunt Louisa ordered, pulling Margaret back so that they could be on their way.

Ainsley stood on The Briar's front step and waved as the carriage jerked into motion. With the carriage's occupants barely out of earshot, Margaret rounded on Ainsley and charged up the steps toward him.

"Was that not enough to convince you?" she asked.

"I saw nothing amiss," he lied. If he were truthful he'd admit to having a lump in the back of his throat and a general unease while in their presence.

"She is a scared girl," Margaret said, turning to watch as the carriage rolled its way down the long lane to the road. "And I'd wager she hasn't a friend in the world."

"I want you to stay away from them, Margaret," Ainsley said without taking his eyes from the carriage. "We can hope they never have need to cross our paths again."

"There's nothing you can do to stop me," Margaret said.
Ainsley lowered his gaze to the ground. "I know."

Chapter 8

Its crowds are solitudes to me.

Not long after Ivy and Garret's departure, Margaret found herself walking the back garden. In the short time since Margaret last lived there the gardens had almost been laid to ruin. It seemed all the work Margaret's mother had done to bring the manor house back to splendor had been abandoned since her death, most likely at the behest of their closefisted father. In the dark regarding the particulars of their family's finances, Margaret was always led to believe the lion's share of funds was reserved for Marshall House in Belgravia, while The Briar was left as a token to their mother, who brought it, and nothing much more into her marriage. She knew her father had a mind to sell it, most likely to pocket the profits and forget his wayward bride ever existed.

Despair overtook her as she took in the half-dead rose bushes and withered ivy that lay brown and crisp in the summer sun. She walked the gravel path toward the covered gate that would take her to the yard beyond the wall.

Once through the garden gate, she headed for the woods, retracing the path she and Ainsley had taken when they found the girl. The heavy rain that had fallen that night washed away any evidence of the struggle but Margaret found the patch of standing water and mud from where Ainsley had retrieved her.

How far had Ivy walked? Had she made the entire journey on her own from Summer Hill Farm? And where could she possibly have been heading? Land belonging to The Briar included a number of acres of forest, and ended somewhere amongst the trees, where other properties bordered theirs. Margaret glanced down the trail that led deeper into the old growth forest. It was possible the girl was heading to town, perhaps with the intent of catching a train. That scenario seemed highly unlikely, though, since she had no luggage or belongings of any kind with her.

A sound in the trees snapped Margaret's attention back toward the house.

Jonas was making his way down the path toward her. "I didn't mean to scare you," he said from the opposite side of the puddle. "Is this where you and Peter found her?"

"I wondered if there was something we were missing," she said, unable to keep eye contact with him. "What was she so afraid of?"

"You believe she needs your help?" Jonas asked, his demeanor soft.

"We all saw the same thing during dinner," she said. "What it was, I don't know—but something isn't right."

Jonas nodded and began to walk around the puddle toward her but Margaret turned just before he reached her. She continued her walk deeper into the woods, unsure if she should invite him along or if she wanted time to herself. She didn't protest, however, when he fell in step alongside her.

"Have you spoken to Peter about it?" Jonas asked.

"Of course," Margaret answered. "He says there isn't a need for us to get involved."

"Perhaps he is right."

Angered but not surprised by his reply, Margaret just shook her head and heaved a sigh. "Something has changed in him. I can see it in his eyes, though I cannot say for certain." An opening in the canopy showered them with sun as they walked. Margaret squinted against the light and relished the warmth. "What happened back in London?" she asked pointedly.

Jonas opened his mouth to speak and then looked back at the house as if it would grant him permission to continue. It was clear their easy friendship was gone, replaced by something far more awkward and methodical.

"Tell me!" Margaret demanded. "He came home battered to an extent I have never seen before. He kept to his room for a week before we set off for the country. I fear he may do himself harm."

Jonas shook his head in weak protest. "That is not Peter's way."

"What are you both hiding from me?"

He averted his eyes, scanning the grass surrounding them, searching amongst the greenery for the answers he could not generate. "There's nothing I can tell you."

"How very cryptic," Margaret offered, ill-amused and her

patience waning.

"It's a delicate subject matter," Jonas called after her as Margaret began walking away. "He would not wish me to tell you, only to say"—Jonas ran to keep her pace—"to say that what is done is done and he is no longer in any danger." Jonas stood in front of her and forced her to stop. "You, as well, are safe."

His eyes dropped to the sheer cloth that covered parts of her neck. Margaret found her hand rising to cover her stitches, worried the fabric was not opaque enough.

"May I see it?" Jonas asked.

Margaret pushed past him. "No."

"I am your treating physician."

The fact did not make her feel any better about him seeing her so mangled. The state of her wound was in no way due to his work with the needle but rather the infection that set in afterward. Julia did her best to keep the skin from going septic but it did not stop the bubbling and curling of the skin around the stitches before it healed. The medicine Ainsley prescribed worked to keep the infection from spreading but as the days passed it became more apparent that Margaret would never wear a traditional bodice again, nothing with a low neckline or flattering sleeves. Despite this, Margaret was far more concerned for her brother, whose external scars healed while his internal ones seemed to be killing him.

"Margaret, please, I care about you." Jonas's words sounded desperate, an attempt to bridge the gap that had come between them. A gap that was becoming more and more difficult to ignore. "Why won't you look at me?"

Since his arrival that morning she had endured a fair amount of mental torment contemplating whether to confront him. The carriage ride from town had been pure torture, filled with pleasantries and small talk that was uncharacteristic to their normally easy conversations. She knew exactly why things had become so strained and she had little doubt that he knew as well. It was time they spoke of it, so they both could go their separate ways. There was no need to pretend anything more existed between them.

"I've decided I have no interest in fighting for your affections," she said.

Jonas's easy stride slowed and he turned.

Margaret stopped and made a point to look him squarely in the eyes. "She may have you. I am not the sort of girl to chase after men. If that is the sort of reaction you are looking for I am sorry to disappoint you."

Jonas licked his lips and slipped a hand into his pocket. Two weeks prior Margaret had gone to visit Jonas at St. Thomas and found him in an embrace with another woman. Her initial reaction was to flee and she did, crying the entire journey home. Now she wished she hadn't reacted so strongly. It revealed her feelings for him, feelings he obviously did not share. She would not make that mistake again.

"Who is she?" she asked, and almost immediately regretted it. Such interest made her appear weak.

"Margaret." He walked the four paces that separated them but she turned and continued walking.

"Peter told me he saw you with her as well." Margaret swallowed as she looked over the trees that created a tunnel for them to walk through. "Do not try to tell me it was only once."

"It is not what it seems," he said, his voice faltering. He followed her but remained a pace or so behind.

"I'm sorry I am not like the other women you are familiar with." Margaret had to speak over her shoulder. "I do not flirt, or tease, or provide…favours."

"I wouldn't want you to."

Margaret turned. "Why not?"

Jonas smiled and Margaret realized her mistake. A few moments passed without them exchanging words. She hated how calm he looked, how couth and self-assured. Nothing angered or rattled him. Tall and wide shouldered, he was just the sort of man she'd hope to fall in love with, but now hated herself for doing so. There was a deep panic inside her, one that mirrored her mood, when she saw him with that woman. The trollop.

"I have too much respect for you," he said, breaking the silence at last. "I would never dream of taking such liberties, especially not when—" His confidence waned.

"When what?"

"When I don't know what you want," he said.

Margaret was floored. How could he turn this about on her?

"What I want?"

"What are we doing, Margaret?" He stepped toward her. "Do you care for me? Love me, perhaps?" He grabbed her hands in spite of herself. The warmth of his touch contrasted against the cool breeze and kept her from pulling away. "Command me and I will do whatever you want."

Margaret shook her head but could not force the tears away. "I want to know who she is," she said, pulling her hands away. She wanted to step back as well, not trusting herself to react with composure once he spoke, but even that was too much for her weakening knees. She decided to continue making her way down the path slowly and hoped that Jonas would follow her.

Jonas nodded slowly and closed his eyes. "When my father abandoned us, my mother and I were destitute. She was forced by circumstance to the workhouse and we were separated. You remember me telling you this."

Margaret nodded. She had heard his background before and at each telling she felt a pang of guilt for having been born to such a well-situated, if dysfunctional, family.

Jonas's mother had been hired on as a maid to the Locke family, which enjoyed a modest income. She cooked and cleaned for them and was soon able to have her son come live with her. He had earned his keep as well and Mr. Locke, a chemist who had no sons of his own, took a liking to Jonas. He often let Jonas work with him and would give him sums and readings to do while business was slow. By the time Jonas was twelve or so Mr. Locke made an arrangement for him to go to school, even after Jonas's mother died.

"Do you remember the family who took me in?" Jonas asked.

Margaret nodded and felt a lump form in her throat. Jonas was such a decent, well-respected surgeon. It was often hard to imagine him in such dire need.

"Mr. Locke had a daughter, Eloise. She came to visit me that day," Jonas said.

"I understand." Margaret worked hard to steady her voice.

"I don't love her," Jonas said quickly. "I never have, no matter what she imagined happened. I made no promise to her."

"She looked quite taken with you," Margaret said, not

believing Jonas was completely innocent.

"She tried to force me to marry her, guilt me into it, as it were." Jonas's expression grew sour at the mention of it. "Told me it was my way to repay the debt to her family."

"Mr. Locke expects you to marry his daughter?" Margaret had lied when she said she wished to end things between them. In fact, a life without him would feel empty and barren. Margaret closed her eyes and turned away so he wouldn't see her tears.

"I had dinner with her once last summer when she was visiting London and since then she's been attaching herself to me. I've caught her following me around London, on more than one occasion."

Margaret's skin crawled at the idea of someone shadowing her in such a way.

"When I saw you at the hospital, I didn't know what to do. If I ran after you she'd know we…that I love you and I couldn't give her any more control over me." He reached out to her and grabbed her arm as she walked, turning her around to look at him. "Please tell me you understand."

It seemed a convoluted explanation, one that Margaret herself would never have come up with on her own. She knew this woman existed and had even heard Ainsley speak of Jonas's reluctance to give in to her advances. That was before he made eyes for Margaret, at a time when she thought he was every bit a rogue as her brother. The tidbit that stood out for her the most, beyond the girl and his excuse for their embrace at the hospital, was that Jonas Davies had just said *I love you*.

From behind her, Margaret heard the sound of hooves galloping along the path. When she turned she saw the horse coming toward them quickly, as if not realizing they were there. Margaret felt Jonas's hand on her stomach just as they stepped back from the centre of the path. The horse reared up, straining its neck against the reins, and let out a long whinny of surprise.

"Whoa, girl." The rider pulled back on the reins, easing the animal away from the pair.

Jonas stepped forward, placing himself protectively between Margaret and the stranger. "You'd do well to look before charging down a footpath," he said sternly. "We were nearly trampled."

Easily controlling his horse, the man on horseback looked

between Jonas and Margaret. "My apologies," he said, before sliding from his saddle on the opposite side. He brought the reins over the horse's head and met Jonas face to face on the road. Margaret stepped out from the bush but kept close to Jonas.

The stranger was similar in height with equally broad shoulders held back in a rigid quality Margaret had only ever seen amongst nobility. His face was soft, though, with full cheeks and an easy smile, and a slightly longer hairstyle than was the fashion. The darker tone of his skin gave away his partiality for the outdoors, riding mostly, Margaret guessed, considering the way the horse stood at his side so easily.

"I ride these paths every day and have never happened upon anyone on foot." He readily offered his hand to Jonas in greeting while trying to steady his breathing after the exertion of his ride. "Brandon Thornton, of Breaside."

Jonas returned the hand shake but did so cautiously.

"Brandon?" Margaret eyed the stranger closely and then smiled. "I'd never have recognized you. It's me, Margaret."

When his eyes turned to her there was no mistaking that he was one of the boys she and her brother grew up playing alongside, in those very woods where they stood now. There was a pause amongst them as he took her in. While the seconds passed the recognition grew until he finally stepped toward her for an embrace.

"Margaret Marshall!"

When they pulled apart they were both smiling. Brandon took a second glance to Jonas, perhaps wondering if he was recognizable as well. "Has Peter returned home as well? I'd love to see him again."

"We've just returned." Margaret turned to Jonas. "Allow me to introduce Dr. Jonas Davies, a family friend who's come to visit us."

Brandon gave a nod. "I've just been out giving my girl some exercise," he explained, nodding to his horse. "I hope I didn't startle you too badly. Like I said, I scarcely meet anyone on these paths."

Jonas slipped his hands in his pockets and looked to Margaret. "You're fortunate Lady Margaret doesn't scare so easily."

A half smile grew on Brandon's lips. "It's good to know you haven't changed much."

"I daresay we've all endured a certain degree of change," Margaret said, hoping her cheeks weren't as red as she believed they were. "I should congratulate you on your pending nuptials. Priscilla is a lovely girl."

Margaret was surprised to see Brandon's face fall slightly at the mention of his intended. He certainly wasn't the first person to look upon marriage so bleakly.

"Thank you," he said. There was a moment of awkwardness before he raised his face to the sky. "Well, I'd best be heading back. I certainly don't want to get caught in the rain. Feel free to stop by the house any time. Bring Peter. I know Blair would love to see him. It would be like old times."

"Of course. Peter and I would love to pay a visit."

His eyes lingered on Margaret for a few second before he turned his attention to his horse. Margaret felt Jonas's hand rest on the small of her back as Brandon lifted himself up into the saddle.

"It was good seeing you, Margaret. Doctor Davies."

Margaret nodded as he pulled his horse around and retraced his earlier gallop along the path, this time somewhat slower, Margaret noticed.

"He seems an amiable fellow," Jonas said as they watched him leave.

"We were all terribly close once, Brandon, Blair, Peter, and I," she said with a breathy air. She felt her heart ache at the memory of it. "And then, with a blink, we grew up."

Chapter 9

O, how I long to be agen
That poor and independent man,

Ainsley winced against the pain in his right knee as he hobbled to his room. He had been able to deny anything was amiss for most of the day but it had caught up to him, and now he could barely bend it. He lowered himself onto his bed and lifted his leg onto the covers. He should have elevated it hours ago but his pride prevented him from admitting injury.

A creak in the floorboards drew his attention to the door, where Julia stood, a pitcher of warm water in one hand and a metal bucket in the other. "I saw you struggle up the stairs," she said, without waiting for him to invite her in. After closing the door, she placed the bucket and the pitcher near the washbasin and then helped Ainsley roll his trousers up so they could look at his knee.

The joint had nearly doubled in width, swollen more on one side than the other. The skin had turned black in places, indicating internal hemorrhaging. Julia's face fell at the sight of it.

"We should apply ice and heat," she said, turning to the pitcher. She poured out the steaming liquid into the basin and used a washcloth to transfer the warm water to Ainsley. The pain was relieved the instant she placed the cloth upon it. "Hold this," she said. While the heat permeated his swollen joint, she turned to the bucket. Using a different towel, she gathered a fistful of ice and tied the towel edges into a knot. Without warning, she exchanged the warm cloth for the iced towel. "Stay still," she said.

Ainsley grimaced but willed himself to relax.

"What other injuries are you hiding?" she asked pointedly.

Ainsley showed her his hands, which had been gouged by the gravel upon his impact with the ground, and then the deep scratches on his elbow. These wounds did not need attention.

Ainsley had already cleaned them and left them to heal but the injury to his knee was far more complex.

While alternating between heat and ice, Julia eyed him sympathetically. "Wounds are not limited to the physical," she said, matter-of-factly.

Ainsley reached out to her and held his hand to her cheek. He hadn't been cared for so lovingly since he was a small boy and while it made him uncomfortable to have Julia fuss so, he enjoyed her attentions and appreciated these windows of time when they could be together.

"My pride, I suppose," he said.

Julia pressed her lips together and nodded.

"Margaret wishes I were more charitable. She says it's our duty to help, and yet I cannot justify further harm to her or anyone else in this house," Ainsley said. "Especially not after what happened."

The warm water grew cold and Julia stopped her treatment.

"How bad is it?" Ainsley asked as Julia gathered up the cloths and deposited them in the washbasin. "Her scar, I mean."

Julia's movements became slow. "Bad enough Miss Margaret wishes no one to see it. She has asked me to alter the necklines of most of her dresses and will only wear others if they can accommodate her scarves."

"Do you think it will improve?" Ainsley asked.

Julia shook her head. "It may lighten in colour but I doubt it will improve much. Her skin did not take to the stitches and—"

Ainsley raised a hand. He could not hear anymore. He felt personally responsible for her injury, for not finding their suspect before he found out who Margaret was. Until then, Ainsley cared nothing for his own safety and naïvely believed he could keep his professional life and family life separate. He had already decided that he would not make such an error again.

"You see then, why I cannot get involved?"

Julia nodded slowly. "Yes, I see."

He knew she recognized the fear he felt, the anguish for not being able to protect Margaret. Julia understood him and all his complexities better than anyone else and that is why she held such a place in his heart. With her he could be both Peter and doctor, neither highborn nor tradesman. To Julia he was just Peter.

Alarm grew inside him as he watched her gather the items she had brought to his room. "Don't leave me," he said. With the bucket and pitcher in her hands, she smiled. "I'll be back soon." She planted a kiss on his forehead and left.

An hour or so passed and she did not return. The house grew quiet and the world beyond the lanterns faded into darkness. Ainsley waited up for Julia for a time but eventually gave into the lure of the sandman. Before heading to bed, he made sure his door was slightly ajar in case Julia came to him in the night. He didn't dare seek her out in the house, not with so many people about. He couldn't compromise her in such a way. He fell asleep easily but awoke slightly when he heard the floorboards in his room creaking.

He smiled into his pillow, thinking Julia had come to him as she had promised. The footfalls stopped at the side of his bed. Sleepily, he waited for her to climb in and moved to the side slightly for her to have room. But there was nothing.

Ainsley opened his eyes and saw no one at his bedside. He sat up and looked about the room. Eventually, his eyes adjusted to the darkness and saw that he was indeed alone. The door was still in the position where he left it and nothing else was amiss.

"Julia?" he whispered, knowing she wouldn't answer. She'd have said something by now if she had come to him. He went to the door and peered out into the dark hallway. All the doors were closed and no light shone from anywhere. The reliable grandfather clock in the hall ticked, ticked, ticked away the night.

Ainsley swallowed nervously and closed his bedroom door. He couldn't see anyone but that did not mean he was alone.

Chapter 10

With labour's lot from morn to night

By the next afternoon, word of the Marshalls inhabiting The Briar once again had spread through much of Tunbridge Wells. Margaret was forced to endure calls from four women she scarcely knew. She remembered enough of them to know they had ostracized her mother while she lived. Lady Charlotte Marshall had never been one to follow rules, and her chosen seclusion in the country had only served to fuel the fires of gossip. Lady Charlotte did not mind the isolation; she welcomed it, actually, but little exposure to receiving guests, attending other manor houses, and behaving with the upmost decorum left Margaret in a terrible position. Even with Aunt Louisa at her side, Margaret felt like an imposter.

"I was very dismayed to hear about your mother," Lady Adele Cole said, placing her teacup back on its saucer daintily. She looked to her daughter then, eighteen-year-old Delilah, who was quick to take her cue.

"Yes, very tragic."

They both looked at Margaret, eager to hear intimate details of Lady Charlotte's untimely demise, details that Margaret was in no rush to relay.

No doubt sensing her niece's discomfort, Aunt Louisa cleared her throat. "I'd heard on my travels back to England that your son will be a father soon." Aunt Louisa looked Lady Cole squarely, with a smile tickling the very edge of her lips. "Does he have plans to marry the girl or will your grandchild be an underservant as well?"

Lady Cole's face turned sour. She stood suddenly, entreated her daughter to follow, and left without a backward glance.

"That is how you put them in their place, Margaret," Aunt Louisa instructed. "A person can only make you feel inferior if you give them permission."

Margaret looked to the empty sofa opposite them as Aunt

Louisa slouched back into her seat.

"How do you do that?" Margaret asked. "How do you say such things knowing you will see them again in the future?"

"People talk. Nothing can be done for it," Aunt Louisa explained, waving her hand dismissively. "The trick is to beat them at their own game. Show them you will not be defeated. The circumstances of your mother's death cannot be changed but the talk"—Aunt Louisa waved a pointed finger at her—"you should have expected."

Margaret nodded. She knew the scandal would follow them for some time.

"Show a little gumption, will you? If I have learned anything from my time in India it's that predators can detect blood from miles away. Those women who just left are no different." Aunt Louisa's face turned solemn. She grabbed a throw cushion and laid it against her body, playing with the trim. "You have to show them you will not be toyed with." A moment of contemplation followed before she finally tossed the cushion aside and sat up.

"Thank goodness, I have no daughters. But I do have a motherless niece"—Aunt Louisa grabbed Margaret by the upper arms and shook her ever so slightly—"and I will teach her everything I know."

Margaret could not help but smile at this.

A faint rap on the door signalled Julia's arrival. She stood to the side very primly before speaking. "Another caller, ma'am," the maid said. "Lady Isabelle Thornton of Braeside as well as Lady Catherine Brundell, and her daughter, Bethany Brundell."

Margaret popped up exuberantly from the sofa at the mention of Bethany's name. The fact that she was accompanied by the Duchess of Sussex and Bethany's mother, the Countess of Lansbury, was almost lost in the excitement. Margaret had known Bethany for a numbers of years and, until recently, Margaret believed her to be silly and spoilt. In recent months, however, Margaret grew to value her familiar face, and was even more thrilled to find that she had escaped to the countryside as well.

Had Aunt Louisa not placed a gentle hand on her niece's forearm, Margaret would have rushed Bethany at the door and scurried her away to some secret corner. Given that she was not the only arrival, any private conversation would have to wait. Margaret watched her aunt step forward, greeting the duchess and countess gracefully before turning to Margaret.

"My niece, Lady Margaret," she said softly, giving a gentle wave of her hand.

After proper curtsies and brief pleasantries, the assembly took their places on the sofas and chairs centred in the room. The picture of grace and elegance, neither the countess nor the duchess made mention of the dated wallpaper or faded furnishings.

"Mother, doesn't Margaret look much better?" Bethany asked, reaching from her chair to take Margaret's hand in her own.

The countess smiled and nodded. "You really do look the picture of health, my dear."

"The country air agrees with you," Lady Thornton said. "I wonder why you and Peter have not called on the boys."

At the mention of Blair and Brandon, Margaret smiled. As children, Margaret remembered Peter casting her aside numerous times, midgame, to chase the boys in the forest that connected both the Braeside Estate and The Briar property. For many summers he seemed to prefer their company over Margaret's, before he caught on that his sister enjoyed a good romp in the woods as well. Margaret distinctly remembered the boys teasing her for having cast off her boots and choosing to run barefoot. Already confined by a dress, the young Margaret was not about to be thwarted further by laced-up boots.

"Peter has been busy hosting Dr. Davies, a prominent surgeon from London," Aunt Louisa offered by way of explanation. "I'm sure he would have come to call had he known the boys were here."

"Oh yes, each summer they come to ride their horses and play at sport. It would seem I can't get rid of them," Lady Thornton said with a laugh. "Not that I'm in any hurry to be rid of them. Brandon's impending marriage has me in such a state. I'm quite happy Blair's heart hasn't been stolen as yet." She offered Margaret an admiring smile. "However, I do believe, Lady Margaret, you could seize it in an instant. You've grown into such a pretty thing."

Lady Brundell eased forward in her seat. "Your mother would be proud, my dear."

Margaret knew the women were attempting to flatter her and she truly wished they wouldn't bother. Thankfully, the conversation turned, never requiring her to reply.

Absentmindedly, Margaret touched the lace at her throat and then, realizing what she had done, began to worry that she had somehow dislodged the scarf to reveal her scar.

When Margaret looked up she found Bethany looking at her sympathetically. She had been there when that monster had attacked her. She couldn't know how much damage he had done, and was most likely thankful that Margaret had not perished while on an outing with her. Margaret felt nothing but guilt for not sharing in Bethany's positive point of view. Margaret felt grotesque and tainted, forever mutilated by a man trying to hurt her brother.

After a time, the women agreed to take a turn around the garden together. Given the amount of rain that had fallen lately, they said, it seemed silly to spend such a sunny day inside of doors. The change in venue presented the perfect opportunity for Bethany and Margaret to separate themselves from the larger gathering. Once out in the garden, they locked arms and allowed their steps to shorten until finally they were a good distance from the older women.

"I'm sorry I did not come to visit sooner," Bethany said, practically pouting.

"Nonsense," Margaret answered dismissively. "You are here now and I am glad of it."

"Peter has not been asking for me?"

Margaret had to bite her tongue to keep herself from laughing. Bethany was happy to set her cap for Peter indefinitely, it seemed. "He is not worthy of your devotion."

"You are right, but I will not give up hope."

Margaret looked away to keep a straight face before deciding on a change of subject. "Are you familiar with the Owens family?" Margaret asked.

"Isn't everyone? Brother has been purchasing his horses from them for years. Last summer he bought a filly that finished the Epsom in third. Grandmama said she'd never seen such a sprint. So many of his friends attend the farm, you know, to train the horses and see the new stock. Mother says they all put money on little races, illegally betting, you know, but it's all for good fun. Are you interested in a horse? Perhaps not for racing, but a bit of riding. This must mean you plan to stay then, and not return to London." Bethany stopped. "This isn't about that fellow, is it?"

Margaret shook her head but Bethany spoke so quickly she was not permitted a word.

"Good. The papers said he had been killed in a brawl or some such thing, so there's no need to worry on that account."

Margaret let out a sigh, quickly realizing that getting information from Bethany Brundell on a single topic was going to be a difficult task. The girl could hardly stay on point longer than two sentences.

"Have you been introduced to Ivy Owen, then?" Margaret asked, raising her voice to halt another round of chattering.

"Delightful girl," Bethany said. "A bit strange, but I suppose who wouldn't be after what happened." Bethany looked to Margaret. "You do know what happened, don't you?"

Margaret shook her head. She'd laugh were she not afraid of what Bethany was about to tell her.

"Her mother died a number of years ago. Ivy was still in nappies when it happened, or so my mother said. They said Annabelle just fell to the floor, suffered some internal ailment."

"Oh dear."

"That's not all."

Margaret closed her eyes, readying herself for the next bit.

"No one was home at the time save for Ivy and her mother, so when Annabelle died Ivy was left for hours with the body just right there beside her. The babe didn't move or cry or anything."

"Now I wish I didn't know," Margaret said suddenly feeling a sunken feeling in her chest. "How dreadful."

"I've seen her a number of times just staring off into nothing," Bethany said, frowning deeply. "She's not soft in the head or anything," she explained, "just not like you and I."

Chapter 11

And books to read at candle light;

Summer Hill Farm was not far from The Briar. Ivy and her family occupied a small acreage at the end of a long gravel road. As the carriage bumped along, Margaret surveyed the land, noting how their fields of hay and pasture came into view long before the modest house. Made of stone, the farmhouse looked centuries old, built sturdily on the sod before time took hold. The ground looked as if it were attempting to swallow the structure whole, gently pulling the house down and in on itself.

The stables gave another perspective on the operation entirely. The expansive structure was three barns connected as one. No expense had been spared during its construction. A maze of fences and paddocks spread from the stables out into the hills beyond, only halted by a standing of trees at the backside of the barn. An ornamental weathervane stood at the highest peak of the roof, a horse galloping into the wind.

Margaret licked her dry lips as the carriage came to a stop near the tall but half-dead sycamore tree next to the pond.

She wasn't the only visitor who had come that day. Teams of horses and riders entered and exited the stable. Farmhands burdened with wheelbarrows and pitchforks made their way to and fro, completing their daily chores.

Margaret hadn't been picturing an operation so lively. When Garret described his family's farm he did so modestly and never hinted at such a thriving operation.

Walter, the Marshall family driver, hopped down from his perch and opened the door for her. He gave Margaret a doubtful look when he offered his hand so she could step down.

"What's the matter, Walter?" she asked, adjusting her gloves.

The driver lowered his gaze. "Never thought I see the likes of you asking to come to a place such as this," he said.

"A place such as this?" Margaret asked.

"Yes, ma'am."

"You mean the gambling?"

Walter nodded hesitantly, perhaps knowing he was overstepping his place.

"I am not here for any gambling," she said. "Only to visit a friend." Margaret checked the placement of her hat. "I think I shall walk home. It isn't far."

"Do you think it wise, my lady?" the driver asked.

"Probably not," Margaret answered honestly. "But I enjoy the exercise."

Margaret began making her way toward the house, scanning the yard for Ivy.

"Miss Marshall?" Garret's voice came from behind her as she crossed in front of the barn. When Margaret turned she saw him walking toward them with another tall, lanky man just behind him. The man walked with a distinct limp in his left leg, scuffing his boot along the gravel and dirt, sending plumes of dust into the hair about his feet.

"Mr. Owen," Margaret said, employing great effort to sound cheerful. "I have come to call on Ivy. I thought maybe she'd enjoy a walk with me."

"Delightful. She'd enjoy that very much. First, allow me to introduce my brother, Samuel."

The tall, lanky man bowed his head slightly as Margaret said hello. "You must be brawn of this operation," she said, noting how much taller and wider Samuel was compared to Garret.

"Yes, ma'am."

And the quieter one, as well.

"I'll take you to Ivy," Garret said, gesturing toward the house.

Garret led the way to the back of the house, where a small gazebo stood with a little round table and a set of two chairs beneath its shelter. "She's been very quiet today, miss," Garret said quietly before they reached Ivy.

"Oh?"

"She will be pleased you are here. It may even lift her spirits." He offered a gentle smile before taking his leave.

Ivy sat in one of the chairs, staring at something in her lap. As Margaret grew near she could see it was a tiny Bible and a small bundle she could not make out. She could hear Ivy muttering to herself.

"Ivy?"

"Margaret!" Ivy jumped to her feet when she saw Margaret.

"Some light reading?" Margaret said, pointing to the palm-sized Bible. She held out her hand, asking to have a closer look at the edition. Thumbing through the thin pages, she squinted at the tiny typeset. A few passages were underlined in pencil.

"Tell me your favourite passage," Margaret asked, smiling at the prospect of having a common ground.

"Oh, I don't read it," Ivy said. "With this in my hands, Garret thinks I am praying and he leaves me alone," Ivy explained. "It's the only peace and quiet I am permitted."

"Dear me," Margaret whispered. Margaret looked to Ivy, who seemed to be avoiding her gaze. She looked back at the dreary house and shuddered at its foreboding. She wondered who spied on them from behind the curtains and shadows of the windows. "Let's walk," Margaret said, standing suddenly. She looped her arm into Ivy's and pulled her up.

For a moment, Ivy looked elated. But her expression betrayed her fear when she stole a glance back at the house. "Father says I'm no longer allowed to go off on my own."

"You're not alone. You are with me," Margaret answered gaily as she pulled Ivy away. "Besides, I already told your brother I intend to take you for a walk." Margaret herself could feel the tension release from her own shoulders as they stepped farther and farther away.

They walked for some time, first through the narrow woods that skirted the Summer Hill property before the path spit them out onto the top of a grassy clearing. A few oaks stood guard over the crest of an embankment, their roots exposed where the sod and dirt had eroded away to the river far below. Margaret and Ivy inched closer, eager to have a look. The waters, swollen from the torrents of recent rain, rushed energetically along, barring access to the meadow on the other side.

"How far down is it?" Margaret asked, using the trunk of a tree to keep her on the top of the hill.

The drop was considerable, as if the earth had been cut away by a giant's carving knife. In front of them, Margaret and

Ivy looked over the fields and forest. A small town could be seen, marked especially by the steeple of a church obscured by a cluster of trees. The sight was humbling, reminding Margaret how insignificant she was compared to the vastness of the world.

Ivy smiled, amused by Margaret's interest. "There's a path," she explained.

Margaret's gaze followed the steep trail, which resembled nothing of a walkable path, and saw a makeshift foot bridge at the bottom that crossed the water amongst some trees.

"Samuel and his friend Matthew tried to scale down it last year," Ivy said, breaking Margaret's reverie.

"They did not succeed?"

Ivy shook her head. "Sam fell and broke his leg. That's why he walks with a limp." Ivy came to the other side of the oak trunk and looked over the edge. "It's his portion of the curse," Ivy explained.

"Curse?" Margaret instinctively stepped away.

Ivy nodded but showed no interest in elaborating. She turned and began a slow walk farther along the path.

"What about Matthew?" Margaret called out against the gentle roar of the wind. "What happened to him?" she pressed.

"He died."

They took a path that skirted the edge of the fields. The crops, sorghum and amaranth, looked to be struggling in the compacted earth. It had been a strange spring with excessive periods of rain and hardly enough sun to complete their circle of life. Margaret fingered the stout plants as they walked by.

"Who tends your fields?" she asked. "Garret?"

Ivy shook her head. "Samuel did but his leg bothers him too much," she said. "We've had to hire some boys from the village. His curse is affecting us all."

"Why do you speak of curses? Surely you can't believe in them?" Margaret asked without bothering to hide her amusement. She knew superstition abounded in the countryside but never met someone who tied so many reasonable events back to one.

"But I do," Ivy said. "We live in a cursed land, afforded by cursed means."

Ivy continued walking and Margaret kept pace. "The

gambling?"

Ivy said nothing.

"What's your portion of the curse?" Margaret asked, afraid of the answer she'd be given.

"Grandfather says I shouldn't talk about it." Ivy said. "I think it will make you even more afraid."

Margaret shook her head. "I'm not afraid."

A smile began to form on Ivy's lips. "Yes, you are."

If Margaret were honest with Ivy she'd have admit that Summer Hill Farm set her nerves on edge. As soon as she had stepped near the house she'd felt the burden of a hundred eyes bearing down on her. She swore she could hear whispers in the wind and cautions amongst the trees. Everything felt heavy on Margaret's chest, ushering her away and back to the safety of The Briar.

"Your brother should have let me fall," Ivy said suddenly, her tone serious. "It would have been better for everyone had I died."

"Why are speaking this way?"

A look of panic came over Ivy as she placed a hand on her lower abdomen and started to walk away.

"Ivy, stop please." Margaret pulled back on Ivy's arm. "Tell me why you are so scared!"

Ivy stopped and turned to Margaret so quickly Margaret was almost knocked back from the shock. "Because I am with child." Ivy's voice faltered slightly before she was able to gain control. "And I would rather die a thousand deaths than bring another soul into that godforsaken house."

Margaret and Ivy made their way back to the house in nagging silence. There were innumerable questions Margaret wished to ask but did not dare. Nothing could have been more impertinent than to ask who the father of her unborn child was, so Margaret kept her questions to herself while hoping Ivy would choose to confide in her. Margaret couldn't imagine she had much support from her family; unwed mothers most often didn't. If Ivy was isolated from her family now, she'd be entirely disowned if her condition were revealed. Death would be very appealing, given the circumstances. Margaret closed her eyes and shook her head, trying in vain to push down a discomfort that churned inside her. She had been right. Ivy was in desperate need.

As they neared the barn, the hooves of a horse could be heard thudding the wooden floor. Seconds later a sleek black horse appeared at the door, led by an older gentleman who held tightly to the beast's harness. Rearing up and pounding his front hooves into the dirt of the road, the horse pulled at his restraints.

The man jerked back on the leather straps and then struck the horse on the neck with an open palm. "Son of a bitch," the man hissed through gritted teeth.

Margaret heard Ivy gasp. "Father."

This time the animal sent out a great whinny of pain and bowed its head, all the while stomping its rear legs. Mr. Owen held fast to the harness with one hand and used the thick leather whip in the other to hit the flank of the horse while he pulled the horse from the barn. The horse turned, pulling his hind legs away from the man who beat him. So the man used the whip on the horse's face, striking him again and again in a needless succession of brutality.

A spectacle now, stable hands and other visitors to the farm stopped their activities to watch, but no one attempted to intervene.

Margaret stepped forward, raising her hands up to halt the abuse before she felt Ivy's hand tightly grasp her own. A sideways look to Ivy revealed a terrified expression and a subtle shake of the head. A warning.

When Margaret looked back she saw Garret and Sam grabbing the reins and pulling the horse from their father's frantic lashings.

"I'll teach you to buck on me!" their father said, taking one last swing, ignoring Samuel's attempts to shield the horse.

CRACK! The whip came down on Samuel, catching his forearm and cheekbone. Ivy gasped and raised her hands to her face to hide her tears.

"Father!" Garret pushed his father back from the horse and placed himself in front of Samuel, who held his arm where the whip snapped on his flesh.

Margaret rushed to Samuel to survey the damage. The flesh of his arm reddened as she watched and she could see an abrasion as wide as her thumbnail on his cheek.

"He's a brute!" Margaret pronounced.

"It's the drink," Samuel said quietly, so only Margaret could hear.

"What's she doing here!" Mr. Owen yelled from behind them. Margaret turned cautiously and saw that Garret had been successful in taking the whip from their father.

"He needs a doctor," she proclaimed, not bothering to hide her disgust. She turned back to Samuel, who was blotting the cut with his palm and then inspecting the amount of blood. "My brother, he can give you a stitch," she said quietly.

"You're the one from The Briar then?"

Margaret stood tall and met Mr. Owen's gaze squarely. "Lady Margaret Marshall, daughter of the Earl of Montcliff," Margaret answered haughtily. Normally, she'd not have reminded people of her father's position in the peerage, but she wanted to use her family's title to ensure the man dared not harm her.

He stumbled as he took a few steps toward her. Clearly, he was inebriated, and Margaret had already decided he was an angry drunk. "Aren't you just like the rest of 'em," he said, sending spittle in their direction, "thinking ye can come here and spy on me and my family." He stopped a pace from Margaret, towering at least a foot over her. He looked far more haggard than one would expect for someone his age. His skin looked dark and crisp due to years of work in the unrelenting sun. Pockmarks scarred his jowls and neck, a condition that made it hard for Margaret to look him in the eyes as she ought. "You think I need you skulking about?"

"Certainly not."

"It's bad enough you try to take my daughter from me, now you want my son." The old man's words ran together into one. Margaret glanced over her shoulder to Ivy, who had taken hold of Margaret's arm. Angry drunk men were immune to soothing tones and attempts at resolution. They only knew pain and fear.

Ivy began pulling Margaret away. "Let's away, Miss Margaret," she said in a desperate whisper.

"Your brother needs a few stitches," Margaret said.

"He'll need plenty more than that when I am done with

him!" Ivy's father charged for Samuel again. Margaret and Ivy tried to run, pulling at Samuel's arm to get him away, but Mr. Owen reached them before they could move. Margaret was pushed to the side roughly. Both she and Ivy fell to the gravel. By the time they scrambled to their feet Samuel and his father were caught in a struggle, each one throwing fists with one hand while holding the other back with the other. It truly wasn't a fair fight. Samuel was taller, bigger, and completely sober. He hit his father reluctantly, obviously not wanting to cause the man harm, but also needing to defend himself against the onslaught. When Garret placed himself between them the struggle ended with a single blow. Mr. Owen stumbled to the ground with blood pouring from his nose.

Garret gestured for some farmhands to come forward. "Take him to the house and clean him up," he said, slightly out of breath. The men obliged and gathered their assignment from the dust.

Margaret found herself pulled away by Ivy but she couldn't take her eyes from the drunken man, now moaning and writhing in pain as he held a hand to his nose. "Grandfather won't like this," Ivy said under her breath.

Garret dusted off his hat on his pant leg as he walked toward Margaret.

"Were you hurt?" he asked.

Margaret shook her head slightly, unable to fully commit to the action because of the shock. She hadn't expected Mr. Owen to react to her the way he did, and she certainly did not see Garret as the type of man who'd be able to defeat a man with one strike, even a drunken one.

"Ivy, see that Lady Margaret gets to her carriage," Garret said, gesturing toward the lane that would take her from the property. Ivy stepped forward, keeping a watchful eye on her father, and looped her arm around Margaret's.

"I told my driver to go," Margaret said, turning in place to follow Garret as he paced.

Garret pointed farther down the lane. Walter was just beyond the barn, running toward the crowd and the dust that had been kicked up. Looking beyond him, Margaret could see the horse team beneath the shade. A look of relief came over the driver when he saw Margaret unharmed.

"Come, miss," Ivy said, her voice shaky.

Seeing the girls coming, Walter turned and hurried back to the carriage to ready the horses.

With each step that took her farther from the house Margaret felt greater relief. The carriage wasn't far and Margaret knew it had just been Garret's way of removing her from the embarrassing scene.

"Would you believe me if I told you he won't remember it in the morning?" Ivy said once they were out of earshot of the others.

"I believe you," Margaret answered. "I am well aware of the effects of drink."

Ainsley's love affair with his flask had taught her a number of things about the effects of alcohol and the various forms of drunkenness it provoked. "Perhaps he grieves for your mother," Margaret offered, remembering what Bethany had told her.

Ivy shook her head. "No, he's always been like this. My mother's death was her reward for having survived this for as many years as she did." She stole a glance back at the house but kept pace with Margaret.

Halfway between the house and the carriage, with Walter preparing the team for their departure, Margaret turned and took both Ivy's hands in her own, a gesture that forced Ivy to look at her squarely and not avoid what Margaret so desperately wanted to say.

"Ivy, have you told anyone of the child you carry?" she asked, giving a quick glance over the girl's shoulder to make sure they would not be overheard. "The child's father even?"

Ivy shook her head slowly. "I have confided in no one," she said, "only you."

Margaret wasn't so sure she wanted such a distinction. "How far along are you?"

Ivy swallowed, most likely unsure. "I don't know. A few weeks I suppose," she offered.

"Is the man in a position to marry you? It can be arranged in a matter of days. No one has to know."

Ivy tried to avoid Margaret's gaze but Margaret moved wherever the girl's eyes went.

"He must be held to account. It is as much his child as yours." Margaret searched Ivy's face but saw nothing. It was if the girl pretended not to hear her. "Very well," Margaret said, her plan defeated.

She couldn't imagine what Mr. Owen's response would be were he to find out. It was still unclear to Margaret whether he intended to do her harm. "I can see now why you are afraid," Margaret said at last.

She glanced over her shoulder to the carriage that waited. Walter was no doubt eager to get Margaret home. Ivy must have seen it as well.

"You should go, Lady Margaret," she said, her voice low.

Margaret hesitated and then nodded but still did not release Ivy's hand. "You will come to me, won't you," she asked, "if there is anything you need?"

Ivy nodded and gave a half smile before pulling her hands away.

Margaret was not ready for their parley to end. There was so much she needed to know: who the father was, how she came to be pregnant out of wedlock, but most important of all, how she planned to hide her pregnancy from her father. She wanted to reassure Ivy that everything would be all right, that she would help and even give her sanctuary should it come to that.

She had an uneasy feeling about leaving Ivy behind, a trepidation that she could not shake even as the carriage rolled down the hill and away from Summer Hill. On her way home, she vacillated between telling Ivy's secret to Peter, to see what counsel he could give, or remaining mum. In the end, she decided it was not her secret to tell.

Chapter 12

That followed labour in the field
From light to dark when toil could yield

Ainsley spent much of the day in his room, a book his only excuse for being such a recluse. The noise of the house did not find him in the confines of his room, his refuge; even still, he could not concentrate on one word in print before him. Mental images plagued him relentlessly, reminding him of the life that waited back in London, the reality from which he was so desperate to escape. He may have escaped judicial repercussions, for now, but his own conscience would not allow him peace. The drink at his side made the pain in his knee tolerable but the pain in his heart was relentless.

He sat in his green, velvet chair, placed next to the windows with the curtains in place. He received just enough light by which to read the pages and no more. His book should have been better chosen, instead of hastily grabbed. He was not in the mood for Thomas Moore.

The doorknob to his room began to shutter, the unmistakable movement of someone on the other side attempting to enter. Ainsley had closed it, preferring everyone believe he was asleep. Ainsley ignored the rattling at first and after a time it ceased before starting up again with greater vehemence.

"George? Hubert?" Ainsley called from his chair.

The doorknob stopped and the room fell silent. No one replied. Ainsley waited, listening intently for the sound of the floorboards outside his door to signal their departure.

Nothing.

Ainsley exhaled and lifted his book to continue reading. He heard a click from the door and looked again, expecting it to open, perhaps with one of the boys asking for him to play. Again there was nothing.

"What do you need, boys?" he asked, amused at their resistance to talk to him.

Finally, Ainsley put his book down, wondering why the boys felt the need to be silent. He walked toward the door in a gentle, easy stride, not wanting to scare them off. Just as his hand reached for the doorknob, it shook violently.

Ainsley jumped back and watched as the door shuddered on its hinges, the knob rattling and turning in its place with such force he knew two young boys could not be responsible. After a minute, everything stopped. Ainsley stood stunned, wondering at what he had just witnessed, and then he flung the door wide open, intent on catching the culprit on the other side.

He was met with an empty hall. "What in—" Ainsley did not finish. Instead, he listened, and heard nothing. He walked the hall, peering in each room, listening for sounds of a prankster. At the top of the stairs he heard a bang, the sound of his book hitting the wood floor in his room, and when he turned around his bedroom door slammed.

"So you just put pins around the wings?" Jonas asked, looking up from an attempt at entomology. "How do you know what will look best?"

Ainsley shrugged from his seat on the other side of the library. "That's what I have been trying to figure out for a week now," he said. "It takes practice." Ainsley lifted his drawing pencil from his sketchbook and looked over. "Don't waste too many of my specimens," he warned. "They aren't easy to find, you know."

"You probably ordered them from a catalogue," Jonas quipped.

A rap on the door signalled Nathaniel's entrance. The young man smiled as he surveyed the room, seeing both Ainsley and Jonas within and most likely delighted with his luck. Ainsley was far less amused. The only thing he hated more than being host was playing nanny for those younger than him.

"I'm not disturbing important hospital business, am I?" Nathaniel asked, genuinely startled at the prospect.

Ainsley snorted. "Yes, of course." Ainsley nodded toward Jonas. "Once he's completed resuscitating that scarab beetle, he'll finally get a chance to amputate one of my left toes. For the sake of science, you see." He flashed the gullible Nathaniel a fleeting smile before returning his attention to his sketchbook. He made no attempts to hide his annoyance.

Nathaniel licked his lips. "I only ask because I find it all so fascinating." He moved farther into the room and stood over Jonas.

"You find it fascinating because you know Aunt Louisa would never allow it nor would my uncle. You are just going to have to stick to more respectable means of earning a living, like gambling or irresponsible speculation." Ainsley didn't bother to look up.

The room fell quiet after that but Nathaniel refused to leave. Eventually, Jonas threw his hands up and pushed himself away from the desk. "I fold," he said, tossing a final pin down with the others. "I haven't the patience for beetles and dragonflies."

"Not enough glory in it for your liking?" Ainsley asked, only half joking. Two years earlier they had both graduated with honours from Edinburgh Medical School. While Ainsley was confined to the morgue by circumstance of his birth as well as the reality of his slow if accurate hands, Jonas was able to flourish as a prominent surgeon, providing services to many noble men and women, the types of people who'd recognize Ainsley in a heartbeat.

"You understand that isn't why I do it," Jonas answered.

"Isn't it why every surgeon does it? So we can put on airs, play God, and woo women?"

Jonas scratched at the side of his nose. Ainsley knew he was right and didn't need any agreement from his friend.

"Embitterment is not a flattering look for you," Jonas said gently. Jonas had a way of making a point quietly. He was couth without being self-righteous and Ainsley hated him greatly for it. "I had hoped my presence here would alleviate that."

"I know why you are here, so let's not bother pretending you visit solely for my benefit," Ainsley said as he looked up sharply. "Margaret fancies herself a bluestocking and so willingness is of most importance. I said my piece on the issue. It's my father you need to convince."

Jonas was quiet for a moment. He rested his knuckles on the desktop and closed his eyes. Jonas and Margaret were too friendly for being so opposite. As a surgeon, even a well-respected one, he'd never earn any favour with their father. Margaret was Lord Marshall's only daughter and it was always expected she would marry well. If Ainsley's father hadn't already picked the lucky man out himself, Ainsley had no doubt he'd steer her toward someone with a title to inherit as well as property and yearly earnings that were too far out of reach for a young, upstart surgeon.

Jonas understood all these things, as did Margaret, but for some reason their liaison continued, drawn to each other like moths to a flame. It was clear things would not end well.

"You intend to ask Cousin Margaret for her hand?" Nathaniel asked excitedly.

Ainsley saw Jonas's gaze fall to the floor. Both had nearly forgotten the boy was still in the room.

Jonas turned from them then, choosing not to answer and walked for the window, perhaps hoping the subject would end there, but Ainsley wasn't about to let things go so easily. He snapped his sketchbook shut and tossed it to a nearby table.

"My friend forgets," Ainsley started to explain, for Nathaniel's benefit mostly, "as much as my sister is fond of him, and clearly she is, she would never be permitted to marry him, by our father or society."

"I thought I'd let Margaret decide," Jonas said, without bothering to turn to look at them.

"How very modern," Ainsley said. He stood then, and walked to the desk and the project Jonas had abandoned. "I think—"

Margaret entered then, without acknowledging that she had interrupted their conversation. She pressed her finger to her lips, a signal for them to be quiet. Walking the width of the room, she passed in front of the fireplace and opened the hidden cupboard along the wall.

Amidst the initial confusion, Ainsley laughed and almost said his sister's name when Aunt Louisa entered the room. "Have any of you seen Lady Margaret?" she asked. Suddenly his sister's hiding spot made sense.

The three shook their heads in near unison. "No, can't say we have," Ainsley answered calmly.

Aunt Louisa's shoulders sank as she exhaled. "Margaret and

I have been invited for tea. I can't stand the thought of taking tea with her all on my own."

Ainsley nodded, as if he understood her plight. "Dreadful," he said under his breath.

"Nathaniel, come help your mama for a moment." She motioned with her finger for him to follow her. He obeyed with only a slight hesitation.

"She's gone," Ainsley said after a time, loud enough for Margaret to hear.

Margaret opened the secret door slightly. "I've never been called upon to entertain so much in my entire life," she said quietly. She looked weary and downtrodden, not the pleasant, even-keeled young woman Ainsley knew her to be.

There was a rap on the door. Reactively, Margaret ducked back into her hiding place before Ainsley could tell her it was only Julia.

"Mr. Garret Owen has come, sir," she said to Ainsley. "He said he'd like a word with you."

Ainsley gave a quick glance to Jonas, who nodded and began to exit the room.

Julia stopped him at the door. "Dr. Davies, he means to speak with both of you."

Garret appeared at the door, hat in hand, and ill at ease. He wore what appeared to be his best suit, clean and freshly pressed, without a speck of dirt or sign of his work in the stables. Samuel stood behind him, even less certain that they should have come. Both Ainsley and Jonas greeted the man with a handshake and that's when Ainsley noticed the open wound on Samuel's cheek.

"Let me offer apologies for our intrusion," Garret said.

"No, no," Ainsley answered, gesturing to the sofa and taking a seat opposite him. Jonas took a seat in a chair to the side. "Julia, some tea for our guests, please," Ainsley said.

Julia nodded and left the room.

"That's one hell of a cut there," Ainsley said. "A stitch or two from my friend here ought to stop the bleeding."

"We've been told you aren't so bad with a needle and thread yourself, Mr. Marshall," Garret said. "Or is it Dr. Marshall amongst friends?"

Garret licked his lips and smiled out the corner of his mouth. "Margaret told us. She said you could give Samuel a stitch or two."

"Jonas, will you fetch my bag?" Ainsley asked, turning to his friend. He couldn't help but give his friend a look of defeat. He had been found out and he needed to tread carefully if he didn't want his secret spread throughout the county. Acknowledging Ainsley's predicament, Jonas nodded and left the room. He returned with Ainsley's medical bag in hand.

Once settled into the desk chair, Samuel positioned opposite him on the settee, Ainsley set about to prepare a needle and bit of thread. Ainsley eyed the cut, and cleaned it with a bit of alcohol and gauze. "I haven't anything for the pain," Ainsley said.

Samuel did not flinch at the suggestion.

"This is not the only reason for my visit," Garret said, rubbing the back of his neck nervously. "My family needs your help."

Ainsley's eyes darted to Jonas, who looked just as unimpressed as Ainsley felt.

"I'm sorry. I'm not quite sure how to say this." Garret stammered and let out along breath. "My sister is with child," Garret said suddenly, his voice cracking midsentence.

Pausing his work, Ainsley held the needle steady, wincing internally at Garret's confession. Two days ago, the girl was perched on the roof wishing for death, and now Ainsley knew why. After a moment, Ainsley resumed work on Samuel's cut. Three stitches finished the job and he was able to snip the thread.

"Don't remove these until the skin has healed," he cautioned as he dabbed an alcohol-drenched cloth on the cut. "Clean it a few times a day with this." Samuel accepted the bottle of alcohol but said nothing.

"No one else in our family knows," Garret continued as Ainsley cleaned up his work area. "I only guessed it when I found her ill one morning." He placed his hands over his face for a few seconds before beginning again. "She'd been known to go missing, sometimes for hours at a time without any explanation as to where she had been. When she disappeared I figured she'd eloped with the child's father."

"That is why you did not raise alarm," Ainsley answered,

closing the clasp of his bag and placing it on the floor next to his chair.

Garret nodded. "Our family is very well-known in these parts. We could not afford such an assignation to our character. If she were found with a man, unmarried, we did not want it broadcast to the town."

Ainsley nodded, aware of the delicate balance between scandal and respectability.

"Your family has shown us such kindness. I hate to ask for further assistance." He used his palm to settle the nervous bounce of his knee. "Are there not means to end an unwanted pregnancy?" Garret asked, meeting Ainsley's gaze squarely. "Medically?"

Ainsley glanced to Jonas uneasily. Procedures to terminate unwanted pregnancies did exist but it wasn't common medical knowledge and it certainly wasn't covered in medical school. Poorly tested and haphazardly documented, the act was illegal and could not only cost a doctor his license but also what little respect he had in the community.

"What you are asking is illegal," Jonas explained evenly. "Any respectable surgeon would never undertake such a task openly."

"Yes but..." The horse trainer hesitated and looked at his hands, which cupped his knees. Suddenly, he raised his gaze and looked Ainsley squarely in the eyes. "No one knows you are a medical doctor, just as no one knows my sister's condition. We will keep your secret, if you keep ours."

Unsure how his medical training had led him to this, Ainsley rubbed his temple with the tips of his fingers. It was indeed unfortunate that Ivy should find herself in this predicament but Ainsley was not in a position to assist, not when so many moral questions already weighed on his heart. "Have you no relatives to send her to for a few months?" Ainsley asked, desperate for an alternative solution. "Until the child is born and can be adopted."

"No, sir," Garret answered. "Our father would become suspicious. He's a difficult man at the best of times."

Ainsley could not explain the discomfort he felt regarding the question put to him. Many young women had been brought to his morgue, dead and found to be with child. It seemed so tragic to snuff a life because of one unfortunate circumstance. Not many choices existed for these women, who were often friendless and alone, having been cast out of their families and unable to support the young life inside them. Orphanages as well were not the best places for a child to grow up. Rife with violence and abuse, death was often a release for the motherless who found themselves there.

He also could not help feeling as if he were being dealt an ultimatum. He could either relieve Ivy of her unfortunate circumstance, and in doing so save her family from scandal, or find himself and his double life exposed, which would bring new scandal down on his family.

Ainsley eyed Garret, trying to read the man, who by all accounts was unreadable. Neither humble nor boastful, the horse trainer was in a class all his own.

"If either of you learned gentlemen could help, my family would—"

"What does Ivy wish to do?" Jonas asked suddenly.

Garret chuckled slightly. "I haven't spoken to her yet."

"Seems presumptuous to arrange this without her knowledge," Ainsley said.

Garret's gaze drifted from Ainsley to Jonas and back again. "I am nearly positive this is what she wants," he said.

"And the father of the child?"

Garret seemed to supress a sneer at the mention of another party involved. "I haven't a clue and my sister refuses to tell us."

Ainsley nodded, though he wasn't convinced of the truth of this statement. "I'll need some time to think it over," Ainsley said as he stood.

"I'll pay you. Whatever you need, it's yours," Garret said quickly, standing and circling in place to follow Ainsley as he moved away from the sitting area. "A horse, perhaps, a thoroughbred racehorse."

Ainsley sighed and placed his hands in his pockets. "I said I would think it over, Mr. Owen," Ainsley said.

"Thank you, sir."

Garret had only been gone a minute before Margaret emerged from her hiding place. Her downtrodden expression bore the weight of Ainsley's heart as their eyes met.

"Did you know about this?" Ainsley asked.

Margaret said nothing to confirm or deny his suspicion. Her eyes fell to the floor as she pressed her lips together. "What are you going to do?" she asked

Jonas began to close the door, just as Julia appeared with a tray for tea. "Oh sorry," she said, as she looked over the room. "Have the guests left already?" she asked.

"Yes," Ainsley answered. "Sorry to have bothered you, Julia."

Julia set the tray down and set about to pour tea for everyone.

"Ivy would rather die than have that baby," Margaret said. "She told me as much."

Ainsley moved toward his desk and plucked a pen from amongst his papers. "I don't want to get involved." His words lacked conviction and he knew it. This was not a conversation about his needs as much as it was a conversation about Ivy's needs. But the law was clear. He could not follow through with Garret's request without jeopardizing himself and his family. "It's just a baby, Margaret," he said. "There are worse things to befall a young woman." He slipped into his chair and leaned back, still twisting the pen with his fingers.

"She's so slight, I believe a full-term labour will kill her," Margaret said.

"It's illegal."

Jonas snorted. "You've never worried about upholding the law before."

Julia placed a cup of steaming tea on the desk where Ainsley sat.

"You can't tell me you support this plan?" Ainsley asked, after pulling the cup toward him.

"You and I both know what happens at the result of untrained hands," Jonas answered. "If you don't do it, they'll find someone else, someone who was probably trained as a barber. She could bleed out or die."

"It's a baby, Jonas!" Ainsley protested.

"Not yet, it isn't," Jonas answered.

Ainsley did not disagree with Jonas, not entirely. Not much

time in school had been dedicated to women's health and what was taught was met with snickers and snide remarks from the male students. In a profession where the line between science and superstition was still being defined, many female ailments were left unstudied, leading doctors to draw their own conclusions about the whys and wherefores. The termination of a pregnancy was not viewed as a decision for women, but rather a decision for the courts.

Ainsley rubbed a hand over his face, secretly wondering how his family had become embroiled in such a debate. "Do you think he is trying to blackmail me?" he said at last.

"I think he was trying to tell you that we all have secrets to keep," Jonas said.

The room fell quiet as the gravity of the situation set in. After a time, Ainsley spoke. "I won't do it," Ainsley said, almost apologetically. "I can't."

Jonas stood taller and shook his head. "Then I will do it," he said. "I'll need someone to help—not you," he said, raising his hand to Margaret, who had been quick to step forward.

"Why ever not?" she protested.

"Do you want me to help the girl or not?" Jonas asked, turning toward her. Ainsley watched from his side of the room as Margaret rolled her hands into fists, angered at Jonas's dismissal.

"I don't see why I can't assist you," she said.

"I'll help," Julia said at last. Everyone had nearly forgotten she was in the room. She stood to the side with the empty tea tray in her hands. "I'll help you with Miss Ivy."

"Julia..." Ainsley could not help but breathe her name as she spoke.

Julia ignored Ainsley's protest. "I've assisted Mr. Marshall with a few procedures in the past and I've assisted with a few births at the orphanage. Will you take me?" she asked, turning to Jonas.

Jonas nodded. "Yes," he said somberly. "I'd be glad of it. Thank you."

"No," Ainsley said harshly. "Certainly not."

"It's decided, Peter," Jonas said sternly.

Julia pressed her lips together and lowered her gaze. She slipped from the room but Ainsley marched after her, pulling her back to look at him once they reached the back hall.

"You don't have to do this," he said, almost pleading with her.

"I know," she answered easily. She met his gaze and offered a soft smile. "I want to do this. For the girl." She smiled slightly and turned to leave.

"What if I said no," he said, crossing his arms over his chest.

Julia stopped her retreat and turned to look at him again.

"You are under my employ. I can stop this entire thing if I had a mind to."

Julia nodded. "You could." She smiled a knowing smile, challenging him and yet knowing he would not do as he threatened.

"The procedure is dangerous," he said, lowering his voice and stepping closer. "What if she can never have another child—or worse." Ainsley swallowed. "Women die on the table all the time. They bleed out or develop infections. Are you prepared to have that kind of blood on your hands?" As if to drive home his point he took her slim hands in his, and felt the slight roughness there from her work about the house.

Julia's eyes searched his face. "We all have blood on our hands," she said after a moment of silence. "Some of us are just better at hiding it than others." She leaned forward then and pressed her lips into his gently. The touch, so openly and freely given, sent a sensation up his spine. "It will be all right," she whispered when she pulled away.

Chapter 13

Real happiness with little gain,
Rich thoughtless health unknown to pain:

For some time after Garret's visit Ainsley had an uneasy feeling in the pit of his stomach. He wondered if this was truly what Ivy wanted and questioned what his answer would have been if Ivy had asked him herself. He worried that the girl was being pressured into an abortion by her brother.

At the top of the stairs Ainsley turned to head to his room but stopped himself. Instead, he turned toward his mother's bedroom at the farthest end of the opposite hall. It was the only remaining room in the house that had not been assigned to anyone and it stood untouched since their mother was last living at The Briar.

Ainsley pushed open the door and felt a sense of relief, seeing it as it was, as he remembered it as a child. Had their mother been alive Ainsley could have, and no doubt would have, confided his predicament to her. It was because of her influence that he was driven to help others. It was a condition that weakened him, he thought, especially in a world as callous as he now understood it to be.

He made his way to one of the windows that overlooked the south lawn. He could not see Summer Hill from his position but he knew it sat just beyond the hills and the standing of trees. A road scarcely wide enough for more than a cart and not maintained in any way skirted the western boundary of The Briar, winding its way over the small mounds. It was from there that he could estimate how far Ivy had walked in the rain to get to The Briar from Summer Hill.

"What do you think Mother would say to us right now?" Margaret asked from behind him. When Ainsley turned he saw her walk into the room and stand at the window alongside him.

Ainsley could not bring himself to answer the question. Any

fear he had of disappointing his mother before was only made worse by the fact that she was gone and he would never know.

"When you were away at school she'd go on and on about what a great man you would be one day. How you'd save countless lives or discover some medical miracle. She knew that you'd sacrifice yourself to save others." Margaret took her gaze from the view and looked at Ainsley directly. "She believed in you more than you ever believed in yourself."

Ainsley smiled. "She couldn't have known what it's really like," he said. "She couldn't have known what it would cost me, what it would cost you."

"This isn't you, Peter," she said. "This moody, irritable, unapproachable man. I just..." Margaret stopped herself and shook her head. "I just wonder what you are afraid of."

"I'm not afraid."

"Yes, you are!" Margaret turned to him. "You're afraid there are other monsters out there preying upon innocent people and you are afraid that you won't be able to do anything to stop them."

"I'm afraid of losing you, Margaret!"

Margaret's face softened as she looked at him.

"I've already lost Mother. If I lose you, what am I left with?" Ainsley charged. "A brother who believes himself better than me in almost every way and a father who'd rather disown me than admit my chosen profession to the world. You are the only one who knows both sides of me and the only one proud of that fact."

Margaret grew quiet, pondering Ainsley's words thoughtfully. Ainsley turned his attention back to the window, wanting to look anywhere but at the sister who had grown so disappointed in him.

But this time the landscape had changed. Instead of the idyllic countryside, he saw a great plume of black smoke wafting into the otherwise blue sky.

Ainsley used the window to brace himself as he leaned in slightly closer. It was coming from Summer Hill.

"Fire," he said instantly. "There's a fire!"

Margaret looked out the window. "It's Summer Hill," she breathed. "That's the only house for miles."

"Gather some blankets and towels. And my medical bag.

And find Jonas!" Ainsley was almost across the room when the door opened suddenly and Julia appeared, out of breath and frantic. "There's a fire!" she gasped. Hurried feet running the length of the hall could be heard behind her as well as shouts from other servants.

Ainsley passed her and followed the movements of servants rushing to the front of the house. At the steps Ainsley could see on the horizon the dark plume of smoke inking the clear sky.

"Jamieson and Maxwell are hitching the horses to the carriage," Julia said, appearing at his side.

"I can ride," Ainsley said, removing his jacket and handing it to her.

"Yes, a horse is ready." She took his jacket and he began to roll up his sleeves.

Aunt Louisa appeared then, rushing down the stairs as servants bounced frantically between each other. "What's going on?"

"A fire, ma'am," Julia answered.

Jonas and Nathaniel emerged then from the library.

"Jonas, Nathaniel, can you ride?" Ainsley asked. Both shook their heads.

"Do elephants count?" Nathaniel asked, a smile curling the edges of his lips.

Ainsley gave him an annoyed look. It was hardly the time for such quips. "You head over in the carriage," Ainsley ordered with a pointed finger. He began to a quick march toward the stables, where a boy was leading a saddled gelding. He heaved himself up into the saddle but before he had a chance to kick the horse into a trot Margaret rushed toward him and took hold of the reins.

"Peter, what do we do?" she asked.

"We need to get everyone over there. Bring blankets, towels, anything we can use to treat the wounded. And don't forget my medical bag."

A bucket brigade had already formed, drawing water from the small pond opposite the barn. The orange flames peaked out from the window openings of the barn's stone foundation, most likely feeding off the dry straw and timber. As Ainsley tethered his gelding to the fence a safe distance away, he saw Garret was trying to calm a frantic horse. The mare was bucking and pulling back on its reins, edging closer and closer to the fire.

"The horse! The horse!" someone yelled.

Ainsley ran forward, urging Garret to drop the reins before hitting the mare sternly on its flank. The horse took off at a gallop, heading down the laneway as if escaping to town.

"We have to get the horses out!" Garret yelled over the roar of the flames and orders from the brigade.

Garret led Ainsley to the back portion of the barn where flames hadn't yet reached. Samuel was already there, opening the stalls one by one, unlatching the iron, and pulling the terrified animals from their stalls by their halters. Ainsley could hear wood snapping above him as pieces of charred roof, still aflame, rained down on them.

The back portion of the barn grew warm and then hot and sweltering. Ainsley could feel the flames growing closer but he dared not look. Like a machine, they went down the line, releasing the horses and praying they didn't get trampled in the chaos of it all.

"Help!"

Ainsley turned and raised his arm to shield his face from the heat of the flames. Unable to see past the bright orange glow, he squinted and realized Garret was struggling with a horse in the opposite stall. The animal had kicked and stomped at the ground in such a panic his halter had gotten caught on a fallen board. Garret was frantically trying to free the mare, which looked to Ainsley with wide, terrified eyes.

The fire was inching toward them, catching bits of straw that littered the ground in clumps.

Together, Ainsley and Garret lifted the board high enough so Samuel could pull the horse free. Without a backward glance it ran for the back door of the barn, disappearing in a swirl of black smoke.

The heat played at Ainsley's throat, sending him into a fit of coughing. He grabbed Garret's arm and pulled him out of the stall, willing himself to ignore the stinging in his eyes. A thunderous crack rang out over their heads.

"It's coming down!" someone yelled beyond the flames.

Garret turned toward the flames but Ainsley grabbed him and thrust him toward the back door.

"The others!" Garret called, as a horse's panic-stricken whinny erupted from the other side of the flames.

"We cannot get to them!" Ainsley yelled. "We are too late."

Nearly dragging Garret from the structure, Ainsley stumbled from the flames, narrowly missing a flaming beam of wood that broke free from the rafters. The three of them ran around the edge of the building to see a larger group of men had formed a line that reached from the pond up the hill to the barn. The slippery mud, left by weeks of relentless rain, made it difficult for anyone to move and only slowed down progress. The sky was a radiant blue that evening without a cloud for miles. There was no hope of rain to help them that day.

"Look out!" a man yelled. "She's coming down."

A loud crack boomed over the chaos as the ridgepole of the barn buckled. Some of the supporting beams collapsed inward but the ridgepole drifted sideways, tilting in the direction of the house.

"The house!"

"It's heading for the house!"

Indecipherable shouts came from all around as the brigade, a mixture of local men who had all responded at the sight of the smoke, rallied to save the home.

A man began pulling a horseless wagon out from the side of the barn and Ainsley noticed the wheels had caught fire from the heat. With each turn the dry grass singed and it was only a matter of time before the embers grew into flames.

"Stop!" Ainsley shouted as he rushed for the man. As he approached, Ainsley saw a burn wound along the man's arm. "We need water!" Ainsley yelled. He pulled the man away from the burning wagon and urged him toward the pond. "Run and submerse yourself," Ainsley said. "I will see to it once the flames are gone. Go!"

The man hurried to the water and eagerly dove in, hissing at the pain that erupted in his arm. Another man appeared with two buckets of water. Together he and Ainsley doused the flames on the carriage and then guided it away from the barn and into the field. When Ainsley turned he saw his family's carriage coming up the lane with marked speed. Inside sat Jonas, Margaret, Julia, Jamieson, and Maxwell, clinging to the side of the wagon as it bounded over the rough ground. Ainsley grabbed the harness as it drew near and guided the horse to where he could fasten it to the fence.

Maxwell and Jamieson ran to join the brigade without saying anything to Ainsley. Julia and Margaret jumped down, carrying blankets and towels to treat the wounded.

"Where's Ivy?" Margaret asked, panicked.

"I saw her near the house," Ainsley said. "Keep her away, Margaret."

His sister nodded as she and Julia bypassed a group of townswomen who'd come to watch, never daring to pass the safety of the fence line, and ran for the house.

An hour passed easily as Ainsley saw to the wounded, aware of Julia's and Margaret's movements and intent on keeping an eye on them. The fires burned so hot many men suffered burns on their arms and faces as they fought the flames. Julia brought him long bandages, ripped from various linens brought to the scene by neighbours. And together they treated the open and singed flesh with a carbolic acid solution before wrapping the wounds.

Periodically Ainsley scanned the yard for Margaret and eventually spotted her close to the house with a full laundry tub in front of her. She was drenching blankets and linens and placing them on the arms and shoulders of the men so they could approach the heat. Behind her stood a woman who looked similar to Margaret but the heat ripples and heavy smoke made it difficult for Ainsley to see properly. Amongst the chaos and smoke Ainsley didn't recognize her at first and then it hit him like a punch to the gut.

"Mother?"

Ainsley swallowed back flooding emotions, a relief sullied by confusion. She'd been dead for half a year and what he was seeing just wasn't possible.

Then he realized she was looking at him, expressionless but certainly registering him. Feeling panic rising inside him, Ainsley turned away, focusing instead on the man in agony next to him. "My friend will bring you a salve in the morning," he said, tying on a strip of cloth.

Grateful, the man nodded, and Ainsley helped him to his feet. Ainsley watched as the man left, wanting a reason to not turn back to Margaret. Curiosity got the better of him, though, and he looked once again. Sure enough, Mother was there, unscathed by the tragedy all around them. She was not truly there, of course. No one else saw her; Ainsley could tell by the way everyone walked by her, directing the questions to Margaret as they approached.

Ainsley rubbed away the beads of sweat cascading from his hairline. She simply wasn't there, no matter how vivid the image. The thought disturbed him tremendously. Ainsley was slowly losing grip on reality. There simply was no other explanation.

"Peter!"

Julia collided with him as she ran and clung to him, pulling him farther from the barn. The barn had buckled and now the mortar between the stones cracked.

"Away! Away!" Ainsley yelled, waving his arms to bring stragglers away from the collapsing building. Julia clung to him, frightened, and he gladly wrapped his arm around her and guided her back from the flames. Within two steps he lifted her into his arms and ran just as a loud crack pierced the air. The world fell silent, offering only harrowing images of everyone running as far from the barn as they could. As the stones and beams tumbled, the roar of the fire subsided. When Ainsley turned back, he saw that the structure had fallen within ten feet of the farmhouse.

He held to Julia, even as her body slid from his arms. They stood embracing for the shortest of moments before Ainsley felt duty-bound to run back to help extinguish the remaining flames. He cupped her face, pressing a soft kiss onto her forehead before running back to the barn.

"They're trapped!" one man yelled, calling everyone to help.

As the day turned to night the frantic search for the wounded began.

Chapter 14

Though, leaning on my spade to rest,
I've thought how richer folks were blest

The stars began to form in the night sky just as the pump wagon arrived from Tunbridge Wells, but it was too late. All the timber had been consumed. The flames had died down, leaving a shell of blackened stone with a heap of charred beams. A few hot spots remained, revealed as beams and debris were shifted while rescue crews searched for bodies.

Ainsley sat in the grass next to Margaret, who leaned into him. He'd suspected she was nodding off, finally able to rest after hours of demanding work. He too felt the lure of bed and rest. Julia had settled in behind them, close enough that Ainsley could reach a hand below her skirt to rest his palm on her bare ankle. In the failing light he saw her smile.

"My throat hurts," Margaret croaked, half asleep.

"That's from the smoke," Ainsley explained. "I'll contact the chemist in town in the morning. I'm sure we will all need something." He stole a glance to Julia, who looked equally as tired as Margaret but who was forcing herself to remain awake. "You should lie down, Julia," Ainsley suggested. "We'll rally the carriage soon."

She took his advice and settled in, using her arm to cradle her head in the grass.

Ainsley pulled his hand away from the maid's leg just before Nathaniel came into view. Aunt Louisa trailed behind him. A full complement of servants from The Briar followed behind her, each carrying an overflowing basket of food or bottles of drink.

"Here they are, Mother," Nathaniel said.

"Oh my word!" Aunt Louisa's exasperated voice caused Margaret to stir. Ainsley could not help but groan. If anyone deserved to rest it was these two women lying beside him. "I've brought sandwiches," Aunt Louisa said, "and some cordial. I threw in a few bottles of honey wine," she continued as if apologizing, "to keep spirits up."

"That is so kind," Margaret answered dreamily. "Garret and Samuel need something to eat..." Margaret pulled herself up and looked around the yard. The moonlight gave depth to little. It was the handheld lanterns that signalled the positions of those who lingered. "I shall find them," Margaret said, moving as if to stand.

"No," Ainsley answered quickly. "You and Julia rest." Ainsley came to his feet and pulled the basket from his aunt. "Can you take them home?" he asked. "I just want to make sure there is no longer a need for a doctor."

"Can't Dr. Davies see to that?" Aunt Louisa asked, following him for a few steps as he walked away. Her tone was sharp, annoyed.

Ainsley smiled at her naivety. "I have treated nearly ten men with burns to their faces and limbs. Dr. Davies has at least matched me wound for wound. Can you expect me to desert him at such an hour?" Ainsley gave her a look of challenge. "What could be so pressing at The Briar at this hour? Save your self-centred commands for your husband or servant, for I am neither."

He left her, slack-jawed and speechless, and slipped into the darkness to distribute the provisions.

Ainsley found Garret at the site where the barn once stood. No lantern signalled his position, just a form made three-dimensional by the full moon and remaining embers of the fire. Ainsley heard a sniffle as he approached and saw Garret raise his hand to his face.

"My aunt brought bread and cheese," Ainsley said, offering Garret some.

"Thank you." Garret's words were almost given as a laugh.

"I also have wine," Ainsley said with greater enthusiasm. He removed the cork and offered it to Garret. "You need it more than most."

Garret took the bottle reluctantly. "I should find my father," he said. "He'll be needing some by now."

The two men stood surveying the site while taking turns at the bottle. Lanterns bobbed in the darkness all around them. A carriage rolled by, two lanterns lighted on either side, signalling their direction of travel. Ainsley hoped it was his sister and Julia heading back home.

Garret handed the bottle back to Ainsley, who found it empty. "I guess your father will have to wait," he said with a laugh.

"I guess so."

"Do you know what started it all?" Ainsley ventured to ask.

"I was in the lower field." Garret gestured in the direction of the road. "I didn't notice anything was wrong until I saw the smoke." Garret hesitated slightly. "Townsfolk were here within minutes and for a time I thought we had it under control, but the flames caught something and took off without warning. Thank you for helping me release the horses from the south barn."

"Any horses unaccounted for?" Ainsley asked.

"I'll know better in the morning but for now I am down eight head."

Ainsley let out a whistle of surprise.

"A barn can be rebuilt," Garret said, "but those thoroughbreds signify twenty years of breeding. It will take us many more than that to fully recover."

"Surely it's not as bad as all that," Ainsley said.

"And more," Garret answered.

"But the crops?"

"The crops are for my brother Samuel," Garret said. "The horses are our bread and butter. If we can't race, we stand to lose everything."

They were invested greatly. The fire represented an even greater loss than Ainsley first realized.

"Garret, if there's anything—"

"Come quick!" a voiced yelled from the darkness at the edge of the woods. Suddenly, a lantern appeared and began waving back and forth, signalling their whereabouts. "I found a body!"

Ainsley arrived first and was led to an area of tall grass where the body of a man lay. Half his face and one arm was severely burned, showing hints of bone beneath layers of charred flesh. The man who had made the discovery held his light over the body so Ainsley could see. He was clearly dead.

As Ainsley knelt down, Garret arrived at the scene and Jonas soon after. Garret was so worn out Ainsley thought it a miracle the man remained upright.

Ainsley brushed away some blades of grass that had fallen over the dead man's face.

"Father?" Garret pushed past Ainsley and fell to his knees. "Father!" Garret placed a hand on either side of the old man's face and began pulling him up from the ground. "No," Garret yelled. "No!" He gritted his teeth and growled before letting out a visceral scream.

Garret eventually laid his father's body down onto the grass, sobbing uncontrollably as he did so. "Take him to the house," Ainsley commanded one of the other men who'd arrived at the scene. Ainsley and Jonas helped Garret to his feet.

"I cannot leave my father like this," Garret said to Ainsley.

"I will see to your father," he said, reassuringly. "Someone must go tell Samuel and Ivy."

Garret nodded, easily accepting his duty.

As the weeping man left, Ainsley took Jonas's lantern and traced the outline of the body. The old man lay perfectly on his back. He looked to the man who'd raised the alarm. "How did he lie when you found him?"

The man nodded toward the body. "Like this."

"You did not move him?"

"No, sir."

"You dragged him through the grass, did you not?" Ainsley pressed, moving to the dead man's feet and shining a light on the trampled grass that was bent over under the weight of the body.

"Absolutely not," the man answered. "I found him like this. I did not drag him from anywhere."

Ainsley huffed as he looked over the scene. "Well, someone did." A clear line of broken blades of grass could be seen from the back of the barn. Ainsley turned to the crowd that had gathered, circling around them in the dark.

"Did anyone drag this man from the barn?" Ainsley asked, raising his lantern so he could look each man in the face.

"No one is in any trouble," Jonas clarified. "As a man of medicine, I wish to know the circumstances of this man's death."

A few shook their heads and turned to the others standing

near them. Everyone expected someone to come forward but after a few moments it was clear no one would.

Ainsley turned to Jonas. "This body has been moved."

"Could he have been crawling to escape the smoke," Jonas suggested, "and collapsed on his back?"

Ainsley knelt down beside the body, this time closer to the legs.

"That wouldn't explain the drag marks." Ainsley gestured with his lantern and pointed out two distinct channels where the man's legs had trailed behind him. "One leg here, one leg here. The grass between the two legs marks isn't as bruised," Ainsley explained, "which means his torso was upright and his legs were on the grass."

"What are you suggesting?" Jonas asked as Ainsley stood.

"Someone moved him after he died," Ainsley said quietly so only Jonas could hear.

"Perhaps someone pulled him from the fire and hoped it would save his life?"

"Why did no one call for help?"

"Do you believe we could have saved him?" Jonas asked, grimacing at the extent of the man's wounds.

"That's not the point," Ainsley explained. "What would you do if you found someone critically injured?"

Jonas raised an eyebrow.

"All right, what would the average person do in this scenario? You remove them from danger and call for a doctor, even if you think the man is beyond hope. No one raised the alarm or reported there was a body."

"So you think someone is behind this?"

Ainsley was quick to shake his head. "I'm saying someone is hiding something and in my experience, it's more than just a body."

Chapter 15

And knew not quiet was the best.

By late morning the next day, groggy and still suffering the effects of smoke inhalation, Ainsley called a meeting of all in the house, servants and guests alike. They gathered in the foyer, pinched in close due to the confined space. Jamieson stood shoulder to shoulder alongside Maxwell, who sported a bandage secured around his left hand. Ainsley noticed a few of the kitchen maids giving him hesitant glances. It was clear the young butler's heroic deeds of the night had not gone unnoticed.

When Margaret arrived she took her place beside her brother, though somewhat behind, while Julia marched the width of the hall and joined the ranks of her fellow servants. Watching Julia do this stirred a discomfort in Ainsley's stomach. He would have preferred she stay amongst the family, Aunt Louisa, Nathaniel, Margaret, and Jonas. It seemed unnatural for her to be separated from Ainsley when all he wanted was to claim her as his own. Her position in the foyer magnified the inappropriateness of their relationship.

Such a gathering hadn't been held at The Briar in a number of years, not since Lord Marshall lived there. Ainsley had vivid memories of his father leading them all in daily prayer before making clear his expectations of the day. Ainsley himself had no intentions of praying, nor did he see the need to exert his power over anyone.

Ainsley cleared his throat and gracefully placed his hands behind his back.

"As many of you are aware, the barn at Summer Hill has burned down and a body was found nearby." No one moved. Ainsley had no doubt the news had already spread amongst the servants, the gossip creating a tiny flame of its own from eager ear to eager ear. "My good friend Dr. Davies has agreed to look over the corp—" Ainsley stopped, suddenly remembering to whom he was speaking, "the body."

"Is it true the body is in the cellar?" one of the young, impertinent kitchen maids asked. She got a sharp elbow to her ribs from the slightly older girl standing beside her.

"Hold your tongue while Mr. Marshall speaks," Mrs. Hoffman, the housekeeper snapped.

"It's all right," Ainsley said, raising a hand to encourage calm. "Mr. Owen's body has indeed been placed in the ice house and the door locked—"

"Locked? Merciless heavens!" Mrs. Hoffman began to fan herself.

"Is he expected to spring back to life, sir?" the second footman asked, inciting giggles from the other servants, save a few who stirred nervously.

"Enough!" Aunt Louisa slapped her hand on the side table, her palm hitting the surface with enough force to cause the vase and flowers to teeter in place. "Never have I witnessed such behaviour!"

The faces opposite them blanched at Aunt Louisa's words. Ainsley did not require blind obedience, but he had to admit in times such as these it proved useful.

"We have offered assistance to the Owen family," Ainsley said, "I have promised them our discretion in all things. I will ask that you refrain from repeating things overheard in these rooms and that you observe silence when someone outside The Briar wishes to speculate. Our intent is to be a help, not a hindrance, to the family in their time of sorrow. I am expecting your full cooperation in this matter," Ainsley said, releasing his hands and placing one in his trouser pockets. "Anyone who feels themselves above these expectations will be dismissed without reference. Is that understood?"

He spotted a few nods from the crowd. "Yes, sir," they said in a disjointed unison.

"Very well," he said with a nod, "you may return to your normal assignments unless otherwise appointed."

There was a rush of movement as the servants retreated from the foyer, scurrying for the back kitchen and beyond, already whispering to each other. Julia, however, skipped upstairs and turned toward Margaret's room. Ainsley hadn't realized he was watching her leave until Nathaniel appeared beside him. "That's the kind of maid you hear tell about," he said suggestively.

Ainsley revealed a stern expression. "Pardon me?"

Nathaniel's expression fell. "I was only saying Miss Margaret's maid is—" Nathaniel stopped abruptly.

"We do not encourage fraternization with our staff," Ainsley said. "Should I catch you engaging in any such activity I shall secure you a stall in the barn where you will be more comfortable."

"I was only commenting…I wasn't saying…" Nathaniel's voice trailed off with uncertainty. Perhaps he had heard of Ainsley's reputation; the young, wild cousin back in England who enjoyed drink, gambling, and women. Perhaps he had pictured a man more willing to bend moral code and look the other way for the sake of another man's sport.

Ainsley did nothing to hide his distaste for Nathaniel's comments as he watched Margaret, Jonas, and Aunt Louisa pass him and Nathaniel, making their way into the library.

"I can tell you are angry about last night," Nathaniel said, calling his cousin's attention back to him. "I would have come to help but Mother wouldn't let me."

Ainsley stifled a laugh. "You are nineteen, are you not?"

Nathaniel nodded.

"Then I should say you have reached an age where it matters not what your mother may or may not let you do."

"That's hardly fair," Nathaniel answered.

"You know what's not fair? Having every man within ten miles risk fire and smoke to save a family who might have otherwise lost their home while one man hides behind his mother's skirts. Last night, I saw men with half their faces burnt and others who won't be able to speak for weeks due to the pain in their throats. But you are all right, and that makes it all better." Ainsley's teasing smile turned sour as he turned into his library and shut the door in Nathaniel's face.

Margaret's shoulders sank. "Was that really necessary?"

"Yes." Ainsley walked past and took his seat amongst his sketches and insects. He hadn't realized how tired he truly was until he leaned into his desktop, slumped his chin into his propped-up hand, and allowed his eyes to drift over his work. That last altercation with Nathaniel was the final straw in a succession of physical and emotional demands.

It did not matter that it was hardly noon. Ainsley opened the top drawer of his desk and retrieved a bottle of scotch he had stashed there. He hadn't the patience for a glass and instead drank straight from the bottle. The liquid was a soothing release, an elixir of painkiller and energy that settled the trembling in his stomach and mind with the first taste.

"Peter, you need some sleep," Margaret said at last.

While everyone else had time to return home to rest and wash, Ainsley remained at the Owen farm for some time, first seeing to the last of the injured and then helping to settle the horses in The Briar's stables and pastures. Sleep seemed like a far off mirage, elusive yet ever so inviting.

"I shall sleep when I'm—" Ainsley stopped, suddenly distracted by movement in the corner of his eye. Instinctively, he turned toward it, expecting to see Margaret or Jonas pacing the room, but saw no one. When he looked back to the others he saw they hadn't moved from their previous places.

"Dead," Jonas finished with an arch in his eyebrow.

Ainsley looked toward him, startled.

"I took Hollinger's class as well," Jonas answered, reminding Ainsley from where he had stolen his maxim. Ainsley could only manage a nod.

"I do believe he has paled," Aunt Louisa said, suddenly getting up from her place and walking toward him. "Have you eaten anything, Peter?"

Ainsley pulled away from his desk and tilted back his chair. He lifted his heels to the desktop and crossed his ankles before taking a long draw from the bottle of scotch.

Aunt Louisa tried to fuss but Ainsley swiped her hand away. "Leave me," he muttered, eyeing the bottle and marvelling at how quickly the liquid had disappeared.

"You need food," Margaret said, moving to the edge of her seat.

Ainsley avoided looking at her and instead focused on the patch of decaying wallpaper in the farthest corner of the room. He was becoming unhinged, separated from reality. The visions were becoming more frequent, the sensations harder to explain. He could feel his mother in the room, lurking like a fly flittering from one spot to the next, begging to be noticed. She was there like every other soul who still haunted his dreams. Training his eyes to the corner prevented him from seeing them but did nothing for the feeling their presence ignited at the base of his neck.

He shook his head slightly, a gesture meant to refocus his thoughts. "I'm heading back to Summer Hill later this afternoon," he proclaimed. "Garret sent me a message that an inspector is expected at the farm today and Garret would like me present, if I were available. I see no reason why I should not attend."

Ainsley saw Margaret and Aunt Louisa exchange glances.

"And we have arranged for Miss Ivy to stay with us for a few days until matters settle down." Ainsley shot a look to Jonas, who nodded his understanding. There was no better way to hide the procedure they planned and Ainsley's offer to conceal it so cleanly was as close to support as Jonas could expect.

"Oh," Aunt Louisa said. She sat up taller and pulled back her shoulders. "Perhaps Mr. Samuel and Mr. Garret would like a reprieve as well. Why should their sister have all the pampering?" She turned to Margaret excitedly. "We could—"

"No," Ainsley answered plainly. "They are to stay at Summer Hill. Once the investigation has concluded, they will rebuild their barns. Ivy will only be here for a few days."

A doubtful look washed over Aunt Louisa's features but she said nothing. Ainsley could see her jaw tighten as she pressed out the folds in her shirt.

"Maxwell has injured his hand," Ainsley said, turning his attention to Jonas. "Make sure he is seen to. Until he heals he'll be little use to us and we are already stretched as it is."

Margaret inched toward to edge of her seat. "I've asked Cook to prepare some baskets of food and provisions that we can take to anyone who is injured. We're headed to town this afternoon for supplies."

Aunt Louisa scoffed. "It isn't necessary for you to go yourself, Margaret," she said with a chuckle lacing her voice. "You prepare your lists and send your staff." Aunt Louisa looked about the room, seeking agreement from Ainsley and the others.

"But why shouldn't I go?" Margaret asked, her marked seriousness contrasting against Aunt Louisa's laughing tone. "Mother and I—"

Aunt Louisa sighed heavily and turned from Margaret. She waved a weak hand dismissively as she focused more intently on Ainsley. "You were saying, Peter?"

Ainsley hesitated. He could see Margaret trembling ever so slightly as she adjusted in her seat, the enthusiasm for her efforts lost. He had no doubt she vacillated between challenging their aunt's officious behaviour and holding her tongue. Everyone was exceedingly tired and anxious.

"I think it is good that you go," Ainsley said making sure to look at Margaret directly. He ignored the look of disdain directed toward him from his father's sister. "Your personal touch will be appreciated by all recipients, I am sure." Ainsley took a moment to steel himself against the next thing he wanted to say. Playing with a pen on his desk, he cleared his throat. "Aunt Louisa, I trust you have more than enough demands on your mind what with hiring staff and seeing to arrangements at your own family's estate. I certainly don't want you becoming preoccupied with our affairs."

Never had Ainsley seen his aunt look so sour.

"I would be remiss if I didn't—"

"Save your mothering. We have little need of it here," Ainsley offered quickly, putting an abrupt end to her needless intrusions.

"I wouldn't be so sure about that." Aunt Louisa sneered as she stood up and pressed the creases from her skirt.

Ainsley watched as she quitted the room, offering one final glance at the threshold before disappearing into the hall.

Ainsley turned back to Jonas and heaved a laborious sigh. "I need to examine the body and perform a quick postmortem. Garret has asked that we do it. Something about the local doctor being unfit for the task."

Jonas nodded. "Of course."

"I'd like to help," Margaret said.

Ainsley looked up from the papers in front of him.

"It's been a few months but I'd like to assist."

"No." Ainsley pulled a notebook from the top shelf of his desk.

"Peter, you can't mean that!"

"I think it's worthwhile to allow her some practice," Jonas

said, coming quickly to her defence.

"Why? So we can both disappoint our father greatly? Is it not enough to have one ne'er-do-well in the family?" He saw Jonas bristle at the accusation that his profession was less worthy of others. "Besides, what good is such practice when no medical school in the country allows female students?"

Ainsley went straight for the cupboard at the end of the hall, knowing that was where Jamieson kept all the keys for any given room at The Briar. Medical bag in hand, Jonas tagged along behind, showing interest in the workings of the back rooms by peeking in doorways and paying close attention to what each maid may have been carrying as they walked by.

"Are the staff always so lively?" he asked as he came alongside Ainsley, who was figuring out which key opened the cellar door.

"I doubt it," Ainsley said, plucking up the one he wanted. "They tend to perk up when one of the family is about. If you think The Briar's kitchen is impressive, you should see the one at Marshall House. Twice the staff without the quiet of the country to contend with. Not to mention my father keeping a close eye on things."

"An exacting man, is he?"

Ainsley tilted his head and smiled. "And so you understand why he and my mother never got along."

The cellar was constructed out of layers of stone, strategically placed and cemented together with thick applications of mortar. The stairs themselves were stone, slick with the damp of the place, which grew worse the farther down they went, guided by the stream of light cascading from the cellar door.

"Mind your step," Ainsley said to his friend as he reached the bottom. A consortium of underservants looking down at them from the kitchen dispersed rapidly when Ainsley looked up at them. Jonas smiled at the ruckus.

"Who needs the post with that lot poking about?" he quipped. "Half the county will know what transpired here by nightfall."

Ainsley chuckled, knowing what his friend said was true.

At the bottom of the stairs was a thin table where two

lanterns were placed. Ainsley lit them both and handed one to Jonas.

A maze of rooms, some with wooden doors and others without, the cellar was more or less empty, save for remnants of the previous years' harvest. Weathered wooden bins and shelving, fastened securely, lined the outer walls. Tiny, ruddy windows let in a small amount of light but not enough to make any sort of difference to the dark atmosphere. Years prior, Mrs. Harrison stumbled upon a vagrant who had breached one of the windows and made a home for himself amongst the food and provisions. Half-starved and maimed by a mining accident, the man was arrested and sent to prison, whereas Lady Marshall said she would have preferred him to be taken to the workhouse. The discovery, however, created such a to-do amongst the staff that the eight-year-old Peter suffered relentless nightmares in which a deformed fiend clawed its way up to Margaret's room while the family slept.

An eerie feeling crept up the back of Ainsley's neck at the memory, forcing him to throw up his hand to massage it away. "I told them Mr. Owen should be brought back here," Ainsley said, leading the way.

Chilled by the lack of sunlight and a generous cache of ice in the back rooms, they could see their breath as Ainsley led them down the centre aisle to the coldest room of all. The body of Mr. Owen was laid out on a long, wide board held off the ground by two columns of ice, one at the head, the other at the feet. A thin sheet had been laid over him, covering the body from view.

Ainsley hung his lantern on a nail in the beam above them while Jonas placed his on a table to the side and proceeded to empty his medical bag of the tools he would need. "I'm afraid I wasn't prepared for this type of work," Jonas said. "I'm not sure my knives will do for breaking the sternum."

Ainsley waved off his concern. "I doubt we will need to, but I asked Jamieson to bring some of the tools from the garden shed." He gestured to the crate at the side of the table.

"Peter, you didn't."

"Why not?" Ainsley asked, pulling back the cloth that covered Mr. Owen's body. "We needn't concern ourselves with infection."

Jonas gave him a disapproving look but did not protest further. "I suppose I am not as accustomed to working with dead patients as some."

"We can't all be perfect," Ainsley answered.

Jonas laughed. "I'm going to miss this," he said as he watched Ainsley lean over the corpse.

"What do you mean?"

"I've accepted a position at Edinburgh," Jonas explained. "I'm afraid the position means I won't have much interaction with cadavers," Jonas said. "My understanding is that it is mostly administrative with some coordination work at the hospital."

The revelation came over Ainsley like a punch to the abdomen he wasn't expecting. Since the first day of medical school they had been as thick as thieves, figuratively and literally. During the day they competed with each other for top marks for most of their courses and then dug up corpses at night from freshly made graves in outlying communities to earn some shillings for Jonas's tuition. Their midnight activities were never detected but the act bonded them like brothers, making them nearly inseparable.

"Don't give me that look," Jonas said, snapping Ainsley from his memories.

"What look?"

"The look that says you are very disappointed in me." Jonas shook his head. "I can't stand that look."

"I did nothing of the sort."

Jonas shook his head in protest and turned his attention to the corpse between them.

"Does Margaret know?" Ainsley asked suddenly.

Jonas looked up, licking his lips hesitantly. "I meant to tell her when I first came but…it never felt like the right time."

"She's not going to like it," Ainsley confessed.

His friend nodded thoughtfully. "Nothing lasts forever."

Chapter 16

Go with your tauntings, go;

The barn was a heap of rubble in an otherwise unchanged landscape. What remained of the stables was charred beyond recognition with only a few skeletal beams, blackened and shrunk, protruding from the mound of toppled stone. From his horse Ainsley saw Garret seated on the grassy hill that overlooked the remaining debris. He dismounted slowly, keeping hold of the horse's reins and leading the gelding to the nearby fence to tether him.

Garret only looked up when Ainsley's shadow eclipsed him and even then his gaze was unsure, his focus distant and soft. Never had Ainsley seen such a mournful creature. Garret looked back to his hands, which were knitted in front of him, propped up by his bent knees.

"Samuel blames me, you know," he said. "Said it was I who drove him to drink." A nervous chuckle escaped his lips, hinting at the audacity of his brother's claims. "As if anyone had such power." He scratched at the side of his face, his nails scraping along the stubble of his whiskers.

Ainsley took a seat beside him, settling into the grass with a thud that highlighted his fatigue.

"I know what you say is true," Garret said, looking up suddenly, squinting against the sun. "Someone killed my father."

"What remains to be answered is how and why," Ainsley said, his tone somber. "I was hoping you could help us sort through this puzzle."

Garret exhaled and returned his gaze to the remains of the barn.

"I can't claim to know how the mind of a murderer works," Ainsley said. "There are murders committed on purpose, they are preplanned and precisely executed. There are murders resulting from passion and uncontrollable rage. And there are murders that could not be foreseen and can be considered purely accidental."

"You are asking me which is more likely in my father's case?" Garret asked.

"Any insight is beneficial," Ainsley said. "The detectives will ask."

Garret nodded. The inspectors were to arrive any minute but Ainsley had an inkling Garret wasn't going to wait to share his suspicions. "Ivy has been increasingly unpredictable," he said as he rubbed his temples. He scrunched up his face as if it pained him to say anything against her. "I've caught her speaking aloud as if engaged in some argument—only no one is there. She cries without cause, at least none that I can see." Garret swallowed. "I've been worried for some time that it may come to this, that she may do harm to herself…or others."

Ainsley shifted uncomfortably. Perhaps he had done the family a disservice by dismissing her erratic behaviour while she stayed at The Briar. Had he told Garret she wished to die, would his father still be alive?

"You cannot be held responsible for the actions of another," Ainsley said by reflex. He did not truly believe the words, however. He blamed himself nearly every day for his mother's end.

"I do not wish to inform the inspector," Garret said as if suddenly remembering, "not yet, at any rate."

Ainsley nodded cautiously. "Do you believe her capable of another crime?"

"Perhaps, though I certainly hope it is truly what you classify as an accident," Garret said. "I'm afraid our family could not recover should she be arrested and tried, even if she were found innocent. Suspicion is enough for people to shy away."

What Garret said was true. Despite elaborate laws governing fair trials and ensuring due process, there were many who would be quick to judge the family for even a hint of accusation. It was a stigma that would haunt them for generations to come.

"I do not desire scandal," Ainsley said. He was in no position to single out another lest he himself be set upon and scrutinized. It was this fear that kept him mentally caged and unable to help in ways that would have come so easy to him as his former self. Judging by Garret's budding smile, however, Ainsley knew his motivations were misunderstood.

"That is very good to know," Garret said. "Very good, indeed. You and your friend have discussed the proposal I put before you earlier."

"Dr. Davies has agreed to it, solely for the girl's benefit," Ainsley said. He scanned the fields that surrounded the barn and marvelled at the empty quiet, a stark contrast to the evening before.

Garret spoke with great relief. "My sister and I are much obliged—"

"I have my concerns," Ainsley said quickly, wishing to forgo any need for exuberant gratitude. He was in no mood to hear how Jonas was, yet again, proving invaluable. "You ask me to open my home and I will do so for the well-being of your sister but..." Ainsley's voice trailed off, unable to bring himself to say he was scared of the possible outcome.

He was never so scared when he and Jonas harvested freshly buried bodies from the city cemeteries, nor had he been as scared when he drank and gambled the weeks away in the illegal gambling dens Jonas had introduced him to. He had been no stranger to illicit acts, either noble or otherwise, and yet for some reason a persistent fear kept a hold of him, tainting everything he wished to do.

In his heart, he believed ending the pregnancy was right for the girl, especially now given Garret's suspicions of her, but that did not ease the worry that plagued him. He had eluded the long arm of the law for much of his life, saved by his rank of birth and his family's fortune, no doubt. He was convinced now that it was only a matter of time before his luck ran out.

"My involvement ends there," Ainsley said firmly. "For my own family's sake."

Garret nodded. "Fair enough."

A few moments later, the police carriage appeared at the end of the lane and began making its way up the slight hill toward the farm. Ainsley and Garret watched as the carriage stopped on the opposite side of the rubble. A single detective slipped from the cab, dressed in a severely starched, navy blue uniform complete with sparkling silver buttons and a crisp notebook in hand. He tipped his hat toward Ainsley and Garret as he made his way toward them. "Good day, sirs," he said. His attempt to sound stern was lost thanks to a smile that curled the edges of his mouth. "Detective Inspector Marley. Would you be a Mr. Garret Owen?" he asked, offering his hand to Ainsley.

"No sir," Ainsley answered, "This is Mr. Owen. I am merely a neighbour assisting."

Garret stepped forward and shook the detective's hand. "Hello, sir."

"May I have your name for my records?" Inspector Marley stood primly, his notebook poised to collect any information they divulged.

"My name is Peter Marshall, sir, from The Briar."

The inspector whistled as he inked the page. "Is that so?" He offered a smile. "How do you expect to assist us then, given you do not live on the property?" he asked. He winked at Garret. Ainsley could already see Inspector Marley was a playful sort, and not at all able to hide his jovial nature.

"I was present when the body was found," Ainsley said. He coughed, feeling the burn from the smoke pull at his throat.

"A body? What kind of body?" Marley asked.

"A human body," Ainsley answered. "Mr. Owen's father. He was found amongst the wreckage." Ainsley gestured toward the heap near them, nearly to the exact spot where the body had been discovered.

The detective whistled again, and shook his head. "Unfortunate, indeed." The detective raised his notebook to write something down. "Smoke inhalation, I image. Overcome by the heat." Inspector Marley gave a couple nods toward Garret as if to reassure him.

"I don't think you understand, Inspector," Garret said. "Mr. Marshall here believes my father was untimely dispatched."

Confused, the inspector raised an eyebrow.

"He was murdered," Garret said, spelling it out plainly.

A stunned quiet blanketed the inspector, who after a moment of thought shook his head. "I highly doubt it," he said. He gave a nervous chuckle as he surveyed the damage.

Ainsley glanced to Garret, who stood expressionless while flexing a fist at his side again and again. Ainsley raised a hand in reassurance and began to follow Inspector Marley through the debris. An aura of heat still radiated from the highest mounds. Ainsley watched as Marley sauntered through the middle of what was once the Owens's barn, mindful of his freshly shined boots and avoiding anything that would tarnish his uniform. Marley paused at one mound of collapsed field stones that had once made up the foundation for the barn. Ainsley saw him looking over the unremarkable stones as he ran his free hand down along the buttons of his uniform.

Standing rigid the inspector mumbled to himself slightly and surveyed the remains of the barn with a fleeting interest.

Ainsley himself had come prepared to shift beams and stones, knowing it would be the best way to determine the cause of the fire. It unsettled him to see the inspector so reluctant to investigate.

"Shouldn't we seek out the cause?" Ainsley asked.

Marley chuckled out one side of his mouth, still fingering his shiny buttons. "I'm afraid the cause has been lost in the heat." The inspector began to walk back toward Ainsley. "We may never know what caused the fire."

Ainsley surveyed the damage. Some of the stone walls remained upright while others had collapsed, either from something falling into them or the beam which held them in place caught. Ainsley saw a tangle of beams and rocks. Beneath he could see the floorboards had been burnt away. However, the floorboards farther into the structure were blackened but not completely consumed.

Something in the coals caught the sun and reflected a beam of light back at Ainsley as he searched. It was only a flash and then was gone. Ainsley stopped midstep and retreated, keeping his eye trained on the spot where he had first seen the glint. After a few attempts he could not recreate the light so he knelt closer and used a nearby stick to sift through the coals.

"What is it, Mr. Marshall?" Garret asked.

Ainsley could hear him drawing closer behind him. "I'm not entirely sure."

Inspector Marley kept his distance and Ainsley wondered if the man doubted his sincerity. Perhaps he was threatened by the prospect of Ainsley finding a lead before he had even decided the fire was worth investigating.

Finally, Ainsley saw the glint of sun again. It was a piece of thin glass, broken on all sides from a larger piece. The piece was partially blackened by soot from the fire. Ainsley lifted it to the sun and found it had a curve to it. "It's from a lamp," he said, turning the piece over so Garret could see.

Garret took the shard and laid it out on his open palm while he fingered it. "The entire barn was fitted with lamps," he said, a look of confusion spreading over his face. "They could be taken down and moved to wherever needed."

"So the presence of glass is not unusual?" Inspector Marley asked, a self-satisfied grin spreading over his face.

"That is curved glass," Ainsley pointed out. Suddenly, he stooped down and pulled an iron frame from beneath a plank of wood. The frame had once been a lantern and, though mangled, it still bore the relative shape of a straight-sided lantern. "I believe the lanterns that outfitted the barn were geometrically straight." Ainsley raised an eyebrow, playfully challenging Inspector Marley's conclusion.

Garret looked from the lantern frame to the glass in his hand. "But it was early evening," he offered. "No one would need a lantern with the sun still so high."

"Not even in a barn sheltered by trees in the west?" Ainsley looked over the outline of where the barn once stood. "By the looks of it we are in the middle of a rather wide building. I'm guessing even in the middle of the day this particular spot would be darker."

"I suppose I never noticed," Garret said, giving a look to the inspector. "I'm only ever in here long enough to retrieve a horse and pitch some hay."

"The lanterns would not have been lit," Inspector Marley said, clearing his throat. "The expense for fuel alone would make that clear. Perhaps folks at The Briar are not accustomed to such...economy."

Ainsley could not help but grin at the presumption. He looked to Garret but the man avoided his gaze.

"The truth is," the inspector began to retrace his steps through the ash, "we may never find a cause. Any evidence was lost in the heat of the fire." Once safe from all hazards he pulled at the hem of his jacket and adjusted his collar before raising his notebook and beginning to write.

"That's not good enough," Ainsley said as he picked his way toward the detective. "We owe it to this family to find out how this happened."

Ainsley watched as the inspector pursed his lips, pressing out air and making an odd sucking sound. "Mr. Owen, you tell me what happened," the inspector said after a moment. "Where were you when the fire broke out?"

Garret bore the look of a whipped dog, unable to look the detective or Ainsley in the eyes. He looked almost apologetic, as if he agreed with the detective that he and Ainsley were wasting his time.

"I was in the lower field," he said, "seeing to a horse that injured his foot in his last race."

"Wasn't Red Runner, was it?" Inspector Marley turned to Ainsley, tapping his chest as if they were old friends. "My wife loves that horse. Wins for her every time."

Ainsley's jaw tightened.

"No," Garret said. "Wasn't Red Runner."

"Who else was here on the property?" Ainsley asked, eager to get to the details.

Garret shrugged. "Everyone. Ivy, Samuel. A few of our farmhands. Mr. Thornton, of course, he came to run Elixir before their hunt next week. He brought his brother as well but he only watched. I could see them from the field."

Inspector Marley wrote feverishly, trying to keep notes as Garret spoke. "Anyone else?"

"I have half a dozen hands on the farm at any given time," Garret said. "And any number of clients."

"Any near the barn?" Ainsley asked.

"I can't say," Garret said. "John was with me. Other than that I can't be sure."

"They should all be interviewed," Ainsley said.

"Well now, let's not be hasty," Inspector Marley said with a laugh. "I couldn't possibly interview them all."

"Isn't that what you are paid to do?" Ainsley asked.

The inspector gave Ainsley a stern look before returning his attention to his notebook. He jotted his notes slowly, which created an agonizing wait for Ainsley, who had seen much better detective work in the city.

"I will see who I can find," Inspector Marley said, heaving a great breath before replacing his notebook in his pocket. "Now, show me this body."

Chapter 17

Ne'er think to hurt me so;

There was a feeling of unease gnawing at Margaret. She found herself jittery and light, which was so unlike her usual assured self. The past year had changed her irrevocably, but she did not like this anxiety that lingered, circulating inside her like a sink of water rushing all at once for the drain. In order to busy herself and distract her churning mind, Margaret tracked Jamieson down in the pantry and asked him to let her into the potter's shed.

The country butler gave her a half smile over his clipboard. "Those doors have not been darkened for some time," he said. "Give it a day and I'll see to it Maxwell tidies it up for you."

"I haven't a care to wait," she said. "A few spiders and such don't bother me in the slightest."

Jamieson lowered his clipboard, holding it primly in front of him with both hands. "What is it you intend to do?"

Margaret was taken aback by his inquisition. Her intention was to tackle the gardens, pull out the dead and crusty remains so that the live plants could have more space and access to the sun. She wanted to revitalize things, perhaps return them to their previous splendor while working out her inner tensions. Hacking and yanking at weeds and overgrowth appeared oddly therapeutic. She may never have handled the task before, but the butler's doubt in her seemed highly unwarranted.

"What does anyone do?" she asked with a shrug. "I intend to do the best with what we have."

There was a time when Margaret would receive anything she asked, especially from the family's servants. A child raised in a noble family with governesses, nannies, and tutors enjoyed concentrated attention day in and day out. Often doted upon for being the only girl, Margaret was given special attention and, for many years, was allowed to do as she pleased.

But as an adult she was coming to realize that she was far

from free. Without being able to call herself mistress, the servants held more power than she. She realized, as the butler stood opposite her, that he was under no obligation to grant her request.

To her relief, Jamieson relented. He called over her shoulder to Maxwell, who looked out of place in the kitchen, an apron about his waist and a generous helping of flour coating his hands. "You there," Jamieson called, "Assist Miss Marshall with the gardens. The set of keys are in the cupboard at the end of the hall."

Maxwell nodded as he wiped off his hands. Margaret swore she saw Cook give a sigh of relief as the city butler removed his apron and exited the room. Margaret followed, a burgeoning smile tickling the corners of her mouth.

"How is the country treating you, Maxwell?" Margaret asked as the butler led the way down the hall.

"I believe the country air agrees with me, miss," he said, looking over his shoulder to offer a smile.

A shallow cupboard hid in the wall nearest the door and housed nearly twenty sets of keys to various locks scattered about the estate. It took some time for Maxwell to discover which ones were intended for the shed.

"And the other servants, have they been agreeable?"

Maxwell licked his lips and Margaret's expression fell. "Tensions are high, miss," he said by way of offering an excuse. "There has been a great deal of stress."

Margaret nodded, recognizing for the first time how the sudden arrival of so many people was affecting the normally subdued country estate. She doubted the dead body in the cold cellar was helping matters much.

"Julia told me some of the kitchen girls refused to work this morning," Margaret said as Maxwell plucked two canvas aprons from a nearby hook.

Maxwell nodded. "Said something about not wanting to share the air with the body, miss."

Margaret nearly laughed out loud at this. "You are far more sensible, aren't you, Maxwell?"

"The air is still a hundred times better than what could be found in the city, even if I do have to share it with the deceased Mr. Owen." Maxwell gave Margaret a funny little nod and wink before opening the door and allowing her to pass through.

The gardens themselves were a collection of slightly raised beds arranged in an ornate, complicated design. Meant to be walked through at a leisurely pace, the garden included flowering plants and medicinal herbs that Margaret remembered her mother installing when she and her brothers were still under the care of a nanny, and not yet the governess. Positioned between the east wing and the kitchen addition, the gardens dominated the courtyard. Though sheltered from the worst of the wind and the harshest afternoon sun, the garden now looked overgrown and neglected.

As Maxwell rummaged through the weatherworn potting shed, Margaret took a survey of the work needed and quickly decided much would need to go. She imagined under some of the bushes and brambles lay hidden plants screaming for sun. A quick rummage through the foliage reinforced her theory and without a moment of hesitation Margaret began a fury of work. She ripped at browned stems and tore through a pile of dead and decaying leaves. When Maxwell appeared at her side he brought a rickety wooden wheelbarrow and an assortment of tools.

"Are you sure you wouldn't rather just watch me do the dirty work?" he asked, slipping on a pair of garden gloves.

Margaret smiled as she wiped her brow. "Certainly not. You can see to the bushes there," she said, pointing a few paces away. "They need to be cut back and shaped, if you have the patience. Mind your hand though," she said, indicating the bandage. "I wouldn't want you aggravating your injury."

"Yes, miss."

After a time Julia arrived to join them. She worked alongside Margaret, though she had trouble matching her mistress's frantic pace.

"Look at this," Margaret said, between puffs of breath. "Look how much we've done." Margaret gestured to the long row of greenery she had exposed under the dead foliage and smiled. "I do believe I have done more work this past hour than I have done my entire life."

Julia smiled and continued her work as she spoke. "That might be a slight exaggeration," she said, glancing to her mistress.

"Perhaps," Margaret answered. She paused for a break and watched Maxwell as he inched along the bushes, pruning with more precision than was truly necessary. "I know now why my mother enjoyed it out here," Margaret said, sitting back on her heels. "In the city, I feel like I am being spied upon every waking moment, where out here I feel free to do as I please." Margaret eased her pace as she spoke but never entirely stopped her progress. "Her friends teased her relentlessly. Father as well. They all asked if she missed good theatre, or visiting the shops. I once overheard Father call her feral. Perhaps he thought it would entice her to return to civilization."

"And you, miss?"

Margaret shrugged. "For many years I held no opinion one way or the other. I preferred my mother's company, difficult as she was in recent years, so I stayed here. Even when Daniel and Peter left for school I stayed."

"That was good of you, miss," Julia said.

A smile touched Margaret's lips. "I think a quiet country life suits me best. Or at least it will once Peter returns to the city. I think I've had just about enough of his sulking."

"Do you think it likely Mr. Marshall will return to the city soon?" Julia asked as she dove under a bush to retrieve a handful of dead leaves.

"Most certainly," Margaret said. "He likes to think he can retreat, forget a world beyond this house exists but I know him better than anyone. One day his sense of duty will return and he'll head back to his morgue, back to those who need him most."

"He's a good man, your brother," Julia said definitively as she pulled back from the bush, "if you don't mind me saying so."

"He was once," Margaret said looking up to the house that loomed over them. "I can't say what he is now."

Margaret saw Julia's gaze drop to her hands as a nervousness overtook her. As if knowing she was being watched, the maid tried to offer a playful smile but Margaret saw through it.

"Shall I start on the other side, miss?" Julia asked brightly, offering an opportunity to change the subject.

There was something happening to Julia that Margaret hadn't noticed before, something about the way Julia's eyes brightened when they spoke of her brother. Even though the maid had always been pleasant and jolly Margaret saw a lightness in her features, a contentment that hadn't been there before.

Margaret could feel her heart rising in her chest as the realization dawned on her. "Please, not Peter," she said, trying to find her breath. "Anyone but him."

Margaret rose suddenly, unable to think or even grasp what had all but been confessed to her. There was no need for Julia to speak because Margaret knew. Perhaps she had known long before that moment and now her inkling had been solidified.

The garden spun as she found her feet and she was forced to stand momentarily as she pressed an open hand into her bodice. She pulled at the lace scarf around her neck, and was thankful for the cool breeze that instantly soothed her.

"Has he shown an interest in you?" Margaret asked, without thinking of the implications. "Of course he has," she said, answering her own question, and resigning herself to the evidence.

Julia scrambled to her feet, a look of panic washing over her. "Lady Margaret… I…"

Margaret shook her head and began rubbing mindlessly at the scar on her neck.

"Margaret?"

Jonas's voice found them from the door to the house. He smiled when she looked toward him.

Julia used the hem of her apron to dry her tears and Margaret scrambled to find her scarf, which she had let fall to the gravel walkway. Hastily, she replaced the lace around her collar, and was slightly assured that she had covered her wound before Jonas could see.

"Jonas," she said, struggling to keep an even tone to her voice. She could feel Julia behind her, tucking the lace around her bodice.

She turned to Julia. "Haven't you something to do in the house?"

"Yes, miss." Julia gave a slight curtsey but avoided lifting her gaze.

Jonas gave a confused look. "I'm not interrupting, am I?" he asked.

Margaret forced herself to look away from the house. She was worried her anger would get the better of her and cause her to do something she'd regret. Her brother, and his flirtatious nature, had compromised her own maid, the only servant she could call friend. She wondered how far they had taken their attentions.

"Margaret, what is it?"

When Margaret looked to Jonas he betrayed his worry. He glanced back to the house just as Julia disappeared through the door.

"How long have you know about them?" Margaret asked pointedly. "About Peter and Julia," she clarified when he didn't answer straightaway.

At first he looked as if he would deny any knowledge but then he lost his resolve. "A few weeks," he said.

"And you didn't say anything to me?"

"You've made it very clear your brother's exploits are of no interest to you," Jonas said, smiling.

"You find me amusing?" Margaret crossed her arms over her chest.

"I find you entirely amusing." Jonas stepped closer, which forced Margaret to raise her chin to look him in the eyes. He placed a hand on the side of her face and rubbed her cheek with his thumb. "You can hardly object to them," he said.

Margaret felt the warmth of his other hand as he pressed it into the small of her back. She closed her eyes and for a moment she was able to find relief from the anxiety that threatened to overtake her. Her fears for Ivy, her distrust of that family, and concerns regarding Peter had a stronger hold on her than she realized. When she was with Jonas, all those worries disappeared and all she wanted to do was live in his embrace. Happy and comforted.

She lowered her face into his chest and wrapped her arms around him. She didn't care if anyone saw them, and cared even less for any repercussions their discovery might bring. Secretly, she hoped Aunt Louisa would spy them. Perhaps her aunt would tell her father, which would effectively force their hand and end this tiresome game of love without a future.

She heard and felt the beating of Jonas's heart through his

chest and smiled because she understood now that it beat for her.

"There's something I must tell you," Jonas said, his tone serious.

Reluctantly, Margaret pulled away and looked up at him.

"It's the reason I came here actually. I couldn't bring myself to tell you before," he said. He exhaled deeply before continuing. "I've been offered a position at Edinburgh. I'm to work under Dr. Tilford. He has undertaken some ambitious projects…" He cut short his enthusiasm when Margaret began to walk away. "This changes nothing about how I feel for you."

She couldn't help but laugh at the sentiment. Edinburgh may as well been as far away as India for all the freedom her family afforded her. There was no hope of her ever being able to visit and she highly doubted a doctor's salary, even one employed by the university, could afford regular visits back to London.

"I thought…" Jonas stumbled, stepping closer to her and looking around to ensure they were not being watched. "I thought maybe you'd like to come with me."

"With you?" She placed a hand on her stomach in an effort to steady her breathing.

"As my wife, naturally." He stammered and looked to the ground. "I'd never dream of implying anything else." He took a breath and closed his eyes for a moment. "It's just that it appears I may be gone for quite some time, years even. I'd never forgive myself if I didn't at least make it known that that is what I desired."

"You desire me as your wife." Margaret could barely get the words out, given the thundering of her heart.

"It's ridiculous, that is, to think that you would ever consider me, not that you marrying me would be ridiculous." He pressed his lips together as if chiding himself for fumbling so with his words. "I love you, Margaret. I have for many months. You are the last thing I think of when I go to bed and the first thing I think of when I awake. If you turned me away now, I will respect that and will nevermore speak of it but…"

Margaret fought hard not to smile. Never had she seen him so unsure. Like her brother in many respects he was intelligent and contemplative but also a bit of an arrogant fool when he wanted to be. He was a man without tethers, answering to no one, not even family, because he had none. When she first met him he was kind but distant, a mystery in his own right. Secretive. Which intrigued her all the more. But this proposal, these confessions, made him into an open book, a condition he readily presented for her.

"I think you love me too," he said, taking another step closer.

She closed her eyes and licked her lips, which had become exceedingly dry. "I do love you."

His smile was short-lived. "Then tell me what it is you wish me to do. I will beg your father if I have to, plea for acceptance into the family."

Margaret could not stop a laugh that escaped. Her father had already expressed concern for their budding friendship. She had no doubt what his answer to Jonas's suit would be. His profession as a doctor, though a noble pursuit, was not suitable for the daughter of a peer. "He won't allow it," she said earnestly. "If he caught wind of our attachment he'd lock me in my room and marry me off to the first nobleman's son he could find, as long as the benefits to him were satisfactory."

"Then let us go without permission," Jonas said, his voice giving way to desperation. "It is Scotland, after all." Jonas offered a light smile and shrug.

Margaret closed her eyes. It seemed impossible that such an answer was required from her so suddenly, giving her so little time. She had spent the better part of three weeks cursing him and his wayward attentions. Marrying him, without anything more than a single stolen kiss to mark a courtship, was lunacy. Defying her father so completely for such a fragile, unsubstantiated love was nothing short of foolhardy.

"Jonas!"

They both turned to the house to see Ainsley stepping out of the kitchen door. He waved his arm for Jonas to come. "Jonas, the inspector is here for the body!"

Margaret met his gaze. Her answer would have to wait. "Go on," she said sternly, "mustn't keep the inspector waiting."

Jonas hesitated. "I'd be obliged for one minute, Peter," he said without taking his eyes from Margaret.

"Come man!" Ainsley pressed.

Jonas stepped toward her. "Margaret, I—"

"Jonas, we need you now."

"Go," she said, nearly pushing him toward her brother. Jonas took a half step toward the house and watched her as he did so. To help his departure, Margaret turned away and began walking through the covered garden gate. She listened to his feet on the gravel as he walked to the house but she dared not turn to see. After the sound of the kitchen door closing reached her ears, Margaret collapsed against the stone wall and did not move for some time. The feeling of elation she felt for having found her match was tempered by the knowledge of what marrying him would ultimately do to her family.

Chapter 18

I'll scoff at your disdain.

The Briar staff looked on in stunned silence as Ainsley led Garret, Inspector Marley, and Jonas through the kitchen to the cellar door. Pushing themselves into the far reaches of the room, each kitchen girl, cook, and underservant who happened to be in the kitchen at the time looked on, a morbid curiosity shadowing their features as the parade of men swept through the room.

At the door to the cellar, Ainsley pulled the key from his pocket.

"And no one minds the presence of a dead body below the kitchen?" Inspector Marley asked with a smirk and a cock of his eyebrow.

Ainsley answered the man's jocular tone with a hardened expression as he pulled the door open with a determined tug. He could hear the staff whispering amongst themselves as the party descended the stairs.

At the end of the dissection Ainsley and Jonas had returned the lanterns to the table at the bottom of the stairs and that is where they remained until Ainsley lit them again. Inspector Marley bristled against the marked decline in temperature and Garret marvelled at the puffs of vapour created by their breath.

"This way, gentleman," Ainsley said, indicating that they should follow him.

Through the depths Ainsley led them, ignoring all rooms that had fallen into disuse. Once he reached the room he gave a quick survey to make sure nothing unseemly remained from the dissection earlier. He wouldn't want to create discomfort for Garret should he see an organ or a generous collection of blood.

Once they were all in the room and gathered around the body, which was concealed beneath the original cloth, Ainsley turned to Garret. "You may prefer to wait in the kitchen," he offered.

"No sir," Garret said with a marked determination.

"Very well."

Ainsley nodded, and Jonas pulled back the sheet to review the corpse from waist up. Despite the distinctive chill in the air the body had started its decomposition, forcing Marley and Garret to cover their noses with their hands as they fanned out around the body. Gas generating in the torso of the corpse pressed outward beneath the skin, making Mr. Owen appear bloated and many pounds heavier than he was in life.

"Let's make this quick, doctor," Marley said, pulling out a white handkerchief and holding it over his nose.

Jonas nodded and went straight to work. "The subject suffered multiple burns on the arms, left side of the torso and the left side of his face." He raised the lantern and used the light to indicate which areas he spoke of. "Just by observing the outer crust, I would say he had been exposed to the hottest heat for less a minute, maybe two." He looked to Ainsley. "The barn was completely engulfed when we arrived, so it is safe to say he was dragged from the fire well before the bulk of the structure caught fire. Drag marks at the scene indicate he was pulled like this—" Jonas laid the lantern aside before positioning himself at the corpse's head and motioning with his arms that Mr. Owen was dragged from under his arms.

"That is an interesting theory," Marley said, lowering his handkerchief slightly.

Jonas stood to his full height and crossed his arms over his chest. As if sensing a challenge, Marley quickly defended his words. "You can't say for sure, can you?" Marley asked.

Ainsley tensed at the inspector's words. Things had been so much easier working with Inspector Simms from the Yard. Ainsley found himself missing the natural way with which they worked. The man himself was unmatched.

"I am sure of the evidence and to the most likely explanation as to what generated it," Jonas said.

"You rely on conjecture."

"We rely on science, Inspector Marley," Ainsley broke in, leaning into the table to catch the inspector's eye. "Science is the next wave of policing."

"Of course." Marley chuckled to himself. "By all means, Dr. Davies, continue."

Ainsley saw Jonas take in a breath as he gathered his thoughts and began again. "In my professional opinion, Mr. Owen was in the barn at the time the fire broke out or shortly after and was removed before the bulk of the heat was able to singe his skin." Jonas grabbed the lantern's handle and waved it over Mr. Owen's face. "I noticed some contusions, some bruising on the face and temple indicating he was hit or—"

"That was me," Garret said, suddenly. "I hit him the day before."

The other three men in the room turned toward Garret.

"He had imbibed a fair amount the day before and was caught beating a horse..." Garret said as his eyes shifted slightly, "and I lost my temper."

"Was anyone witness to this?" Ainsley asked.

"I regret to say Miss Marshall was present," Garret answered, unable to meet Ainsley's gaze. Jonas gave a sideways glance to Ainsley but neither one said anything.

A sigh escaped Inspector Marley. "You see, gentlemen, there isn't anything here. This man died from the heat of the fire—"

"Pulled from a fire a man can live for days with burns such as these. He will be in abject agony but he will live. In a fire it is the smoke that kills, not the burns." Ainsley realized he was flexing his fist at his side as he spoke.

"So he died from the smoke," Marley offered, his voice rising.

Jonas moved the lantern again and used both his hands to open the mouth of the corpse. "Smoke inhalation causes swelling, and leads to airway collapse in the chest. This man's airways were constricted at the throat."

"These contusions are far too deep to be the result of a single tussle," Ainsley explained, looking to Garret. "I believe there was another altercation, one that led someone to hold your father by the throat, here." Ainsley positioned his hands over bruises at Mr. Owen's throat.

"Away with the theories!" Inspector Marley waved his hand dismissively.

Ainsley could not say why it mattered so much to solve this man's murder. Everything Margaret had said about him led Ainsley to believe he was a bully, leading his family with a fist of iron, governing with fear and loathing. During his life, Mr. Owen garnered no empathy. In death, he didn't deserve an ounce of mourning, but for Ainsley, he could not turn his back to injustice.

"This man was dead before the fire started," Ainsley said, pounding his fist on the board holding Mr. Owen's body. "Someone killed him!"

"Mr. Marshall, you are not a doctor!"

Ainsley stood to his full height, staring down the inspector who dismissed his learned observations. It seemed foolish to have dedicated so much of his life to medicine, yet not be able to utilize its worth to the full benefit. If Ainsley was to be a doctor, a surgeon entrusted with cases such as these, what good would it do to hide in the shadows, dodging would-be blackmailers and avoiding scandal? If he wanted to practice medicine, Ainsley would have to come clean, work openly, and endure any disgrace that came his way for doing so. But not yet.

"I am Peter Marshall, second son and heir to Lord Abraham Marshall of Montcliff." Ainsley ignored the confused look on the inspector's face and angrily replaced the sheet over the body. "If you lack the competence to find this man's killer then don't stop an attempt from me!"

Ainsley left, finding his way out of the cellar without the aid of a light, and stormed through the kitchen, ignoring the gasps from the unsuspecting staff. He stood his ground, made his decision to leave the shadows but all he could think of in that moment was how much he needed a drink.

Walking past the parlour, Ainsley noticed a dark figure standing by the window. It was Ivy, looking out over the yard, her cream-coloured dress made black by the sun's rays on the other side of her. He heard faint muttering, the pieces of a conversation, and soon realized Ivy's lips were moving.

"Ivy?" Ainsley drew near, eyeing her. There was no one else in the room. "Is everything all right?" he asked.

Her murmuring stopped. Another moment passed before she turned from the window to look at him. "Grandfather says I should not speak with you."

Ainsley stopped himself from laughing. "Yet here you are." He was in no mood to pander to such a family, not when he had already overstepped his own imposed limitations. By all accounts, he should wash his hands of them, have them sort out their own affairs. But that chivalrous side of him, that side that his mother saw in him at an early age, bid him to carry on. In the end, the opinion of Ivy's grandfather mattered little to him.

Drawn to a small cabinet at the side of the room, Ainsley poured himself a glass of scotch and then began to fill his flask for later. "Care to tell me why your grandfather thinks so little of me?" Ainsley asked, returning to stand before her with his glass in his hands.

"Because you lie," she said without inflection.

A smug smile tugged at the corner of Ainsley's lips.

One of the servants appeared at the door. "Your room is ready, Miss Ivy. I'll show you the way."

Before Ivy could sidestep Ainsley, her head low and gaze avoiding him, he stepped into her path. "What exactly does your grandfather say I have lied about?"

Ivy raised her chin and looked him squarely in the eye. "That night in London."

There was something about her eyes, the deep recesses behind their glossy sheen that held more than the typical soul. She read him, knew him, even though her answer was exceptionally vague. She challenged him and hid behind her grandfather to do it.

Ainsley turned in place as Ivy skirted him and watched through the open doorway as the servant led the way up the stairs. Ivy gave one final glance to him as she ascended the stairs, but this time her gaze was different, her demeanor more like the Ivy Margaret described. He pulled at the stubble on his chin and downed the final gulp of his scotch before returning to the cabinet to pour himself another.

Chapter 19

Cold though the winter blow,

When Ainsley entered The Briar's stables he found Garret saddling his horse, readying him for the ride back to Summer Hill. As Ainsley neared, he held out a hand and rubbed the gelding's nose, cradling it as came closer with his arm. The horse nudged him and huffed as it savoured the attention. "You and your brother breed gorgeous animals, Garret Owen," Ainsley said as he peered around the animal.

Garret lowered the stirrup on one side, buckling the leather strap before walking to the other side. "He's fast on his hooves, let me tell you," he said with a laugh.

Ainsley watched as Garret adjusted the strap on the underside of his horse and then tested the stability of the saddle by pulling down on the seat. "Inspector Marley has gone then," Ainsley said.

An amused look spread over Garret's face. "Aye, none too pleased neither." They both chuckled. "Do you always stand up to others like that?" Garret asked, feeding the loop of the reins over the horse's head as Ainsley stepped aside.

"When I have to," Ainsley answered honestly. "I haven't any patience for incompetence."

Garret nodded thoughtfully. "My brother and I appreciate your efforts," he said. Leading the horse out the stable doors, Garret and Ainsley walked side by side into the evening sun. Ainsley saw Garret give a glance back to the house. "With everything," he said when he turned his attention back to Ainsley. "I don't know what my brother and I would do with her if your friend hadn't agreed to help."

Ainsley nodded, though he wasn't entirely sure what to say.

"I must confess, now with our father gone, how we will manage her. We haven't the authority over her as our father did and I fear she may be"—his voice trailed off for a second—"losing touch."

"In what way?" Ainsley asked.

"My sister is a willful girl."

Ainsley scoffed at the word. Agreeing completely.

"But there is more to it," Garret continued. "She speaks to herself. Mutterings that neither myself nor my brother understand. She conducts entire conversations on her own, without any help from Samuel or I." Garret rubbed the back of his neck with his free hand. "And there are frequent outbursts, screaming and lashing out." He exhaled nervously. "Are you familiar with any doctors at St. Andrew's House?"

Ainsley feared this was coming. Putting his own experiences with Ivy aside, he had heard a number of questionable tales regarding the girl's conduct. Perhaps there was more as well, things even Margaret dared not reveal. Even so, the asylum for the insane was not an institution to be considered without care.

"I can't say that I am," Ainsley confessed. "Alienism is an entirely different science."

Garret nodded but his expression was grave.

Ainsley kept his gaze trained on Garret for a long moment before speaking. "You mean to have your sister committed to the asylum?"

"We don't know what else to do," Garret said. "We can't risk another fire."

The pain in the man's eyes was evident. He had lost his father and was facing the progressive loss of his sister.

"All right," Ainsley said. "I'll make some enquiries."

"Thank you, Mr. Marshall!" Garret breathed a sigh of relief and shook Ainsley's hand in gratitude.

As Ainsley watched the man mount his horse, and guide it down the lane to the main road, he wondered at the wisdom of his agreement to assist.

The next morning Ainsley was able to slip away from The Briar unnoticed, coaxing Walter to take him to Barning Heath with a promise not to utter a word to Margaret about it. St. Andrew's House, which stood four storeys high, was tucked back from the road, hidden by a stand of trees and a long laneway that wound its way to where the asylum stood. The yard, extensively fenced with black iron, looked well maintained though stark and devoid of life.

The secretary at the front desk eyed him shamelessly as he signed his name in the ledger. "How long do you plan on staying with us, Dr. Ainsley?" she asked as she pulled the book back toward her.

"Not long," Ainsley said. "I just wanted to enquire about your facility while in the area."

"You haven't a particular patient in mind, then." She smiled awkwardly as she tucked a tendril of hair behind her ear.

Ainsley hesitated. "I have one patient in mind but I'm not convinced she would be a good fit for your"—Ainsley glanced around him at the concrete walls and stark hallways—"establishment."

The secretary stifled a laugh, which spurred a quizzical look from Ainsley. "Forgive me," she said quickly. "There aren't many people who show such concern. Many families are just happy to be rid of their burdens." She snatched up a clipboard from her desk and hugged it her chest. "I'll take you for a tour," she said cheerily, with a forced smile and playful expression.

"I'm sorry, what did you say your name was?" Ainsley asked as she slipped past him.

"Grace," she said over her shoulder.

Ainsley followed her down a long hall on the first floor made dark by the line of closed doors and noticeable lack of windows. Near the end of the hall, she turned, leading him into large common room lined with tables but no chairs. Along the tables stood women, some in groups, others alone. Between them on the tables sat great piles of linen. Though many had stopped to look at Ainsley and Grace, others continued their task of folding, meticulously lining up corners and pressing down on the creases.

"A few of our patients are of stable enough mind to contribute to our upkeep. Those who have gained our trust are allowed out of their rooms to meet here," Grace explained. "Unfortunately, most of whom we treat are not suited for such work."

Ainsley approached an empty space at the table to get a closer look. The thick, coarse fabric was grossly wrinkled and required a good ironing.

"We don't allow them irons anymore," Grace explained

when she came alongside him.

"He looks like my husband," a woman near him hissed to the others. The hardened expression on her face led Ainsley to believe her husband was not missed. The girl who stood beside her spat toward him from the other side of the table.

"That's enough of that!" Grace snapped with a pointed finger and sour expression. The girl pulled back but did not look the least apologetic. Grace made a gesture with her hand, beckoning him to follow her to the other side of the room. "Shall we continue our tour?" she asked, returning to her light tone.

"Mary's husband brought her to us last month," Grace explained when they were a few paces away from the tables. "She had had a baby and wasn't adjusting to motherhood as well as other women. He said he found her listless and inexplicably fatigued most days. It's not uncommon amongst new mothers but her husband felt it was best if the child wasn't exposed, you see."

As they neared the door, a patient with an oddly large face, slanted eyes, and protruding tongue approached from the other side. Hunched over slightly, he pushed past them brashly, knocking Ainsley in the arm as he lumbered by. "That's John," Grace said. "He's been with us since he was a baby."

Ainsley watched him as he shuffled toward the table.

"Was he born that way?" Ainsley asked.

"Yes," Grace said. "His mother passed away and there was no one else willing to take him." Grace began walking again.

"That woman. Is her husband permitted to visit?" Ainsley asked as they neared the door.

"Dr. Kingsbury discourages visits from family members. He says it inhibits the patient's ability to adjust to their new lives. In many cases, it's better if the family limits contact."

"But surely they resume their lives with their families at some point."

"I'm sorry to disappoint you, Doctor," Grace said. "But that simply isn't the case. Many times they are brought back to us, only worse."

They walked a flight of stairs and entered a long corridor with a number of doors on either side, each evenly spaced. Some were opened, revealing a small room with a cot low to the ground, a greying mattress, and a single sheet. The rooms had small windows high off the ground and were lined with bars on the outside.

"We have a few ward rooms but Dr. Kingsbury finds they only upset the patients unnecessarily. He thinks isolation is best and because we haven't many staff we lock their rooms at night." Grace marched quickly, not allowing Ainsley much time to take it all in. A porter nodded toward them but did not stop the sway of his mop as he moved out of one of the rooms.

Halfway down the hall, a young woman about Ivy's age exited an open door. She kept her head bowed, but Ainsley could see she was eyeing them as the approached. "Good morning, Lola," Grace said.

"Good morning, Miss Grace."

By all accounts, nothing looked amiss with this girl and Ainsley wondered why she had been brought to such a place as St. Andrew's. Lola smiled as they passed.

"Are there many girls like—?" Ainsley asked. He glanced over his shoulder as he spoke and saw that the girl had collapsed to the floor and was convulsing.

"Miss Grace!" The porter dropped his mop and ran to Lola's aid just as Ainsley reached her. Lola's body went rigid and shook as her eyes stared blankly to the ceiling.

Grace positioned herself at Lola's head, cradling it in both her hands. "Lola, stop this!" she yelled. "Stop this, this instant!"

Ainsley took the girl's pulse, and then lowered his ear to her chest to listen to her lungs and heart. "What's happening?" he asked.

As suddenly as it began, the tremor in Lola's body stopped and when Ainsley looked to her face again he found her blinking. Two more porters arrived and together the three of them lifted the now-confused girl and carried her back into her room.

On her feet again, Grace let out a deep huff and brushed a strand of hair back from her face. Ainsley bent over and picked up her clipboard, which had been tossed aside in the scuffle.

"Thank you, Dr. Ainsley." Grace straightened her uniform. "Lola hasn't had an outburst like that in two months. Dr. Kingsbury will be disappointed to hear this."

"What's wrong with her?" Ainsley asked.

"Nothing."

Ainsley raised an eyebrow.

"Dr. Kingsbury says she does it for attention," Grace explained. "She could end it if she wanted to but she remains obstinate."

Through the open door of Lola's room, Ainsley watched as the porters secured her to the bed, lashing her ankles and wrists with buckled straps attached to the metal frame.

"Come, Dr. Ainsley. We have a very large facility here and much to see."

At the end of the tour, Ainsley was escorted to a room on the third floor with windows that overlooked the front of the building. Dr. Emmet Kingsbury arrived a few seconds later and greeted Ainsley warmly with a handshake. "Dr. Ainsley." He gestured for Ainsley to take a seat near his desk. "I understand you have a young lady you'd like to join us." Dr. Kingsbury sat down and snatched a pen from its stand.

"No, sir," Ainsley said, a bit startled by the suggestion. "I've made an acquaintance with a family who are enquiring and, as I don't have any knowledge of your practices, I thought I'd come and see for myself."

Dr. Kingsbury set down his pen and knitted his fingers as he leaned into his desk. "Of course. What is it you are most interested in?"

"Your criteria for admittance, for one," Ainsley said.

"Well, it's quite broad. We have a mandate to accept patients from all over Kent. You will be happy to know our cure rate is above the national average." Dr. Kingsbury pursed his lips and leaned back in his chair. "We do have a fair number of permanent residents who are quite comfortable with our treatment and care. I can't offer anything more specific unless I know more about your potential patient." He eyed Ainsley, who felt surprisingly nervous. "What is your general complaint?"

Ainsley shifted and swallowed. "Outbursts mostly."

"Willful disobedience? Stubbornness? Hysteria, perhaps."

"I have safety concerns."

"Ah yes." Dr. Kingsbury stood then and went to his bookshelf, from which he pulled down a thick, leather-bound volume and placed it in front of Ainsley. He opened the book to a marked page and tapped a finger.

Ainsley leaned forward and looked over the page, which had an illustration of a man, presumably a husband, pulling his unruly wife, untamed hair and ill-fitting dress, toward the doctor and nurse. The caption read *Female Hysteria* and listed a litany of symptoms—insomnia, loss of appetite, nervousness, and heaviness in the abdomen. On the opposite page was a picture of the same wife with well-coiffed hair and a hospital gown seated sedately at a work station amongst other patients in the same state of dress. The husband looked on alongside the doctor, both of the men smiling.

"It's not uncommon. Idle women, usually due to a lack discipline and structure, become unruly. We find they fit in quite well here, adapting to our routines. It's a common condition amongst women in the middle and upper classes. Tell me, Dr. Ainsley, does your patient fall into this category?"

Ainsley hesitated, unsure if his account was justified. He had witnessed Ivy's outbursts firsthand but wondered if they could be attributed to hysteria or something else. He turned the page to see more illustrations of a woman receiving hydrotherapy, water massages to the abdomen. Another illustration showed a doctor massaging a woman's genitals.

Seeing the illustration that had caught Ainsley's attention Dr. Kingsbury tapped a finger on the top of the book. "Symptoms are instantly relieved," he said.

"This is effective?"

"The majority of my hysteria patients visit me once a week," Dr. Kingsbury said, "on an outpatient basis. However, if you are having safety concerns, it may be best if she come to stay here at St. Andrew's House at least until we are satisfied with our method of treatment." Dr. Kingsbury cleared his throat and raised his eyes to meet Ainsley's gaze. "Tell me, Dr. Ainsley, is the patient married?"

Ainsley shook his head.

"Sexually active then?" He raised a hand, anticipating Ainsley's protest. "I only ask because it is common for women with hysteria."

"I have evidence to suggest she is," Ainsley said, somewhat reluctantly.

"Then tell her family I know the treatment for her," Dr. Kingsbury said, tapping his desktop twice.

Ainsley exhaled and closed the book, unwilling to look at the pictures any longer. Ivy's outbursts were only part of the problem. Ainsley suspected she suffered from delusions, seeing things that were not based in reality.

He also feared that he suffered from the same ailment as Ivy.

"Tell me about your patients who suffer hallucinations," Ainsley said.

Dr. Kingsbury raised his chin and pressed his lips together. "Delusions?" He nearly smiled at the suggestion. "That is an entirely different matter. Not uncommon," he said as if to reassure Ainsley they were up for the task, "but certainly more difficult. Can you describe the visions?"

Ainsley rocked his head back and forth, searching for the words to best describe what he was speaking about. "Seeing people who are known to be deceased." He realized he spoke more of his own experience than Ivy's.

Leaning back in his chair, Dr. Kingsbury whistled as he picked up his pen and began playing with it in both hands. "Apparitions." The doctor closed his eyes, a gesture denoting the seriousness of the diagnosis. "We have treatments, but they require time and a conviction from us doctors. Cases such as these rarely cure themselves."

"Do they require admittance?"

"Most certainly, yes. They often remain for years."

Ainsley's heart began to quicken and he could feel his throat growing dry.

"The young woman is suffering from powerful, internal conflicts. Reality and fantasy collide, forming a world only they are privy to. It's in everyone's best interest to treat these patients away from the rest of society."

Ainsley could barely look at the doctor as he spoke. His mind reeled at the memory of his own delusions, the visions that caught the corner of his eye and interrupted his attempts at normalcy. The doctor said he should be institutionalized for them, segregated from society and branded a lunatic.

It took concentrated effort for Ainsley to smile, thank the

alienist for his insight, and leave the asylum. It was only when the carriage rolled through the iron gates that he allowed himself a breath and a silent prayer of deliverance.

Ainsley asked Walter to leave him at the side of the road and then ordered him to return to The Briar. From there he was allowed to take a slower pace, sauntering along a well-worn path through the woods before finishing his journey at Summer Hill. It gave him no joy to relay what he had learned to Garret and Samuel and his recommendation reflected that. The brothers accepted his counsel with even nods and few questions. It was a great relief when Ainsley was finally able to part ways. There was no place he wished to be more than home, away from St. Andrew's House and the Owen family.

Ainsley made his way up the centre stairs but hesitated in the hall as he neared his room. Someone was in there, walking away from his window toward his bookshelf on the opposite wall. He felt unease creep over his skin. He closed his eyes and ran a hand through his hair. He drew in a deep breath to steady himself before walking through the door. "Julia?"

The maid stood in the doorway, her face flush and eyes pleading. She looked as if she had been crying. "I haven't slept all night. She knows," she blurted, gulping for air. "Margaret knows. I did not tell her, I promise you." Her voice rose in a panic and Ainsley pulled her inside.

He closed the door behind her.

"I swear, Peter, I said nothing. You must believe me."

"I believe you," he said softly. Already his mind raced, questioning the possible repercussions. Of all the people to find out, he was glad it was Margaret. He had said nothing of her ties to Jonas and his discretion was sure to win him favour.

"I'm going to lose my place," Julia said, breaking into sobs. "I'll lose my reference."

Ainsley shook his head and stepped toward her, ready to take her in an embrace. "Certainly not."

"Do not laugh!" she said, brushing away his attempt to comfort her.

He had not realized he laughed, nor did he think he was

making light of the situation. She paced the floor and stopped at the window. "I should have known better than…" she stopped short of finishing her sentence and Ainsley was afraid to press her.

Julia wiped the tears from her cheek, sniffling gently. "We should end it."

His stomach lurched, and the heavy feeling that had been building steadily began to turn and fumble in his midsection. He wanted to go to her, to plead with her to be reasonable, but for some reason his feet were locked in place. He could hardly find the strength to breathe, let alone walk the width of the room.

"No," Ainsley snapped. "Absolutely not."

"Peter, I can't. It's not right."

"According to who?" Ainsley asked sharply. "I don't care what anyone else thinks."

He watched as a single tear slipped from her lower eyelid, leaving a trail down her cheek as it dropped.

How could he have not seen this day coming? The outcome was inevitable. But for a time he believed, as many young people do, that good times have no end and that things will progress in the same manner with which they began. He had fought his desire for her for many months, allowing his passion to build before acting upon his urges and discovering she wanted him just as desperately. From the beginning, he could offer little more than late-night trysts and stolen kisses. His position in the family and hers amongst the staff held them prisoners to their secret.

From his father he faced a scolding, perhaps a loss of trust, or a tarnished character. She, however, faced much more dire consequences and had taken on the majority of the risk affecting both her reputation and her future prospects. He realized, as he stood in the middle of his room contemplating all of this, that loving her should have meant protecting her from such risk, not placing her in it.

"I will speak to my sister, make her see reason. She will be on our side."

There was a long pause as Julia regarded him. "What is *our side*?" she asked, giving a slight tilt to her chin. "We do not belong to the same side. We never have and never could." She licked her lips. "I will accept my role in this but my willingness is the only thing separating you from the type of employer the orphanage warned me about."

Ainsley suddenly felt ill. The notion that he had taken advantage of her desire to please, or even that she had no choice in the matter because of her position, was monstrous. It had never occurred to him that he might be using his position to coerce her.

"I never—" Ainsley stepped forward, wanting to pull her toward him, but he stopped suddenly when his aunt appeared at the door.

"Peter, may I speak with you a moment?" Aunt Louisa asked.

Julia hastily wiped her cheeks with the heel of her palms before turning to face the doorway. Something must have been evident in Julia's expression that alerted Aunt Louisa's suspicion. "What's happening in here?" she asked, pointedly. Her gaze shot to Ainsley specifically. From behind her Ainsley could see Julia's head bow in defeat.

"Julia inadvertently let some of my sketches fall into the fire while looking for Margaret's book," Ainsley said without missing a beat. "She was just apologizing for her blunder."

Julia raised her eyes from the floor when Aunt Louisa turned to her.

"Is this true, young lady?"

"Yes, ma'am."

The older woman clicked her tongue in disappointment. "Oh my goodness. Where did your father find this girl? I hope they were not of any great significance."

Ainsley shook his head. "No, ma'am. All are reproducible."

"Good." Aunt Louisa stood tall as if she alone had been responsible for the solution. "Well, off you go, child," she said, waving Julia out of the room.

Head bowed slightly, Julia stepped toward the door, but Aunt Louisa stopped her. "The book?"

Ainsley grabbed the only book on top of his desk. "Nearly forgot," he said, stepping forward to deliver it to Julia's grasp. "Tell Margaret I'm very interested in hearing what she thinks of it and that I look forward to discussing it further." Julia and Ainsley's eyes met as he handed her the book.

"Yes, sir," the maid said, with a gentle nod, before quitting the room.

Aunt Louisa raised a hand to her forehead and closed her eyes. "This is exactly why good help is so hard to find."

"I'm afraid I am very busy, Aunt Louisa. You wished to speak with me?"

His aunt bristled at the abrupt change in their easy conversation. "Well, yes." She stopped. "Follow me, will you, Peter?"

Moments later they were standing, shoulder to shoulder, looking to the set of three windows that overlooked the west lawn.

"It's horrific," she said disparagingly.

At first, Ainsley wasn't sure what he should be looking at, but when he stopped focusing on the property outside, he saw how the wallpaper was bubbling around the window. He drew nearer for a closer look and noticed that the wood frames and walls that surrounded the windows were waterlogged. His pointed finger quickly tore through the paper. Without thinking he grabbed one of the edges of the wood and was able to break a sizeable chunk free.

"Water is the enemy of any house," Aunt Louisa said, looking toward the ceiling.

When Ainsley glanced up he saw the ceiling tiles appeared loose, while the edges appeared grey compared to the white plaster colour it was supposed to be.

"I will write to my brother," Aunt Louisa said. "But I'm afraid we don't have much time to wait for a reply. We can live at the London house for a time while the work takes place." Aunt Louisa turned and bent over the desk to make a few notes. "We'll need to spend a good deal of money if the house is to be saved. I daresay there is more rain in our future. We should see to it that this gets taken care of. I doubt these walls will last another winter."

Ainsley shook his head, the shock still setting in. "There is no money," he said quietly.

Aunt Louisa huffed. "What do you mean, there is no money?"

"Father only sets aside a minimum to take care of Jamieson

and the others. There is no capital available for the house," Ainsley said.

"But all houses need capital to pay for repairs." Aunt Louisa nearly laughed at the predicament. "Goodness, how does your housekeeper afford new linen, or polish for the silver?"

"We don't live here," Ainsley said. "Mother was the only one who lived here."

It was then that Aunt Louisa nodded, understanding setting in. "Well then," she said. "I'll keep a tally then. We can approach your father when he returns."

Seeing no other way, Ainsley nodded. Satisfied, Aunt Louisa made for the door but turned before exiting the room. "How long is Miss Owen planning to stay with us?" she asked.

Ainsley, Margaret, Jonas, and Julia were the only people who knew the true reason for Ivy's stay at The Briar. To everyone else she was seeking respite after the fire and nothing more. Ainsley shrugged in answer to his aunt's question. "A few days, I suppose," he said.

"Perhaps I shall take this opportunity to introduce her to a few of our close friends. We can pay some calls—"

"Given the circumstances, I doubt she will be doing anything beyond resting," Ainsley said earnestly. "The woman is traumatized."

Aunt Louisa nodded slowly. "You are quite right," she said. "Perhaps I should arrange for a special meal, a little taste of India to spice things up."

Ainsley relented. His aunt was so much easier to get along with when she was busy and if these were the types of projects she took pride in, who was he to stop her?

Chapter 20

When hills are free from snow

Margaret made a point to bring Ivy's breakfast to her room the next morning. Maxwell stood beside her, tray in hand, as she rapped a knuckle on the door to the room that used to be her mother's. After a moment, a tiny voice invited them in. There was no key in the lock this time, no apprehension, only the unmistakable cloud of tragedy and fear that resonated between Margaret and Ivy.

"Thank you, Maxwell," Margaret said after the butler slid the tray onto the small table in the corner. He nodded and left without a word.

"Good morning, Ivy," Margaret said to her friend, who sat on the edge of the bed

"Hello, miss," Ivy answered. Their greeting was muted, their happiness at meeting subdued.

"Breakfast?" Margaret gestured for the table. "I brought enough for both of us."

Ivy smiled but shook her head. "No thank you, ma'am."

The girl looked distant, not altogether aware of where she was or why. She avoided looking Margaret in the eyes and kept glancing to the dark corner of the room.

Margaret looked over, wondering if there was something she was not seeing, but there was nothing. When she looked back Ivy was staring at her.

Margaret plucked a deck of cards from the tray. "How about another game of Piquet?" she asked.

"Later, perhaps." She pressed a hand into her stomach and Margaret felt her own stomach lurch. She couldn't imagine the emotions running through Ivy's head.

"You don't have to do this," Margaret said suddenly, and then wondered if she was just making things worse. "If someone is forcing you—"

"No one is forcing me to do this," Ivy said suddenly.

"That is good." Margaret swallowed down the lump in her throat. "Perhaps you need more time then."

Ivy shook her head. "I know what I need to do."

"Does the baby's father know that you are doing this?" Margaret asked.

"I do it for him." Ivy twisted her fingers in front of her, dividing her attention between them, Margaret, and the dark corner of the room.

"So he is aware you are with child?" Margaret asked. "I can go tell Jonas you are unsure."

"No, Miss Margaret!" Ivy nearly jumped up from her place on the bed. "I thank you for your kindness. But I need to do this on my own now."

Ivy's gaze drifted to the corner again before she gave a marked nod, as if agreeing to something. Margaret looked again but still, nothing was there.

There was a gentle rap on the opposite side of the door and a moment later Jonas slipped into the room, Julia at his heels. The doctor brought his bag and the maid carried a second washbasin, a heap of towels, and a pitcher of water.

"Morning, Miss Ivy," Jonas said, remaining on the opposite side of the bed. Nodding toward the doctor, Ivy kept her expression steady even as Julia began preparing for the procedure.

Chapter 21

It will be spring again.

Ainsley wasn't quite sure how to respond when he came upon Margaret in the upper hallway. Exiting Ivy's room, Margaret appeared defeated and withdrawn, as she pulled the door closed behind her.

"Jonas has begun then?" Ainsley asked, somewhat uneasily.

Margaret nodded. "He wished to take advantage of the light coming in the windows." Margaret looked back to the closed door before speaking again. "I offered to stand guard at the door to make sure no one disturbed them but he said no. Julia would lock the door."

Ainsley waited nervously, wondering if she would choose to bring up her new discovery of him and Julia. Mentally he readied himself, preparing to defend his indefensible actions against any onslaught. He needn't have bothered. Margaret was in no mood, and seemed to have a number of things on her own mind. He turned to the stairs but stopped himself.

"I'd planned to go to Breaside today," he said. "Pay a visit to our old friends. Perhaps you care to join me," he offered. "You are probably busy helping Aunt Louisa repaper the library—"

"I'll come!" Margaret cut in quickly at the mention of their aunt. "I'm not much use to her, in any case."

The carriage ride to Breaside Estate look less time than Ainsley remembered. A landmark on the Kent countryside since the reign of the Tudors, the estate once encompassed three thousand acres of forest and fields, enough property to host king and countrymen should they venture to the area for fox hunts and horse races. In recent years, since the reign of George III, the estate had been reduced to less than a quarter of its original size. One of the severed plots became The Briar, another was transformed into Summer Hill Farm. And others still that skirted the town had been passed down between families and claimed over the last hundred years. It was their rich history, as much as the property lines hidden deep in the woods, which connected them.

They arrived in their carriage just after luncheon. Both Ainsley and Margaret would have preferred to walk, but arriving slightly out of breath and more than slightly rumpled was not how guests were received by a duke and duchess.

They were escorted to the parlour, where Lady Thornton waited for them. She rose to greet them, shaking each of their hands in turn before gesturing to the sofas and chairs. "I am delighted that you both decided to come and pay me a visit," she said, after they all took a seat. "It's been far too long since you last called. My pantry shelves have never been so full."

Ainsley answered her joke with a laugh. "I expected the boys to take up my slack while I was gone."

So many years had passed since Ainsley haunted those rooms. Being back felt as if the memories belonged in another lifetime, certainly not the one he found himself entrenched in now. Lady Thornton's sons, Blair and Brandon, were like brothers to him at a time when his own brother wanted nothing to do with the young Peter and Margaret.

Lady Thornton looked to Margaret. "My apologies, my dear, Priscilla is under the weather and wished to stay to her room this day." Without missing a beat, she turned to Ainsley. "Did Miss Margaret tell you we met in the shop the other day?"

Ainsley raised his eyebrows in surprise.

"You were looking for a scarf, yes?"

Margaret nodded sheepishly.

"You always were ahead of the fashions." Lady Thornton patted Margaret's knee playfully. "Looks lovely, my dear."

Steps were heard just outside the parlour and a pair of male voices grew louder as the footsteps drew closer. Lady Thornton heaved a sigh and looked to the door in anticipation.

"Certainly not," Brandon said to his brother, Blair, as they rounded the threshold. "Mother, we are heading for the stables for—" The playful look on Brandon's face evaporated when he saw Ainsley and Margaret. "My apologies. I had not realized you were entertaining."

Ainsley, Margaret, and Lady Thornton rose as the boys walked toward them.

Brandon stepped past his brother and stretched out a hand to greet them. "How many years has it been, Peter?" he asked.

"Too many," Ainsley answered. "You remember Margaret."

Brandon's exuberance was muted by his brother's subdued greeting. Although happy to see Peter and Margaret, his confidence waned and he was happy to let his brother take the lead. Ainsley saw him take in a calculated breath before reaching his hand out to them.

Margaret allowed Blair to take her hand but instead of shaking it, as he had done with her brother, he lifted it to his mouth and kissed her fingers just below her knuckles.

"Lady Margaret," he said calmly.

"Mr. Thornton."

Ainsley saw Margaret give a playful smile as she pulled her hand away.

"How long have you been back?" Brandon asked.

"Not long," Ainsley answered.

"We were heading to the barn," Brandon said, "for our afternoon ride. You are more than welcome to accompany us, if it's agreeable to Mother."

Lady Thornton waved off their concern.

"You are more than welcome to join us, Lady Margaret," Brandon said.

Blair's eyes brightened. "Please do," he said. "We have a side saddle."

"Oh heavens, no," Margaret said. "You won't find me on a side saddle ever again." The room erupted in joyous laughter at Margaret's jest and, when the gathering quieted, Margaret spoke again. "Besides, Lady Thornton and I have yet to exchange any gossip."

"Go, my dear," Lady Thornton said. "It will be good for you all to get reacquainted." She gave a light kiss to Margaret's cheek. "We shall catch up on all the gossip another time."

Together they walked the gravel path through the trees to the modest stable beyond. "We are expanding the barns, you know," Brandon said as he walked slightly ahead. "Making way for our team of racers."

"My brother has many grand designs pertaining to our

horses," Blair said from beside Margaret, who could not help but walk slowly due to the confining nature of her dress.

"Racehorses, big brother," Brandon corrected.

Braeside always had a good variety of equine on the property, used mostly for carriages and pleasure riding, but this endeavour into racing was new, and it was clear Brandon was very enthusiastic about it.

Once they cleared the trees they could see the expansion project underway. Slightly farther away from the main stable, workmen were busy constructing a similar though substantially bigger version of the outbuilding. "They will connect, you see," Brandon said, indicating with his arms how the buildings would be joined. "We'll be able to fit thirty more thoroughbreds."

"Surely he cannot race them all at once," Margaret teased, directly her words to Blair at her side.

Blair laughed. "No one said he could not try."

Within twenty minutes, four horses were brushed and prepared, a saddle secured on each. Never comfortable riding side saddle, Margaret was pleased when no one chided her for insisting on riding astride. There was a time when her riding coach made her, citing dignity and ladylike manners, but she felt like she were going to fall off at any moment and couldn't find a proper posture that did not cause pain in her back. Two hours riding in such a manner had been enough for her entire lifetime and she was thankful when the Thornton brothers did not give her a hassle for breaking from tradition. It certainly wasn't unheard of for a female to ride astride like men, but it wasn't entirely befitting of her station.

"Lady Margaret." Blair stood at the horse's shoulder, the reins in his hand.

Margaret wanted to disregard Blair's offer to help her in the saddle. She was more than capable of hoisting herself into place, but his offer was sincere and avoiding him would be considered inexcusably rude.

"Is there no mounting block?" she asked, doing a visual search of the yard.

Blair gave an apologetic shake of his head before lowering his hand, flattening it to create a step. She tried not to blush as she placed a hand on his shoulder while she lifted her boot into his hand. They moved swiftly, Margaret throwing her right leg over the horse while Blair steadied her left foot. Once seated, he slid her boot into the stirrup and handed her the reins. He lingered at her side a few seconds longer than required, ensuring she had control of the horse and rechecking the position of her feet. His close proximity brought warmth to her cheeks and also brought pangs of guilt to her heart.

"Are you always this thorough, Mr. Thornton?" she teased.

"Only for the things which pique my interest," he replied sincerely.

The flirtatious exchange went unnoticed by Ainsley and Brandon, who were only just then leading their horses from the barn.

"Where shall we ride?" Ainsley asked once they were all secured in their saddles.

Brandon looked between Ainsley and his brother and smiled. "Everywhere."

It was clear from the start that Brandon was a man who enjoyed riding at considerable speeds. For a time, Blair held back, perhaps expecting to help Margaret gingerly maneuver her way through the forest trails. She laughed internally, thinking about the look that must have been on Blair's face when he realized she was as good a rider as any man.

They barreled through the forest trails, skipping streams and rounding stumps as the foliage turned the world around them into an indecipherable green haze. After a time, the forest morphed from luscious and light to almost dark as night as the canopy grew thick overhead. The trail was well maintained and the group was able to keep a quick pace.

It had been a number of years since Margaret enjoyed rampant pleasure such as this. Civility had little place in her younger years. Her mother allowed her the freedom to ride and run with the boys without recourse. This did not satisfy her father, though, who in recent years attempted one last push to civilize her. Still awkward and ill at ease in formal settings, her father's enterprise only managed to instill guilt and a hearty dose of anxiety. She felt as if she would never grow accustomed to the ways of society; never know exactly what to say or how to behave. The Briar was her sanctuary from the weight of her family's title and fortune. The woods were her closest connection to her childhood, the only time when she ever felt truly free.

Once the trees opened into a clearing, Brandon took off with Ainsley, charging behind him to keep the pace. Margaret nearly forgot that Blair was behind her and she slowed her horse's pace. She knew she could never keep up to them, certainly not with her stays digging into her ribs.

"My brother flirts with death," Blair said, bringing his horse alongside hers. "He believes himself invincible."

"Don't all men of means?"

"Certainly not. I cannot afford to, I'm afraid," Blair said in earnest. "Father has been hammering a sense of duty into me since the time I could write my name."

Margaret nodded, his words reminding her of her own family's expectations.

They sauntered along for a time until Blair began to lead his horse slightly quicker than Margaret's. Sensing a bit of fun, Margaret picked up her pace until Blair guided his horse in front of her, preventing her from passing. He looked back with a playful smile, which faded when she finally overtook him. Not willing to be usurped, Blair started into a gallop and soon he and Margaret were racing each other. Margaret's hair came loose, trailing behind her in waves of chestnut brown.

When she looked back she saw Blair trying to keep pace, kicking his horse and slapping the reins. But it was clear Margaret was riding the racehorse and it moved instinctively, as if knowing the other horse was not so far behind her.

They finally caught up to Ainsley and Brandon, who were dismounting their horses near a fence along a line of trees. Brandon smiled as Margaret approached. "We thought we'd lost you," he said. He stepped forward and grabbed the harness of Margaret's horse, steadying it while she dismounted. "But I see you haven't changed a bit."

Margaret could see Ainsley smirk as he tended his horse. "She's stubborn like that," he said.

She wiped her brow and pulled the last few pins from her hair, deciding not to care about the untameable curls.

"There's a river near here where we can water them," Brandon said.

Margaret looked back and saw Blair leading his horse toward her. She smiled, remembering how the girls clamoured over him at parties, and wondered if the younger girls still gasped when he entered a room dominated by females. To her, he had always been Blair, as kin and no more. She'd heard a rumour once that he had promised himself to some lesser noble's daughter, a girl that Margaret remembered meeting only once. At the time, Margaret hadn't the chance to confirm what she had heard and that was some time ago. No nuptials had been announced and she wondered if it were safe to say the rumours were unfounded.

He said nothing as he walked closer and then grabbed the harness of her horse. For a moment, Margaret wasn't sure what he was doing, and even thought he may try to kiss her, but then realized he was allowing her to walk without having to lead her horse. She hesitated to give him a smile, afraid it would only encourage him.

By the time Margaret made her way to the river, Ainsley and Brandon were leading their horses to the water by perching themselves on some boulders jutting from the calm water. She stood at the water's edge while Blair led the pair of horses to the bank, where the water was shallow and the current less threatening. She felt a rush of cold air swoop down upon them and she raised her face toward the sun. That is when she realized they were standing beneath the cliff at the farthest edge of Summer Hill. She saw the oak tree where she and Ivy stood peering down at the eroded earth.

A chill sent a quiver over her body as she looked over the steep, eroded hillside and the large boulders that waited at the bottom on the opposite bank. An image of a man splayed out over the rocks flashed into her mind. Matthew, Samuel's friend. Margaret closed her eyes and willed the image away.

When the queasiness left her, she opened her eyes to see Blair leading the two horses away from the water and tying the reins to a tree not too far from where they stood.

Margaret decided to settle herself on a large rock at the water's edge. From her vantage point she could just see the surface of the water as it coiled and danced around the other larger rocks at the river bank. She could feel Brandon eyeing her, hesitant to speak.

"I hear Miss Ivy Owen has been spending a great deal of time at The Briar," he said.

Margaret saw Blair give his brother a slight shake of the head but Brandon ignored it.

"I was sorry to hear her father passed away," Brandon said, leading his horse away from the water. He tied her to a tree next to the others.

"No great loss, I'm afraid," Blair said unflinchingly. "He was a drunkard and brute. Not many will mourn his passing," He licked his lips and lowered his gaze, perhaps second-guessing his harsh words. "How is Ivy?"

"She is in shock, for the most part," Margaret explained. "She's staying with us for a day or two. Until things settle down." Of course she would not say the real reason why the girl was staying at their home.

"A lovely gesture," Blair said.

"They lost a great deal of horses," Brandon said. "'Tis a shame. Many of them were practically born in the winners' circle—"

"I heard you were there the day the fire broke out," Ainsley said suddenly. The men turned to Ainsley, surprised by the abrupt manner with which he spoke. Margaret was the only one who wasn't surprised. She had seen Ainsley use the technique before. He wanted to catch them off guard, and force a response before they had a chance to collaborate their stories.

The technique worked for Blair, who hesitated and shot his brother a look before answering. "That's right."

"I was present when Garret spoke with the inspector. He mentioned your name, so I thought I would ask," Ainsley explained, taking on a much lighter tone.

Brandon returned Ainsley's stare. "Did he tell you it's not unusual for my brother and me to be there many times in a week? Garret has been boarding a number of our horses while our stables are being constructed. Thankfully, none of our horses were affected by the fire."

"Interesting how that happens. You board a number of horses there and yet they all escape injury." Ainsley held a blade of grass in his hands, twirling and then knotting it with his fingers.

Margaret found herself becoming increasingly uncomfortable. Interrogating anyone would have put her on edge, but these men were sons of a duke and held a higher place in society than the Marshalls. "Peter, is this necessary?"

"It's all right, Lady Margaret," Brandon said, offering a smile. "Your brother is doing right by the Owens. I was there in the early morning," he said, heaving a sigh of resignation. "I took some of my horses for a morning ride. If I can't attend I send one of our stable boys or grooms. I was home before luncheon, as always. And from what I understand the fire broke out closer to four."

Margaret gave Ainsley an imploring look that went ignored.

"Perhaps you noticed something," Ainsley pressed.

Blair laughed then. "I had not realized you now work for the constabulary. If investigators wish to come speak with us they are more than welcome."

"There will be no investigation," Ainsley said. "Inspector Marley feels Mr. Owen succumbed from smoke inhalation, nothing more."

This news startled Margaret. When she spoke with Jonas on the subject he had been very convincing. She knew Ainsley, as well, believed Mr. Owen had met an untimely end. The Thornton brothers were quiet for a moment, eyeing each other on the opposite sides of the gathering.

"You disagree?" Brandon asked, squinting against the sun breaking through the foliage.

"I do," Ainsley answered. "And I would appreciate it if you and your brother were honest with me." Ainsley raised his head to look Blair in the eye.

Brandon nodded soberly but Blair had grown agitated. "Are you accusing my brother and me of being less than honest?" Blair asked, his face twisting harshly at the insult. He stepped forward, forcing Ainsley to stand, readying for a fight.

Brandon crossed between Ainsley and Margaret to push his brother back. "Calm down," Brandon said.

Margaret stood so she could step back from any ruckus that erupted.

"The interesting thing about secrets, Peter Marshall, is that they don't stay hidden for long, not in the counties," Blair said steadily while his brother stood between them. "Everything comes to light sooner or later."

Margaret saw her brother smile. She wasn't sure if Blair hinted at Ainsley's position in medicine or something else entirely.

"Brother, this isn't wise," Brandon cautioned.

"Hasn't he any clue who he's speaking with?" Blair asked, his anger growing. "How dare you assassinate our characters in such a way? Who else have you spoken to?"

Margaret came to his side. "Blair, we only ask to put the pieces together. We weren't accusing you or Brandon of anything."

Blair looked to her as if surprised to see her there. "You knew he intended to do this? That he intended to corner us, ask impertinent questions?"

"You are hardly cornered," Ainsley said, a little more harshly than Margaret would have expected.

Blair moved as if to charge Ainsley but Brandon held him back. Throwing his brother's hands from him, Blair turned and marched toward the horses, holding his hands in fists at his sides.

"We do not mean to insult you," Margaret said to Brandon, trying to regain peace. "Miss Ivy is becoming a dear friend, and I would never forgive myself if we did not fight for justice for her family."

Brandon's face seemed to soften at this. He nodded quickly and ran up the hill after his brother. From their place beside the creek Margaret could see them speaking and arguing but she could not hear what they were saying. She turned to Ainsley and crossed her arms over her chest. "You haven't any tact!"

"You wouldn't either if you had seen what I've seen," Ainsley answered unapologetically. "For all we know there could a grudge between the two families. They could have killed Mr. Owen when an agreement went awry, something about a racehorse or even a poorly placed bet. Men have killed for less."

"Peter, hold your tongue!" Margaret could not fathom one of their closest childhood friends having any sort of mind-set to do a thing such as Ainsley was suggesting.

"You saw the way they looked at each other each time before they spoke." Ainsley drew closer, lowering his voice so only Margaret could hear. "What do we know of them? Truly? Men like this believe they are above the law. We've seen it before, Margaret. I will not blindly look the other way simply because they were friends or because they have a title."

Margaret knew what her brother said was true. Their involvement with the Owen family could not be discounted, but she doubted they'd get any further knowledge by addressing them so abruptly.

A few moments later Brandon returned and when Margaret looked past him she saw Blair mounting his horse and quickly galloping for the trail, heading farther from the house and deeper into the woods. It was not the way she had wanted to say goodbye.

"My brother regrets that he must depart," Brandon said, slightly flustered but gaining composure.

Margaret stepped forward. "Brandon, we never intended—"

"It's quite all right," Brandon said, raising a hand to halt any further explanations. "He's just overtired. You understand."

Margaret nodded, though she wasn't entirely sure that she did.

Chapter 22

So go, and fare thee well,

"What did you expect would happen?" Margaret asked as she charged along the trail, Ainsley trailing behind her. "Must have learned such interrogation tactics from the Yard."

After Blair's outburst, they helped Brandon return the horses to their pasture before offering a few awkward goodbyes. There was no longer a need to keep up appearances so they choose the trail through the woods to take them home. And it was better this way, Ainsley decided; he and Margaret had much to talk about. He couldn't decide, however, whether Margaret was upset at his brazen line of questioning or at the abrupt end to an afternoon with someone who was clearly smitten with her.

"Really, Peter, have you lost all sense of propriety?"

"My questions weren't unreasonable," he answered in self-assured protest.

"If you were an officer of the law they wouldn't be," Margaret answered. "We aren't in the city anymore. It won't be so easy to hide your involvement in cases if you insist on acting like the inquisition."

"I wouldn't need to act like the inquisition if people were straightforward and truthful," he said.

Their pace was quick and the trail overgrown. Walking single file, they dodged low-hanging limbs and trailing undergrowth.

"You saw how quickly Blair grew to anger. Innocent people don't behave like that."

"I think you may have truly offended them," Margaret answered.

"So what if I have?" Ainsley said with a shrug. "I'm in no great hurry to align myself with murderers or arsonists. And you shouldn't either."

Margaret stopped. "I won't believe it," she said. "When we were children—"

"We were all different people as children, Margaret. You, me, them. Everyone changes. The sooner you realize that the better."

She stopped suddenly. "What's happened to you? The brother I know would never be so bitter, so untrusting."

Ainsley turned and gave a pointed finger to her. "You brought me into this! A week ago ignorance was my closest ally."

"Is this your way of punishing me then? This is your defence against an uncertain world? Push everyone away until they can no longer stand it to be near you?"

If Ainsley didn't know any better he'd swear he saw his mother standing opposite him, imploring him to answer. Margaret resembled their deceased matriarch in nearly every way. There were times, while their mother lived, when he couldn't rightly say who held his heart more and, now, with their mother gone, all his love and protection fell onto Margaret, who deserved far better than what he was able to provide.

"Perhaps," he said.

"I didn't push you out the door when we saw the smoke. I didn't make you stay even after the flames were out. Your own conscience wouldn't let you look the other way. You are a good man, Peter. A brave man. A righteous man. I only wish you saw yourself as I do." Margaret's eyes glistened as she chided him. She wiped her cheeks and turned away, perhaps hoping he hadn't noticed.

It was clear she believed the words she spoke, misguided as they were. She saw him in a much fairer light than he ever could, not after what he had done. If anything, he sought absolution for his misdeeds, and hoped that in some way he could right the scales that he had set off balance that fateful night back in London.

After a long pause he spoke, offering a heavyhearted breath before shattering her illusions. "You are wrong. I am none of those things." He raked his hand through his tussled hair. "I am just a man. There's nothing special about Peter Marshall and certainly nothing special about Peter Ainsley."

The Briar appeared through the trees, bringing with it a great sense of relief to Ainsley. They had walked for the better part of an hour in an uneasy silence and the house represented an opportunity for reprieve for both of them. Margaret skirted ahead, charging for the covered garden gate, leaving Ainsley to make his way up the hill alone.

As he came to the gate, a figure in one of the upper windows caught his attention but he refused to look. He ducked back behind the gate as a sense of unease crept up over him. He felt the hairs on the back of his neck stand on end. It seemed silly to be so frightened, so ill at ease when it was most likely a trick of the light or his mind making something recognizable out of something lacking definition. That's all it was, he tried to convince himself, a mundane, commonplace thing that his mind made into something else.

When he finally brought himself to look he saw Hubert staring at him from the same window. When George appeared at his side they both waved energetically and then darted away.

That was real, he told himself. And that is what he should focus on. Only what was real.

By the time Ainsley entered the house he found Margaret, Nathaniel, and Aunt Louisa sitting down to tea in the parlour as he passed in the hall. He regretted not being swift enough to pass by unnoticed.

"Peter?"

Aunt Louisa's voice found him just as he reached the bottom of the stairs. He placed his hand on the bannister and lowered his head in defeat. For a second he pondered the repercussions of pretending not to hear her.

"Peter." She appeared at the door to the parlour and looked out over the foyer. "Do come join us."
She gave an amused smile as she called him with a single finger. Knowing he would do as she commanded, she did not wait for his reply and retreated back into the room.

A tray of tea, cups and saucers, cookies, and other treats had been placed on the table at the centre of a small sofa and two chairs. Jonas stood near the window, a teacup and saucer in his hands.

"We've received an invite," Aunt Louisa said, popping a remaining bit of cookie in her mouth. She picked up a card and envelope that had been slipped beneath her teacup. "The Duke and Duchess Thornton are hosting a dinner the day after next and we have all been invited. Including Dr. Davies, it seems."

Ainsley gave a sideways glance to Margaret, who did not flinch at the news. She raised her teacup higher to take a sip.

"Lady Thornton has handwritten a note asking us to join them for a fox hunt the following morning as well." Aunt Louisa lowered the invite. "My, my, Lady Thornton is not known for hosting many parties. Seems whatever transpired this afternoon has made an undeniable impression on her. Perhaps she means to make you her next daughter-in-law."

Margaret nearly spat out her tea. The effort to keep herself from doing so sent her coughing uncontrollably. Jonas stepped closer as Ainsley handed her a napkin. Once composed, she patted her chin and gave a look of embarrassment to those watching her. "My apologies," she said, looking to Jonas, who stood over her. "I'm not quite sure what brought that about."

Aunt Louisa furrowed her eyebrows before relaxing as she looked back to the invitation. "Your attempts at refinement lack…refinement," she said, clearing her throat. "Perhaps we should review some skills before the dinner." Aunt Louisa pressed out the skirt of her dress, as if drawing attention to her posture. "Dr. Davies might benefit as well."

Ainsley cleared his throat and placed his teacup and saucer on the table. "I'd promised Jonas I would accompany him to town to see some of the burn victims," Ainsley said, feigning regret. "And Margaret, didn't you promise Miss Ivy that you'd show her a few dresses you've grown tired of?" Ainsley said.

Margaret looked at him surprised. "Yes, of course. How remiss of me to forget." The pair stood up in unison, both eager to be free, as Jonas placed his teacup and saucer on the table.

Ainsley and Jonas stopped a pace short of the door and allowed Margaret to walk through ahead of them. In the hall, she turned to Ainsley slightly as they walked. "Do you think the duchess will rescind her invite?" Margaret asked quietly as they approached the base of the stairs.

"She risks committing a calamitous *faux pas,* if she does," Ainsley answered. "I doubt she would risk drawing such attention to herself."

Margaret nodded. "She may not even know. Suppose Blair

and Brandon did not say anything to her about this afternoon."

"All the more reason to believe they have something to hide."

Chapter 23

Nor think ye'll have to tell

Jonas had been curious to see the hospital in Tunbridge Wells and his intended professional visit presented Ainsley with a convenient excuse to gain access to the patients who were admitted after the fire. The nurse stationed at the front door of the hospital wasn't surprised to see Ainsley and Jonas when they first walked in. When they introduced themselves she smiled politely and led them down the main corridor to one of the ward rooms. A burst of coughing erupted in one of the rooms before becoming muffled and then subsiding completely.

"I'm afraid Dr. Hollingsworth is not here," she explained, glancing over her shoulder. "I know he would have liked to hear any insights you have regarding our treatment methods."

"I'll be sure to inform him should I notice anything," Jonas said humbly.

The nurse slipped through an open doorway to one of the ward rooms and stood to the side as Ainsley and Jonas filed in. The room was open, with wood floors, high ceilings, and rows of metal beds spanning the entirety of the space. Between each bed was a small table that held glasses of water, books, or a patient's spectacles. Most beds were occupied by patients, all of whom were male. Metal frames had been erected around certain cots, with white fabric curtains stretched between to offer a modicum of privacy.

A solitary nurse attended to them all. Ainsley watched as she slipped between the beds with a pitcher of water, refilling glasses, and for the first time he noticed how both nurses were dressed primly in gleaming white and heavily starched uniforms, a stark contrast to what awaited them back in their London hospital. At St. Thomas', only the head nurses had such pristine clothing, while the younger and less experienced girls wore the stains of their trade.

"We have a handful of patients from the fire," the nurse at

the door said to Ainsley and Jonas. She gestured to the sectioned-off cots hidden behind the curtain before guiding them down the aisle toward them. "Most of the men were treated and sent home. These men are at further risk if they return home, so we opt to keep them here, where we can best protect them from further infection. Helen can answer any of your questions," she said, nodding to the attending nurse. "I'll let Miss Diane, our head nurse, know you are here."

Jonas nodded their thanks while Ainsley scrutinized the beds closest to the burn victims.

Helen smiled as she approached with a basket of clean, rolled bandages. "I was just about to change this man's dressing," she said. The nurse slipped between an opening in the curtain frames and Ainsley took the liberty of following her while Jonas fell into conversation with another patient.

The young man who lay in the bed tried to sit up when he saw Ainsley, who immediately recognized him as the man who led the wagon from the back of the burning barn.

"Sir," the man said before stopping suddenly and hissing against obvious pain. Ainsley noticed the man's right arm was limp on the bed beside his torso and he was very reluctant to move it.

"I'm sorry, Alistair," Helen said, setting her basket of clean bandages down on the table beside the bed.

The man grew alarmed when the nurse approached and looked to Ainsley imploringly.

When Helen pulled back the white sheet Ainsley saw that the bandages on his one arm had been nearly soaked through with blood and pus, staining the white cloth. Alistair used his free arm to cover his face and then pull his black hair into a tight fist. It was clear the procedure was a painful one and the man would have done anything to avoid it.

"Isn't there's a better way?" the patient implored. "A medicine or something I can take?" He looked to Ainsley and then back at the nurse, fear evident in his eyes.

Helen looked to Ainsley as she knelt beside the bed. She filled an empty washbasin with fresh water before untying the first of two knots in the wrapped bandage. The man stiffened before she'd barely touched him.

It was the smell that hit Ainsley first, ripe with the unmistakable pungent aroma of rot. She worked quickly, pulling back the layers of cloth that the wound was slow to release. Once finally exposed, Ainsley was able to see how the burn had become infected after only two days and would continue to do so until it was successful in taking the man's life.

When she reached for a clean bandage roll Ainsley held out a hand to stop her. "Are those treated with carbolic acid?" he asked.

At first startled, Helen looked to the bandage in her hand and then to the basket. "I don't know," she said with reluctance.

Ainsley peered out from their curtained enclave and called to Jonas. "Dr. Davies, your medical bag, please." A moment later Ainsley had retrieved a palm-size bottle labelled "Carbolic Acid" and began to prepare a solution that would sterilize the cloth.

Ainsley did not doubt the quality of care offered at the hospital, but after seeing the man's wounds he was glad he had come. Alistair's arm was already showing signs of a severe infection. If it continued unabated, there would have been no choice but to amputate, which often ended in death. Dressed properly, employing every measure of infection control, the patient would have a chance at recovery.

Jonas went to the opposite side of the bed and looked over the patient while Ainsley slipped the bandages into the carbolic solution.

"You told me to go to the pond," the man said suddenly, eyeing Ainsley as he worked at the table. "The water felt good for a while, like the flames hadn't even touched me. It was only after that my skin started"—Alistair hesitated and looked to the nurse—"you know."

"I doubt there is anything you could say to make this woman squeamish," Ainsley said without taking his eyes from his task. "She's a nurse, after all."

The man nodded but chose to end his story there.

"It's called hydrotherapy," Ainsley said, pulling one of the bandages from the water basin. "It's proven very useful for burns and other injuries." He wrung out the strip of cloth and turned to the bed. "Can you hold his arm?" he asked the nurse.

With Alistair's arm suspended off the bed slightly, Ainsley

coiled the wet bandage around the burn wound. The patient braced himself for pain but relaxed after a moment and even began to watch as his wound was dressed.

"Now," Ainsley said, carefully tying off the cloth, "what were you doing in Mr. Owen's barn?" Ainsley grabbed a dry bandage and began a second layer of dressing.

"I work for the Owens, sir," Alistair said. "I share a room above the kitchens with two others."

Ainsley nodded. "So you were there when the fire broke out?"

"I was at the house, sir. Seeing to some things for Mr. Owen..." Alistair licked his lips and pulled his gaze away. "I didn't know what to do when I heard the screaming."

"Screaming?" Ainsley perked up at this.

Alistair swallowed and glanced to Jonas. "Miss Ivy, sir, running from the barn screaming. I'd heard tell of her, tried to avoid her if I could. She's unpredictable, you see. By the time I got outside, the barn was filled with smoke black as tar." Alistair exhaled as Ainsley tied off the dry bandage and replaced his arm onto the top of the bedclothes. "Scariest day of my life."

"I can imagine," Jonas said.

"So you ran for the barn?" Ainsley pressed.

"Yes, sir. I thought I could get it out with the water from the trough but the flames reached the roof and I knew we had to get the horses out of there."

"We?" Jonas asked.

"Samuel and I."

"A portion of the roof caved in shortly after I arrived," Ainsley said.

"Yes, sir. I was just about to go back for another horse when it did. I tried pulling the wagon away but something fell on my arm and burned right through my shirt. That's when you told me to go to the pond."

Ainsley nodded and turned the events over in his mind. The sequence of events he suggested made sense and was easily combined with what Ainsley had witnessed himself.

"Did you see anything else?" Ainsley asked. "Anything strange or out of place?"

Alistair shook his head.

"What about Miss Ivy?" Jonas asked. "You said she is unpredictable."

The patient nodded. "I heard some of the other hands say things, you know, say she was damaged in some way. Not quite like the rest of us."

Ainsley and Jonas exchanged glances. "Do you happen to know if anyone said anything about Miss Ivy having a male friend?" Ainsley asked cautiously.

"Perhaps one of the farmhands showed a particular interest in her," Jonas suggested.

"No, sir. We all keep our distance, if you know what I mean. Mr. Garret would not like anyone making eyes at his sister. He's very protective of her, he is."

Ainsley nodded.

"This is about Mr. Owen and them that killed him, isn't it?" Alistair asked suddenly.

Jonas and Ainsley didn't answer.

"I wish I could be more help. It all happened so fast. I've had a lot of time to think about it too, and all I remember is the roar of the flames and the fear in the eyes of those horses." The man looked as if his soul had been chilled by the memory of that night.

"Thank you, sir," Ainsley said, laying his hand gently over Alistair's.

Ainsley stood and handed the corked bottle of carbolic acid to Helen. "You need to treat everything, bandages, clothes, tools with this, just as I have done, especially for this man. That infection cannot be allowed to get any worse, understand?"

Helen nodded as she accepted the bottle. They left the curtained area and walked the aisle of the main room.

"And we're going to need the list of all patients who came here seeking treatment after the fire," Ainsley said. When the nurse left, Ainsley saw the quizzical look on Jonas's face. "We're going to need to see if anyone has any injuries not relating to the fire. Bruises, contusions, that sort of thing," Ainsley explained.

"You mean to see if anyone fought with Mr. Owen before he died," Jonas said.

Ainsley nodded.

"And Ivy? What do you make of her?"

"I'm not entirely sure," Ainsley answered. "That girl is the real mystery."

Chapter 24

Of wounded hearts from me,

Margaret was thankful to not have to spend her afternoon refining her decorum alongside Aunt Louisa. After the previous week at The Briar, Margaret was feeling gluttonous for breathing room, given all the people crammed into what was intended to be a small country cottage, not a sprawling estate suitable for numerous guests. The presence of Aunt Louisa and her boys was really beginning to grate on her and Margaret could tell Ainsley was even more displeased.

Despite her desire for some time alone, Margaret had a duty to check in on Ivy and, regardless what Aunt Louisa might think of her, she wasn't about to neglect the woman, who was becoming a fast friend.

They had given Ivy their mother's room, though there had been some debate regarding its suitability. Ainsley suggested Lady Charlotte's room outright because it had not been used in many months and was probably one of the most hospitable rooms in the entire house. Margaret fought against the suggestion, however, and in the end she lost. There was no particular reason for her resistance other than her own desire to keep it as it was, tainted though it may be.

Just before Margaret reached the closed door Aunt Louisa's voice found her in the hall. "Oh Margaret," she called out in her signature singsong tone. Margaret could feel herself bristle at the sound and very much wished her aunt had not cornered her so. How much longer would Ainsley and she have to suffer under such close scrutiny?

"I've decided I won't be joining you and Peter for the dinner at Breaside. Nathaniel is keen to go but the boys, however, are still not used to their nursery here. I should like to stay close by for their sakes." Aunt Louisa tilted her head to the side and gave a closed-mouth smile. "You understand, don't you, my dear?"

"I'm sure Julia could give them some extra attention,"

Margaret offered.

"No, no, unfortunately the boys have developed quite an attachment to me. Excellent governesses were terribly hard to find in India, you understand. Much of their upbringing was relegated to me in the end and, well, this has been the result." Aunt Louisa's smile faltered slightly and her eyes glistened with threatening tears before she blinked them away. "I fear I may worry for them all night and I do not wish my motherly doting to impede on your budding friendships." She winked at Margaret then, hinting at the relationship she imagined Margaret and Blair were forming.

"Very well, Aunt Louisa. We shall offer your regrets."

"No need. I have already sent a note to Lady Thornton, who I am sure will understand."

Rendered speechless, Margaret nodded and simply watched as Aunt Louisa walked down the hall to her own room, closing the door behind her. She couldn't pretend to know the woman, but she couldn't agree that the boys were as attached to her as she claimed. The entire time the Banks family had been there both Hubert and George frolicked about without much care or concern for their mother. It was Nathaniel who appeared to have a special bond with Aunt Louisa. So overly concerned was he for his mother's wishes that even Peter had noticed.

Alone once again, Margaret gave a dainty knock and only pushed the door open when she heard Ivy's tiny voice inviting her in. Ivy was standing at the window, her arms crossed over her chest. She would have been looking out over the front lawn and would have seen Ainsley and Jonas leave in the carriage.

"Miss Margaret." Ivy said the words as a breath, barely loud enough for Margaret to hear. Even their growing attachment did not erase the fact that the girl was somewhat odd.

"I just wanted to ensure everything was all right," Margaret said, walking into the room.

"Oh yes," Ivy answered. "Quite all right."

It was then that Margaret saw it, the hurt and mourning in Ivy's eyes. Whether she had agreed to the procedure out of coercion or desperation, the girl would never be the same. Margaret took a seat at the edge of the bed and decided she would sit with Ivy, completely silent if need be, to show her she would not be alone.

"It is done," she said. "And we cannot go back."

A single tear rolled down Ivy's cheek before the girl was able to look away.

"Ivy, are you regretting your decision?" Margaret crossed the room and positioned herself so Ivy could not avoid looking at her.

"What kind of person am I?" Ivy gasped, releasing a torrent of sobs. She slipped into Margaret's arms easily, burying her face in Margaret's welcoming arms. Margaret tried to soothe her as best she could, rocking her and holding her tightly. "I almost couldn't do it. I was so scared." Ivy sniffled loudly. "I love this baby's father and I know he loves me."

"Oh, Ivy…" Margaret wasn't sure what the girl said was true.

"But he cannot marry me." A wail grew from Ivy's throat before she was able to choke it back. Ivy lifted her face, revealing bloodshot eyes and tearstained cheeks. "I don't know what's going to happen now. I'm so scared, Margaret. So very scared."

"Everything will be all right," Margaret said, almost forcibly.

Ivy gave a slight sniffle before pulling away. She wiped the crests of her cheeks with the heel of her hand. "Your mother said the same thing." Ivy looked up and offered a weak smile.

Margaret felt her heart slip from her chest to her stomach. "My mother?"

The girl did not flinch, not even when Margaret's body stiffened against the shock of what Ivy had just told her. Margaret licked her lips, which had suddenly become excruciatingly dry. "Ivy, this is not funny." She couldn't help but recoil at the shock. When had Ivy become so cruel as to bring up her mother, who had been dead for nearly five months?

Ivy frowned. "I'm sorry."

Margaret took a step back, and placed her hand over her mouth. She could feel her chin trembling as a chill ran the length of her body. "You shouldn't say such things," Margaret said, willing herself not to cry. She began to pace the room, a hand at her stomach, which was ready to lurch.

"You are right, Miss Margaret," Ivy said rather compliantly. Margaret saw Ivy close her eyes and mutter something to herself that Margaret could not hear. Her anger grew steadily, a sudden flood over an unsuspecting landscape. Within two paces Margaret crossed the distance between them and grabbed Ivy by the shoulders. "Look at me!"

Ivy complied but a fear overshadowed her face.

"Why are you saying such things?"

"I don't know." Ivy's response was so quick, so rehearsed, Margaret knew she must have said it many times before. "I'm sorry."

Again, Ivy's gaze darted for the window, searching the yard for a way out of her predicament. Margaret watched as panic overtook the girl. Suddenly, Margaret felt ashamed of her outburst, the distrust she had displayed for the sincerity of her friend. It was clear others had doubted Ivy as well.

"No, I'm sorry," Margaret said, softening her tone considerably. With a hand at her forehead, Margaret steadied her breathing with a few regulated breaths. The last thing Ivy needed was another person who distrusted her and made her feel ashamed.

Margaret placed a gentle hand on Ivy's. "You have to admit, what you said was quite shocking. What were you trying to say?"

During Margaret's entire apology Ivy did not meet her eyes and then when she did she feigned ignorance. "I'm not entirely sure," she said with a slight laugh. "Mustn't have been important."

"No, no it was," Margaret said, bringing Ivy's hand closer. "Please, I won't get mad. Tell me what my mother said and I shall try my best to hear it."

Ivy let out a huff then, smiled, and shook her head. "How should I know? I never met the countess."

Margaret grew stern but recognized her own part to play. Her eyes threatened tears and her gaze fell to the ground. She sniffled as she brushed the hair from her face. She wanted to leave, to hide in her room, but she hesitated. She felt the tears coming, but her feet seemed rooted in place. She did not want to turn her back on Ivy and yet how could she believe what Ivy herself struggled to acknowledge?

Chapter 25

Locked up in your hearts cell.

Once the sun went down Ainsley and Jonas were forced to work by lantern light. Diane, the head nurse, had shown them to an office with a desk and chair in the middle. She brought them an extra chair and the hospital records for the previous week and then left them alone, saying if they needed her she'd be in the office next door.

The hospital drew quiet as the sun went down, with only intermittent fits of coughing reminding them where they were. Every so often the sounds of a nurse's boots walking the length of the hall could be heard outside the door, the speed indicating their degree of urgency. Together, Ainsley and Jonas sat at the table, opposite each other, scanning the record book and reading the accompanying reports in search of any ailment that could be attributed to an altercation of some sort.

"Perhaps we should ask for a record of Dr. Hollingsworth's house calls, as well," Jonas said, flipping the page of the report he was reading.

"This is going to be more difficult than I had originally thought." Ainsley was reading his fifth report, another burn victim suffering from the effects of the smoke and a burn on his left leg where a smouldering wood plank had fallen on him. The man indicated he was from two farms away and ran toward the blaze when he saw the smoke, just as Ainsley had.

"Hollingsworth lists abrasions on this man's arms and face." Ainsley flipped the page to show Jonas a rudimentary sketch indicating the locations of the man's bruises. "How is that any different from any of us present that night?"

"If Dr. Hollingsworth was processing a number of new patients specifically from the fire he'd be flustered, acting hastily, perhaps not even noticing minor wounds. Certain injuries may have gone unnoticed," Jonas offered.

Ainsley was forced to nod. "I doubt he would have noticed

anything amiss. If he had, I doubt he would have had the wherewithal to write it down in the report."

Ainsley slapped the file closed and leaned back in his chair, running his hands through his hair. "We know Mr. Owen was in the barn prior to the fire," Ainsley began, indicating with his index finger his first fact. "We know he was dragged from the blaze."

"We know he wasn't breathing at that time, though we don't know if he was dead."

Ainsley nodded. "I highly suspect it was an overturned lantern that caused the fire," Ainsley said, "And I further suspect it was overturned during the altercation between Mr. Owen and our killer."

"So what makes you believe our killer elected to stay to assist the bucket brigade?" Jonas asked.

Ainsley shrugged, "I don't, but I can guess that by the time Mr. Owen was dragged from the barn the fire would have caught that straw. People would have already been running toward the scene. How likely would it be that everyone running to help put out the blaze wouldn't see that single person running in the opposite direction?"

"He stayed to help."

Ainsley smiled. "Precisely. No one questions why he's there and everyone is too busy nursing their injuries to see him leave."

A murmur of voices grew outside in the hall. There was a hint of hostility that drew Ainsley's attention.

"It could be anyone," Jonas said, tossing a report in his hand down on the desk. "We're looking for a needle in a haystack."

Ainsley raised a finger to his mouth, indicating for Jonas to be quiet. He pointed toward the door with his chin and then noticed the voices had stopped abruptly. Ainsley made a circular motion with his hands and looked to Jonas. "You were saying, Dr. Davies."

"I was saying…" Jonas fumbled his sentence and looked to Ainsley imploringly.

"You are discouraged," Ainsley prodded. "I am as well." Again, Ainsley made a circular motion with his hands, encouraging Jonas to continue while he stood up slowly from his chair.

The voices began again, and as Ainsley inched toward the door he realized it was two women engaged in a hushed yet heated exchange. One of them was Helen, the attending nurse, and the other was Diane, the head nurse. He heard Jonas shuffling papers behind him as he made his way, gingerly, toward the door.

"You have to tell him," Helen said in a near panic.

"Certainly not," Diane answered. "He isn't the physician here!"

Ainsley pressed his ear up to the door, concentrating hard so he could make out the nurses's words.

"What are you doing?" Jonas asked from the desk.

Ainsley gave his friend a wide-eyed look and told him to hush. A bout of coughing erupted, muffling the women's next words, but Ainsley could hear enough to know they were arguing about his and Jonas's presence.

"They are looking into the fire," Helen said, "and they deserve to know!" Her voice grew markedly loud then and was followed by quickening footsteps along the corridor.

The footsteps stopped abruptly and then there was a tiny yelp.

Ainsley was out the door and halfway down the hall before he could piece together what he had heard. The head nurse held the younger nurse to the wall, her hand pressed into her shoulder.

"What is the meaning of this?" Ainsley asked as he watched the head nurse take a step back.

"Nothing, sir," she said. "Miss Fitch here was being reprimanded. Nothing you need to be concerned about."

Jonas appeared at Ainsley's side then.

"What do we deserve to know?" Ainsley asked, looking to the younger nurse, who adjusted her uniform and bit her lower lip. After a moment's hesitation, she spoke. "A patient died this morning," she said, giving a sideways glance to the head nurse. "He was injured in the fire. Dr. Hollingsworth hasn't had the time to write a report yet."

Ainsley nodded slowly and looked to Diane. "Is that so?"

"You didn't need to know, sir," she explained.

He raised a single eyebrow. "I know now, so you might as well take me to the body."

Begrudgingly, Diane led them down the back stairs of the building to the basement and, after opening the lock, showed them into a dark room.

"I don't see how Mr. Fitzpatrick's death is any of your concern," she said, leading them to the table where a body lay beneath a white sheet. "This is a matter for Dr. Hollingsworth."

"We are investigating the death of a local man, anything that can be linked back to that case is a concern of ours," Ainsley explained unapologetically. He no longer had patience for people who stood in his way. After his encounter with the local constabulary he knew he was the only one asking questions and attempting to fit the pieces together.

Jonas pulled back the sheet while the nurse lit an overhead lamp. Ainsley noticed straightaway that the man was older, older still than Mr. Owen himself. At first glance, his injuries appeared minor. The skin on his arms was pink, indicating damage to the dermis, but it did not penetrate the deeper layers of skin. Ainsley leaned close to the man's face and studied his lips before prying the mouth open.

"Dr. Davies, the lamp, if you don't mind."

Jonas pulled the lamp from the hook above them and brought it closer.

"Would you say this man's esophagus is severely damaged?" Ainsley asked. He looked to the nurse, who did not flinch.

"Smoke inhalation," she said.

"You suspect that is what killed him?" Jonas asked.

"Yes," Diane answered. "We have no way to treat it once it gets to the lungs."

"What did Dr. Hollingsworth order for his treatment?"

"Laudanum." She shifted where she stood, as if caught by the headmistress at school. "We were just trying to make him comfortable."

Ainsley nodded. He knew nothing else could have been done to prevent the outcome. A slight injury to the lungs, indicative by coughing and painful breathing, could heal in time, but any greater degree of damage could not be healed. Experimental procedures did exist but were only available in London and Edinburgh, not the Kent countryside.

They looked over the man's body for half an hour, searching for anything out of the ordinary. The search was fruitless, leading them down no new avenues of investigation. He could have been one of the first on the scene or one of the last. The only thing they could decipher was that he had been there and was close enough to inhale a fair amount of hot smoke.

"There are no signs of struggle either," Jonas said, paying special attention to the man's hands, which bore no signs of injury or assault. "It is very likely he had nothing to do with Mr. Owen's death."

"Do we have an address for this man?" Ainsley asked, turning to Diane. She hesitated before giving a slight nod. She left a moment later. Her steps could be heard climbing the stairs to the main floor.

"Plan to interrogate his bereaved loved ones?" Jonas asked without jest.

"I want to know why he was there," Ainsley explained, giving one last look over the body before covering it up with the sheet once again. "You know how country people talk. Someone is bound to know who had a grudge against Mr. Owen."

The next day Ainsley skipped breakfast and spent his early morning hours in the library before readying himself for Mr. Owen's funeral. Margaret had made it known that everyone in the household was expected to attend. "For Ivy," she said when she appeared at Ainsley's door the evening before. He had no intentions of protesting, though her continued care of Ivy left him dumbfounded. More than one person had placed a doubt in him regarding her sanity and his own experience with her did nothing to help alleviate those impressions.

Their finest open-air carriage was waiting at the base of the front steps when Ainsley stepped out. Jonas and Nathaniel had already gathered at the front of the house and looked as if they had been waiting for some time.

"I was beginning to think you weren't coming," Jonas said. "Did you sleep well?"

"Why do you ask?"

"I heard footsteps in your room," Jonas said, "thought you were having—"

"Gentlemen, please, help an old woman." Aunt Louisa stood at the top of the steps calling to them with an outstretched hand. "These steps do not agree with this footwear."

Jonas overtook Ainsley and hurried up the steps to offer assistance. Moments later, Margaret and Ivy appeared at the door. Ivy had borrowed one of Margaret's mourning gowns and looked entirely uncomfortable in the finery as she clung to Margaret's side.

Ainsley offered a hand to both as they approached the carriage and assisted Ivy with the many layers of her skirt that prevented her from stepping up easily.

"I'm impressed," Margaret said behind him. "You and Aunt Louisa managed to hide your contempt for a few minutes at least."

"Margaret— " She did not let him finish. She raised her hand to Jonas beside her, indicating that he should help her into the carriage and was nestled in her spot beside Ivy before Ainsley could say another word.

Once everyone was seated, the carriage jerked into motion, taking them in the direction of town. They sat quietly for some time with only the odd remark from Aunt Louisa breaking their reverie.

"I do hope it's a short service," she said, pulling on her tight-fitting gloves, "Goodness knows how the country parsons love to prattle on so." She chuckled slightly to herself and looked about as if expecting everyone else to appreciate her jest. No one was in the mood. Margaret managed a tight-lipped smile but quickly turned away.

Ainsley wasn't sure if Jonas had told her about his plans of enquiry but she left little doubt that she was angered with him for questioning the Thornton brothers. Exhaling, he leaned back in his seat and gazed out the window. His efforts to escape the vile nature of the city had backfired. Not only did he find himself in the middle of a quagmire of murder and enquiry but one of the dearest people in his life reviled him for his suspicions.

A number of people were already gathered at the grave site by the time they arrived, but the most surprising guests of all were Blair and Brandon Thornton. Ainsley exited the carriage first and remained at the carriage doors to help the women step down.

He wanted to pull Margaret aside to speak before the service. But by the time he assisted Ivy he turned to find Margaret had already been cornered by Brandon and Blair.

"Good day, Miss Marshall, Miss Owen," Blair said. "It appears we could not have asked for a better day to honour your father."

"Thank you, sir," Ivy said, somewhat awkwardly.

Garret approached them. After acknowledging Ainsley and Jonas, he turned to his sister and motioned for her to join the family. "Come Ivy, everyone is waiting."

Margaret turned back to the Thornton brothers. "It was good of you to come," she said in a whisper. "I'm sure the Owens appreciate your presence…as do I." She spoke as if offering an apology for their last meeting, but as always with the upper classes no one spoke of such unpleasantness unless absolutely warranted. Brandon looked disinterested next to his brother, who kept his gaze on Margaret.

"Think nothing of it," Blair said. His gaze lifted to Ainsley, full of contempt and loathing, before returning his focus to Margaret. He offered his arm to Margaret and the two of them headed to the graveside.

"Who is he?" Jonas asked, appearing alongside Ainsley.

"Blair Thornton," Ainsley answered discreetly.

"Is he a good man?"

"I haven't decided yet."

To Aunt Louisa's delight, the service was short and before long they were offering their final condolences. It was planned that Ivy would return home with her family that day following the service. Ainsley watched as Margaret hugged her for a long time, longer than what was viewed as appropriate. "Feel free to visit any time," she said as she pulled away.

Ivy nodded quickly. Ainsley thought he saw her eyes well up as Margaret spoke.

"Come, Margaret," Aunt Louisa said quietly beside her. "We must leave them to their grief."

Glad that their liaison had finally come to an end, Ainsley offered a hand to Samuel and then Garret. "Gentlemen," Ainsley said, "send word to The Briar once you decide to erect a new barn.

I'm sure we can spare a few bodies to assist."

"Thank you, sir," Samuel said. "You have been most helpful."

Before the brothers turned away Ainsley saw a smile curl the edges of Samuel's mouth as he bowed his head. There was a mischievousness to it that drew all Ainsley's blood to his feet.

"Peter." Aunt Louisa beckoned him from behind, already settled in the seat of the carriage. "Peter!"

Ainsley ignored her and watched as Samuel finally released Ivy's arm so she could climb into the carriage. Contrasted by the girl's usually pale tone, her skin burned red where he brother had grabbed her so forcefully.

Chapter 26

Mine still at home doth dwell
In its first liberty.

Mr. Fitzpatrick's house was near the centre of the village. His door was one of seven that adorned the same low-rise, orange brick building, with a single window between the doors for each separate dwelling. A solitary step led to each tenement from the cobblestone street. Ainsley knocked with purpose and looked farther down the lane while he waited. At the crossroads, carts wheeled by and pedestrians hurriedly crossed the street. But where Ainsley stood the birds sang a calming tune while the wind rustled the leaves in the trees at the back of the property.

The door groaned as it opened and a slight, older woman appeared. "Yes?"

"Ma'am, my name is Peter Marshall, my friend and I are looking into the circumstances of the barn fire at Summer Hill. I was wondering if I may speak with Mrs. Fitzpatrick?"

The woman nodded as she pulled the door wider, revealing herself in a black mourning dress. "I am Mrs. Fitzpatrick," she said as she stepped out of the way to allow Ainsley to enter.

The home Mrs. Fitzpatrick shared with her husband was modest in space and furnishings. She led the way through a sparse sitting room at the front of the house, to the equally sized kitchen at the back. A slim set of stairs leading to a half storey above was situated against the farthest wall in the kitchen.

"I was just 'bout to sit for a spot of tea," she said meekly. "Would you care for some?" She placed her hands on the back of one of the chairs at the table as she looked at him.

"Thank you, ma'am," Ainsley said with a nod.

"Have a seat then," Mrs. Fitzpatrick ordered before turning to the stove.

"First let me say, Mrs. Fitzpatrick, how very sorry I am for your loss," Ainsley began as he settled himself in at the table. He saw the older woman slow her movements slightly, bowing her head as if in prayer.

"Thank you," she said before continuing to prepare the tea. A moment later, Ainsley was presented with a lovely china teacup with a chip in the saucer. "I hope you like honey. I'm afraid it's all we have at the moment." Once she spoke, regret overtook her features. "It's all I have, I should say."

"Honey is fine. Thank you."

When Mrs. Fitzpatrick took her seat, she pulled a handkerchief from the sleeve of her dress and dabbed her eyes. "Pardon me," she said, sniffling. "It's all very new."

"Shouldn't someone be here, sitting with you," Ainsley said, "at such a difficult time?"

"Oh, I have a very good neighbour," she said, her expression livening slightly. "Such a dear she is. She sat with me well into the night after they brought me the news. I expect she'll be home any minute now from work." Mrs. Fitzpatrick smiled as she pressed down the creases in her tablecloth. "I have friends, many lovely people who will look after me," she said, as if trying to convince him further. "You wanted to ask me some questions about Rolland?"

"Was he a farmhand at Summer Hill?"

"Oh no, no," Mrs. Fitzpatrick looked as if she could laugh at the suggestion. "He is a railway man. Works at the yards carting things and moving things. He's done right by me for nearly thirty-five years now, he has. I don't think he ever set foot on that farm until the day of the fire. Not my Rolland. No, sir. He's not a gambler."

"He must have seen the smoke then, and ran to help?"

"Yes 'em, he did. Always very helpful he was. I don't doubt it was he who told the others to go too. That was my Rolland. Always the first to help. That fire must have been a dreadful sight. All those horses." Mrs. Fitzpatrick clicked her tongue and shook her head. "He ran for those horses, so they tell me. He cared little for the men at that farm but he would have given his all to save them horses."

Ainsley saw Mrs. Fitzpatrick stiffen slightly at her own words. She pulled the handkerchief from her sleeve again and raised it to cover both eyes. When she pulled it away, her nose appeared red and her eyes moist.

Ainsley reached over the small table and squeezed her hand.

She smiled. "Thank you, deary."

"You said he cared little for the men. Why might that be?" Ainsley asked.

Mrs. Fitzpatrick huffed. "Well, on account of their unchristian goings-on, that's what. My Rolland was a God-fearing man, Mr. Marshall."

"What sorts of 'goings-on'?" Ainsley asked, using her own words.

"Oh, he'd never tell me for sure. Only said those men would face God's judgement before long for what they done." Mrs. Fitzpatrick waged a stout, crooked finger at him. "It was only a matter of time. He never wanted me to concern myself with them. He told me if I were to ever see them in town I was to cross the street or pretend I never seen 'em. And I did. My Rolland has never steered me wrong."

Ainsley nodded as he allowed her words to soak in.

"Seems a shame he had to go on account of that farm." She sniffled loudly as she raised her handkerchief. "More tea?" she asked from behind the cloth.

"No, ma'am. Thank you for your time."

As Ainsley closed the door behind him his heart felt heavier than when he first arrived. He kept finding himself at an end to the clues, yet no further along in his quest for answers. It seemed logical that a man with as good a heart as Mr. Fitzpatrick was said to have would rush to the aid of his neighbours in need. What seemed illogical was the level of loathing he had displayed in his life for a family farm whose worst trespass, as far as Ainsley could tell, was gambling. Unless there was more to it than that.

"Blast!" A woman at the neighbouring door was struggling with her key. Even with her back to the street Ainsley could tell her arms were burdened with a package, books, and a small basket. She pushed on the door, growling at its refusal to budge and then her books toppled to the step. Ainsley hurried to assist.

He pick up one book and was about to snatch another when he realized the woman was Diane, the head nurse at the local hospital. He plucked the book from the pavement, without taking his eyes off her. They both stood at the same time but it was clear Diane couldn't bring herself to look at him.

"Thank you, Mr. Marshall," she said curtly. She collected her books and turned back to the door, probably hoping Ainsley wouldn't say anything more.

"Why didn't you tell me Mr. Fitzpatrick was your neighbour?" he asked. He pushed himself closer and took the books and package from her to ease her burden. He saw her exhale before turning the key in the lock. It worked.

"As I said before, it's nothing to concern yourself about," she said, making a point to look him in the eye as she collected her books and package. She turned to go inside but Ainsley pulled the door closed. A look of resignation fell over her features as her shoulders sank. "Mr. Fitzpatrick was a good man, the best I had ever met, and I didn't want him maligned with the likes of them." Her mouth twisted into a scowl as she spoke.

"You need to tell me why. What is it about these people?"

Diane bit her lower lip and looked farther down the street. "Come inside."

Her home was an exact copy of the Fitzpatricks's, only with less furnishings and knick-knacks. She dropped her books and basket on the table in the kitchen before returning to the sitting room. Ainsley closed the door behind him before he spoke. "Are you the neighbour who has been sitting with Mrs. Fitzpatrick?" he asked.

"Yes. I slept on their couch last night so Maggie wouldn't feel alone." Diane pulled her hatpin and placed her straw hat on the hook near the door. "They are like my parents and I always said I wouldn't know what to do if anything happened to either of them." Diane placed her hand on her forehead. "I know he was old but he didn't deserve to die like he did. He should have died in bed, at home with Maggie at his side."

"What about the Owens?"

Diane took a breath and eyed Ainsley across the cramped room. "My father used to work at Summer Hill. Said it was the best job he'd ever had working with them horses. Could never say anything negative about the place that was so good to him. Even then people in town would talk, about the boys and their father, but my father would put them in their place. Said Summer Hill was as good a place as any and then some." Diane's face soured. "And then one day about three years ago everything changed. He became moody, wouldn't come home at the end of his shift, spent more and more time at the public house. He wouldn't talk about it, to Ma or me. Said he understood what the men were about. That some things, once seen couldn't be unseen."

"What do you think he meant by that?"

Diane swallowed. "I don't know. My father wasn't the same any more, that was clear. He grew more and more agitated. Ma said he should find another place but no one would hire him without a reference and he needed to pay for my schooling." Diane closed her eyes and shook her head slightly. "Then one day I came home and Samuel was here. He had my father pressed up against the wall with his fist holding his collar really tight. I only heard a few words before they saw me. He left shortly after. I'll never forget the look that man gave me as he passed me on his way out. I swear he looked as if he could eat me alive."

Ainsley felt a shiver go up his spine. He wondered if the look was similar to what he'd seen at the cemetery.

"There are many in this town that would love to see the Owens run out and I'm one of them. No better than gypsies."

"Can I speak with your father? Maybe he'll tell me what happened."

"He passed away last August. Dr. Hollingsworth said it was his heart."

Chapter 27

Bees sip not at one flower,

The smoke woke Ainsley first, circling in the air above his head and attacking his lungs as soon as he drew breath. Coughing did little to relieve the struggle for air and when he opened his eyes he found his room engulfed with smoke and ash.

Another breath, deeper than the last, brought heat down his throat and nearly choked the life out of him. Each movement was a struggle but he somehow made it to the door. Rushing into the hall the flames and heat hit him, trapping him at his doorframe.

Through the orange glow and plumes of smoke, Ainsley saw an empty hallway. No shouts or screams escaped Margaret or Jonas, Hubert, George, or Nathaniel. Flames licked the wood frames around their closed doors.

Ainsley pushed through the pain of the heat that singed his pants and lapped at his skin underneath. He began going door to door only to find each room empty. All the furnishings, draperies, and remembrances of the family that were there once were gone. The fire remained in the hall, warming his back as he darted from room to room, finding each one barren.

Ready to make for the front door a form caught his attention at the end of the hall. A person sat on a chair as the flames grew large around him. As Ainsley ran toward them he found his father, Lord Abraham Marshall, seated as easily as he would have in his study at the London house.

"Father?"

His face looked vacant as he stared past Ainsley, unaware of the flames and heat engulfing everything around him.

"We have to go!" Ainsley shouted over the roar of the flames. "Follow me!" Ainsley turned to the stairs, expecting his father to follow.

Lord Marshall did not move.

Moving closer still Ainsley saw a wide swath of fabric sewn tautly over his father's mouth. Ainsley tried to pull his father's body from the chair but it would not move. He checked for rope or anything that could be binding his father in place.

"The house is going to collapse!"

He pulled on his father's body, which remained rigid and unaware until suddenly Lord Marshall's eyes snapped wide and stared at Ainsley imploringly.

"I'm trying to help you!" Ainsley said, almost crying. "Why won't you let me help you?" Ainsley clasped his father's shoulders and shook him angrily, crying against the angst. He could not leave him. "Father, please!"

His head on his pillow, Ainsley drew in a long, exuberant breath, gasping as if he hadn't taken in air for days. He sat upright in bed, his heart still racing from his dream, and realized it was morning and his room looked just the same as it had the day before. He closed his eyes, attempting to relieve the panic that vibrated inside him.

A tiny rap sprang from the other side of his closed door. "Mr. Marshall, is everything all right?" one of the maids asked.

"Quite all right," he answered steadily.

"Do you want me to summon Maxwell for you?"

"No. I'm all right," Ainsley answered with a little more strain. "Thank you," he added as an afterthought.

Chapter 28

Spring comes not with one shower,

As the carriage rolled up the lane at Summer Hill Farm a chill went up Margaret's spine. Two days had passed since she last saw Ivy and she still wasn't quite sure the girl would want to see her, not after what last happened between them. But Margaret could not keep the girl from cropping up in her mind. She felt herself becoming deeply fearful.

The horses were grazing in the lower pasture, farthest from the house, which gave the property a sparse, almost abandoned feel. There was a stark difference between that day and her first visit the week before when stable hands, grooms, and trainers riddled the property. Now it seemed almost too quiet without a sign of life anywhere.

An uneasy feeling washed over Margaret as she stepped down from the carriage. A knock at the front door went unanswered. Stepping back, Margaret looked up to the dark windows of the second storey, perhaps hoping to catch a glimpse of Ivy. A form did appear at the window, pulling back the curtain to look down at Margaret, but it was not Ivy.

"Hello?" Margaret called out feebly.

The figure withdrew, allowing the curtain to fall back into place.

It was the steady *chop, chop, chop* from behind the house that drew Margaret's attention away from the window. She found Samuel just outside the back door, chopping charred bits of wood, presumably some of the remains from the barn fire, into pieces small enough for the kitchen stove. When he saw her he drove the ax into the stump he had been using as a pedestal.

"Good morning, Samuel," Margaret said, somewhat shakily.

He did not look at her and stood, hands on hips, surveying his progress. "What can I do for you, Miss Marshall?"

"I saw a face in the window just now," Margaret said pointing to the upper windows.

Samuel squinted as he looked up. "You must be mistaken. I'm the only one home," he said with a shrug.

"I thought it may have been Ivy," she pressed.

Samuel smiled out the corner of his mouth but said nothing more on the subject. *Chop*.

"I've come to visit with her," Margaret said.

"She's isn't here," Samuel answered, his breathing laboured.

Margaret smiled in an attempt to soften the evident tension in the air. "Do you know when she will return?"

"I can't say she will return," he answered, rearing his ax. *Chop*.

A chill washed over her. "What do you mean?"

Samuel gathered up his ax and balanced the handle on his shoulder as he positioned the next piece of wood to be splintered. "Garret took her this morning to St. Andrew's house. She's been committed. We don't think she's ever coming home."

Chop.

Climbing into the carriage, Margaret told Walter to drive as fast as he could to Barning Heath and he obeyed, but not without a great deal of coaxing. "Are you sure we shouldn't inform Mr. Marshall?" he had asked, swallowing hard and glancing around the empty farm lane.

"Yes," Margaret answered angrily. "He needn't know everything I do."

Walter pressed his lips together and took a deep breath. For a second, Margaret thought he wouldn't comply. But then he gave a quick nod and clasped the carriage door shut.

Her conviction left her only once when she peered out the window just as the carriage rolled through the gates at St. Andrew's House. She had heard stories about the asylum since she was a child—that it was like a prison for women who had never learned their place. She once heard boys taunting a young village girl by telling her they'd have her thrown in the asylum with one word to their fathers if she didn't do what they said. Thankfully, Margaret was able to convince Daniel to intervene while Margaret waited on the stoop of the teashop. She'd been told the rules had changed considerably in recent years but the foreboding remained. No one ever walked through the front doors willingly.

Walter helped her down the carriage steps and lingered behind her as she stepped forward. "We can come back, miss," he said, "with Mr. Marshall. No need to go in yourself."

Any other time Margaret would have accepted his reasoning and relented, but that day she knew she'd have to get herself up those steps and through the arches on her own.

"Wait for me," she said without looking back. "I shouldn't be long."

She did not see his face as she made her way toward the front door, but she imagined he was just as nervous as she was. The secretary scowled at her, the dent between her brows deepening as Margaret approached. "Can I help you?" She looked up at Margaret without lifting her chin.

"Yes, my name is Margaret Marshall. I'd like to enquire about Miss Ivy Owen," Margaret said, keeping her voice steady. She clasped her hands together in front of her to keep them from shaking.

The secretary said nothing but Margaret could hear her flipping pages in a book behind the partition that separated them. After a time the woman looked up. "She's already had two visitors, which is our daily limit."

"Oh please," Margaret said without thinking how desperate she must look, "she must be so scared."

The woman looked as if she would laugh. "She has her friends to keep her company."

Margaret's face fell and tears stung her eyes as the woman spoke. "What do you mean?" Margaret asked in challenge.

"That's why she's here, isn't it?" the woman asked. "Imaginary friends."

Margaret pulled her shoulders back and vowed not to give the woman an inch of ground in that respect.

"Certainly not. Now are you going to let me see her or should I return with my father, Lord Abraham Marshall, Earl of Montcliff?"

Her father was nowhere near Kent County nor could he be at a moment's notice. She was relying on this woman's fear of authority and her respect for the peerage.

The woman glanced left and right and leaned closer to

Margaret. "I'd be more inclined to break protocol were you willing to"—she uncurled her hand with her palm facing the ceiling—"make a donation."

Margaret did not hesitate. She'd do anything for Ivy. She opened the string of her reticule and pulled out all the notes she had and presented them to the secretary.

"James!" the nurse called out as she stuffed the money into the breast pocket of her uniform. A young man looking through a cupboard behind her perked up at the mention of his name.

"Escort Miss Marshall…forgive me, *Lady* Margaret, to Miss Ivy's room."

Margaret smiled. "Thank you."

"You will only be permitted fifteen minutes," the secretary said, turning her attention back to the books opened in front for her. "And I wouldn't go in farther than the door, if I were you," she mumbled.

"Pardon me?" Margaret asked.

"Follow me, ma'am." James appeared beside her then and gestured for the double doors that would take them down a long corridor.

Margaret walked alongside him as he led the way to the third floor. Room after room passed, none empty and most with occupants desperate to leave. "It's all right, ma'am," James said once as they passed a particularly agitated patient who screamed through the heavy door. "They cannot get through those doors."

His words gave her no comfort against the dread that rose up inside her. How would she find Ivy? Certainly not like these others.

Finally, James stopped at a door and pulled a key from his waistband. The metal door opened with a shrill creak and Margaret stepped toward it. A musty, damp smell greeted her as she stood in the doorway, and then she saw Ivy lying on the bed, cocooned by what looked like a backward-facing waistcoat with straps and buckles fastened at her sides. Shocked, Margaret took a step back. "Goodness. Take her out of that contraption at once!" she commanded.

"My apologies, miss, but I cannot. She became violent," James answered.

"Margaret, is that really you?" Ivy wriggled on the bed in

order to see Margaret at the door.

Seeing Ivy looking toward her, Margaret gave a relieved smile but her elation was tempered by the circumstances she found herself in.

"It is in her best interest and yours that she remains restrained," James explained. "I will return in fifteen minutes."

Margaret took two steps for the bed before the heavy door was closed behind her with a thud.

"I never thought I'd see you again," Ivy gasped. Margaret could see Ivy had been crying, and had been for a good long while as well.

"What happened?" Margaret asked, slipping onto the edge of the low bed. She pushed some strands of the girl's blond hair from her face and tucked it behind her ears. She could not stand the sight of the confinement, the room, and the contraption holding Ivy steady, so she decided to focus on her friend's face. "Did Garret do this?"

Ivy nodded. "Yes. They told the doctor that I have been hysterical since Father died. They can't control me."

The accusation was almost laughable given how little time they actually had spent with her since that horrid night.

"You must help me get out of here."

Margaret had never seen a person's spirit so beaten. Ivy gazed up at her like a wounded animal begging for her suffering to end. Margaret felt a lump at the back of her throat pushing against all her efforts of composure. Surely this wasn't the way to treat a human being. "I don't know how," Margaret answered honestly.

Margaret placed her hand gently on the side of Ivy's face and saw her friend instantly relax from the touch. A single tear released from her eyes and trailed down the side of her face and into her hair.

"They won't visit me here. They helped me keep the sadness away for years but they won't come here," Ivy said, inching closer to Margaret despite her restraints. "But you came, didn't you, Margaret?"

"What are you talking about?" Margaret managed, stroking the side of Ivy's face with the hopes of calming her down. "What friends?"

"My friends, Margaret. All my friends."

"Ivy, stop," Margaret said sternly. She glanced to the closed door and wondered how far the porter had gone. "You have to behave or they will never let you out."

"I'm not doing anything wrong. Mister Marshall sees them too, though he doesn't listen to them like I do—"

"Enough," Margaret said quickly, bowing her head in defeat. "You have to stop talking about those friends. They cannot help you anymore." It pained Margaret greatly to keep up the charade, to feed into Ivy's delusions, but her time was running out and she couldn't bear the thought of Ivy crying herself to sleep that night, believing she was all alone. "I will do the best I can to help you, but you mustn't give them any more reasons to keep you here. You must take your medicine—"

"I don't need any medicine."

"Take your medicine!" Margaret said more forcefully. "I can't help you unless you do this."

At Margaret's insistence, Ivy nodded in agreement. "I will do what you say, Margaret," she said quietly, "because I love you like a sister."

Margaret smiled and tried hard not to cry.

The metal door opened and James appeared, the keys clinking together in his hands. "Ma'am," he said.

"That was hardly five minutes," Margaret said, nearly growling.

James straightened his stance and avoided eye contact. "It is time."

Margaret lowered her voice and drew closer so only Ivy could hear. "Do not speak of your friends again, not here," she said. "Pretend you are"—Margaret paused, unsure what to say—"pretend you are me. Mind your manners and do as you are told."

"Be strong."

Margaret started at the suggestion and Ivy smiled. "That is what you are, Lady Margaret," Ivy explained.

Margaret nodded, unable to fight back a flood of tears. She leaned in and gave Ivy a soft kiss on her forehead. "I will be back," Margaret said, "I promise." She gave Ivy a long hug and was reluctant to let go. It was when James inched closer to them that she relented and backed away.

Margaret charged down the corridor while James closed the metal door behind them, securing the lock. Margaret would have run if she could. She'd have run the entire distance home if only to rid herself of the heartache that was nipping at her heels. The rumours were true, Margaret realized. Though soft-spoken and friendly, Ivy was slipping into madness.

Ignoring the budding rain, Margaret charged for the carriage, each step cementing her determination. "Take me back to The Briar," she said to Walter as she approached. "I've had enough of this place for one day."

"Yes, ma'am," he replied taking hold of the carriage door and holding it open for her as she climbed in. "I daresay, I never thought I'd be standing in its shadow twice in as many days." He snapped the door shut. "I'll be happy to stay clear of those gates the rest of my life."

"What did you say?" Margaret leaned slightly out the window just as Walter turned to climb to his perch. He stopped at her words and looked to her.

"I said I'd be happy to stay clear of those gates for the rest of my days, ma'am," he answered, his words less assured.

"No, the other thing. Have you been here before?"

The driver swallowed. "I brought Mr. Marshall here yesterday, ma'am. He made me wait just as you have. I don't mind it at all," he said quickly, as if to reassure her he wasn't complaining. "It's just not the sort of place I would've expected to be bringing a woman like yourself to, is all."

He looked nervous and ill-prepared for Margaret's scrutiny. He couldn't have known the meaning behind his confession. If Ainsley had visited the asylum the day prior, Margaret knew he must have been involved in Ivy's admittance.

"It's all right," she said with a forced smile. "Something you said just caught my attention."

Walter nodded and climbed up to his bench. A few seconds later, the carriage began its journey back to The Briar, giving Margaret plenty of time to ponder her brother's involvement with the Owen family.

Aunt Louisa and Ainsley were standing at the front door

when Margaret walked in, dusty and dishevelled from the long journey from Barning Heath. Her aunt, who had been adjusting Ainsley's bowtie, smiled out one side of her mouth as she took in Margaret's state of dress. "I do hope you clean up well," she said as Margaret passed, heading straight for the stairs.

In her concern for Ivy, Margaret had completely forgotten about the dinner at Breaside.

"Margaret?" From the corner of her eye Margaret saw Peter attempt to follow her up the stairs. "Where have you been? Is everything all right?"

She couldn't bring herself to look at him. "Excuse me," she said curtly, jogging up the steps as if to put as much distance between them as she could. "I must dress."

"May I suggest some rouge for those cheeks," Aunt Louisa called up as Margaret reached the top of the stairs. "Men don't like their women to look sickly."

She could feel Ainsley at her heels as she went. "Margaret?"

She slammed the door when he tried to enter, and supressed the guilt she felt for doing so. She strongly suspected he was involved in Ivy's current state and for that she was prepared to be done with him entirely.

Julia was already in her room, laying out a line of lavender ribbons on the arm of the settee, no doubt intending to use them in her mistress's hair. "Lady Margaret—"

"We must be quick," Margaret said. "We wouldn't want to keep any of the family waiting." Margaret laced her words with enough derision to hide her contempt. She was just about done with balls and fancy dinner parties. She felt an anvil of guilt weighing her down as she thought of Ivy freezing in that small cell while she was preened for a lavish dinner filled with flirting and useless conversation. Everything—her family's wealth and the role she was expected to play to secure more of it through marriage—seemed useless in comparison. It was all Margaret could do to not to hurl her silver-plated hairbrush at the looking glass.

The dresses, the finery, and the relentless expectations agitated her to the point where she could barely stay seated in the chair. She wanted to cry for her friend and scream at her brother for what he had done to her at the same time.

Without a word of warning to Julia, Margaret rose and bounded from the room. She stormed the hall, paying no heed to anything else, and marched right into Jonas's room. Nearly ready, he was buttoning the cuffs of his jacket when he turned at the sound of the door.

She must have looked a dishevelled fright, her hair streaming down her shoulders, her attire still dusty from the roads back from Barning Heath. And she had little doubt that the look on her face would have sent anyone who did not know her into a corner. Jonas, however, smiled as he turned. "Margaret."

Closing the door behind her, Margaret crossed the floor, grabbed his hand, and kissed him. There was no protest. Jonas returned her affections with greater enthusiasm than Margaret anticipated and soon was holding the side of her face with one hand while the other encircled her and brought her body closer. He leaned into her, nearly scooping her off her feet as they kissed.

When they pulled away, Jonas smiled lovingly as he stroked the side of her face.

"When do you leave?" Margaret asked, nearly out of breath.

"I head back to London in the morning," he said, lowering his forehead into hers.

"No, for Scotland. When do you leave for Edinburgh?"

"Two weeks' time."

Margaret nodded. "Take me with you."

"Margaret—"

"I can't be without you," she said, nearly crying. "Whenever I think about it my body shuts down from the pain." She would have collapsed then, crumpled in a heap on the floor, had Jonas not been holding her so close. Her body shook as she sobbed, grateful for the man who held to her. Grateful for his steadfast devotion and unwavering support. He was, without a doubt, the rock she had been seeking in the turbulent world that was her life.

"What is it? What's happened?" Jonas asked, as if knowing her cries were rooted in something else. He attempted to pull her away so he could look at her, but she kept her head bowed as she clung to him.

"The world is just so horrible, so cruel." Margaret pulled in the scent of Jonas's jacket as her fingers curled around his lapel. She closed her eyes against the memory of what she had seen that afternoon. "They put Ivy in the asylum."

"The asylum?"

Margaret nodded slowly and tried to steady the quivering in her chin. "In a suit with arms tied behind her, secured to the bed! I've never seen anyone so scared." She lifted her gaze then, aware that tears were spilling over from her lower lids and streaming down the crests of her cheeks. "I have to help her. Once I know she is free I am going with you to Edinburgh and I won't look back."

"But Peter wouldn't—"

"My brother is the one who put her there." Margaret brushed back a tear as she spoke the words. "And I will never forgive him."

Chapter 29

Nor shines the sun alone
Upon one favoured hour,

Ainsley, Margaret, Jonas, and Nathaniel arrived at Breaside after a somewhat cramped journey in their carriage along waterlogged roads. A break in the rain allowed them to exit their conveyance at the base of the front steps with gratitude for the space to move about and the notably fresher air. Eager to accept Nathaniel's arm, Margaret led the way up the damp and slippery stairs, allowing Ainsley and Jonas to follow behind them.

"Come now, cousin," she said, cheerily, "We shall see how a duke and duchess throw a party."

Nathaniel gave a look of confusion to Ainsley as he was ushered up the stairs toward the front door.

With Margaret a few steps ahead of them, Ainsley saw her take a quick glance over her shoulder before quickly averting her gaze. She had said very little to him as they prepared for their outing and he couldn't fathom why.

Once in the foyer, they were invited by the staff to remove their coats and were escorted to the parlour, where Lord and Lady Thornton greeted them exuberantly.

"I cannot tell you how pleased I am you could come," Lady Thornton said, planting kisses on Margaret's cheeks. "Blair hasn't stopped asking me questions about you," she said in a low voice, though still loud enough for Ainsley to hear.

Margaret smiled demurely, but Ainsley saw her smile quickly melt away once the duchess turned.

Lord Thornton approached Ainsley and Jonas then, effectively removing Ainsley from the conversation.

"So you are the doctor, then?" Lord Thornton asked, shaking Jonas's hand excitedly. "Please to meet you, good fellow. I hear you are making quite the impression amongst my friends and colleagues, saving the House of Lords one by one, I see." Lord Thornton slapped a hand on Jonas's back in congratulations.

"Well, I wouldn't say that—"

A footman appeared with a tray of champagne. Lord Thornton grabbed two glasses by the stem and presented one to Jonas and one to Ainsley.

"Everywhere I go, your name comes up," Lord Thornton continued. "Dr. Davies this and Dr. Davies that." He laughed heartily and pulled on the bottom of his lapel. "When my son Brandon told me that you were staying at The Briar I told my wife you mustn't be excluded from our guest list." Lord Thornton turned slightly and gestured to another couple. "Allow me to introduce to you Sir John Stratton, and his elegant wife, Lady Stratton."

Ainsley and Jonas greeted them warmly, shaking hands in turn as Lord Thornton spoke. "My son, Brandon, has proposed marriage to their daughter, Priscilla, you see," he said, rocking back and forth on his feet. "A finer match there never was, if you ask me."

Jonas lifted his glass of champagne. "Congratulations," he said before looking to Ainsley, who could only muster a smile. As the introductions continued, he stole a glance across the room and saw that Blair had approached Margaret and they were now invested in a conversation, though Margaret seemed deeply distracted.

"Mr. Marshall."

Ainsley turned to see Lady Thornton approaching him slowly. "They looked well-suited, do they not?" she asked, gesturing with a slight nod of her head toward Blair and Margaret. "I understand your aunt was unable to join us this evening, and so I ask you out of my own curiosity, has Margaret been approached by anyone in particular?" Lady Thornton was careful to keep a smile on her face and her voice low.

Ainsley worked hard not to glance to Jonas, standing beside him.

"Marriage prospects, you mean?" he asked.

"Naturally."

"Not that I am aware of," Ainsley said with a closed-mouth smile.

He noticed Lady Thornton's eyes light up. "Excellent."

Before long, dinner was ready and Lord and Lady Thornton entreated the guests to follow them to the dinner hall. Ainsley kept to the side as everyone filed out of the room before pulling at Margaret's arm at the last moment.

"Peter!" She looked as if she could strike him.

He glanced over her shoulder to make sure everyone was still making their way down the hall. "You cannot keep ignoring me," he said in a whisper.

"Why not?" she asked, nearly hissing. "As far as I see it, you are my least favourite person in this house at the moment."

Ainsley's shoulders sank. "What have I done to spur such venom?"

Margaret let out a stunted laugh. "I went to visit Ivy today at St. Andrew's House," she said, scowling so deeply Ainsley thought she might spit at him. "They have her tied in this suit so she cannot move."

Instantly, Ainsley grew lightheaded and his heart quickened. "Certainly not."

"Don't play coy with me. You were the one who had her admitted." She raised a hand to her forehead as if fending off a headache. "If you think there is any forgiveness in your future you are sorely mistaken." She turned to leave but Ainsley pulled her back.

"Peter, Margaret. We are waiting." Lady Thornton appeared at the door to the dining room farther down the hall.

"One moment, please," Ainsley asked before noticing Margaret turning from him and progressing down the hall. Ainsley chased after her and grabbed hold her arm so she would look at him.

"It wasn't me," he said quickly. "Samuel and Garret must have taken her there of their own accord. You have to believe me."

Margaret pulled her arm away abruptly and met his gaze with anger. "Quite frankly, I don't know what to believe anymore."

A few minutes later, they were all seated in the dining hall, a vast room elegantly adorned with hanging chandeliers and massive bouquets of flowers at each pillar. The table had been set for twelve, with Margaret and Blair seated opposite Ainsley. Jonas was given a more prominent seat toward the head of the table. Priscilla Stratton, who was hardly over the age of twenty, was seated next to Ainsley and almost immediately proved herself incapable of meaningful conversation.

One chair at the table beside Margaret was notably empty and that's when Ainsley noticed Brandon was missing from the gathering.

Lady Thornton, seated next to her husband at the head of the table, looked apologetically to her guests. "Please forgive my son's absence," she said. "We hold on to the hope that he will be joining us shortly."

Ainsley noticed a dejected look come over Priscilla's face as the news was told to them.

"Will he be present at the hunt tomorrow?" Lady Stratton asked expectantly.

"He better be," Ainsley heard Blair say quietly from across the table. When Ainsley looked to him he found Blair taking a sip of his wine.

"Most certainly," Lady Thornton said, looking to Priscilla specifically. "He will not want to miss any more of your visit with us."

"I'm sure that whatever may be keeping him is a responsibility which cannot be ignored," Sir John said.

Lady Thornton bowed her head gracefully, thanking him for a tactful response.

"My brother thinks himself different from all this," Blair confessed to those at his end of the table.

"He doesn't enjoy hosting dinners and the like?" Margaret asked, as the first course was placed in front of her.

"Not in any way," Blair said. "He has many grand ideas on the way things should be."

Margaret stole a glance to Ainsley, who as well wished to be free of his role as second son.

"Do you know where he is?" Ainsley asked, quiet enough that only Blair and Margaret could hear.

"Sadly, I do not," Blair answered primly. "Surprisingly." His attitude remained cold toward Ainsley, a condition that matched Margaret's entirely.

"You both are quite close, I understand," Margaret offered.

"Extremely."

Blair continued to drink eagerly throughout all courses, signalling the butler each time his glass was empty. Ainsley watched anxiously as the final dishes were cleared and the women withdrew. He expected Lord Thornton to give his son a reprimand once the ladies had cleared but no such admonishment came. The eldest Thornton only gave a look of resignation as they exited the dining hall and made way for his study.

Lord Thornton poured a glass of port for each of the men, Ainsley, Jonas, and Sir John, but his son waved it away and headed for one of the other bottles.

"Should we be alarmed by Mr. Thornton's continued absence?" Sir John asked as they gathered round the fireplace, glasses in their hands.

"No, no, certainly not," Lord Thornton said. "He has done this quite often and always returns home."

"I can't imagine he has gotten himself into any sort of trouble out here, so far from the diversions of London," Sir John offered.

"My boys have always behaved properly," Lord Thornton said. "I have no need to worry on their account."

Ainsley looked to Blair, who hovered over the bottles of alcohol, avoiding the conversation.

"My daughter tells me you have an impressive collection of horses," Sir John said. "I should like to see them."

"You shall have your fill of them tomorrow at the hunt," Lord Thornton said, placing his empty glass on the mantel. "Peter, you and Dr. Davies are both coming, yes?"

"Unfortunately, I must leave tomorrow. I begin my tenure at Edinburgh in a few weeks and must prepare."

Blair turned. "Edinburgh?"

"I am to work under Dr. Tate, a professor at the university."

Blair raised the tumbler to his lips in an effort to mask his smile. "Godspeed."

Lord Thornton clasped a firm hand on Jonas's shoulder in approval. "Top notch, Dr. Davies."

"I'm quite looking forward to the hunt," Nathaniel interjected, offering an eager smile. Lord Thornton and Sir John turned to the young man, perhaps surprised he was still in the room. Lord Thornton gave an awkward nod, acknowledging Nathaniel's comment before moving on to other topics. Ainsley was amused by his cousin's attempt to garner attention. His family was unknown in England and would suffer a hard time of it if he expected to meld in with society so easily. Favour was often accomplished with difficulty, relying heavily on luck and circumstance rather than presence alone.

"I don't understand," Nathaniel said to Ainsley as he came alongside him. "What did I say?"

"Perhaps if you were less intrusive," Ainsley said quietly. "When they get to know you they will accept you," Ainsley said quietly. "But it takes time."

Nathaniel nodded, eager to take his cousin's advice but then blatantly disregarded it when again he tried to plant himself into another conversation between Lord Thornton and Sir John.

"And I thought I looked foolish," Jonas said to Ainsley.

"He'll learn," Ainsley answered. He kept his gaze trained on Nathaniel, and found it very difficult not to find his blunders amusing.

After handing each of the men a cigar, Lord Thornton led a toast in Jonas's honour, congratulated him on his new position, and wished him the best of luck with the Scots. Everyone seemed generally happy for the young doctor, but all Ainsley could think about was the loss of a dear friend. A year prior, Ainsley would have lamented not being picked for the position himself, but that day he was saddened at the prospect of returning to London and St. Thomas without the aid of his closest ally. He wasn't so sure he could do it alone.

Chapter 30

But with unstinted power
Makes every day his own.

Margaret couldn't remember playing a more boring match of Whisk in all her life. Lady Thornton nearly won each trick while Priscilla fumbled with her cards, asking a great deal of bothersome questions and distracting Margaret considerably. She'd have walked away from the table were there anyone else to speak with but given that their party was so small she couldn't very well do so without causing offence.

"I'm not talking your ear off, am I?" Priscilla finally asked.

"Of course not," Margaret lied.

A moment later the men returned, filing into the room and disrupting their card game. When Margaret looked up she saw Nathaniel heading straight for them at the table.

"Enjoyed your time with the men, have you?" Margaret asked, taking in the unmistakable scent of cigar from Nathaniel's collar as he knelt between her and Priscilla.

"Yes, of course," Nathaniel said, somewhat taken aback. "Your father is a very interesting man," he said directing his attentions at Priscilla.

"Did he bore you with tales from the Crimea?" Priscilla asked. "Daddy is always doing that."

"No, it wasn't a bore at all," Nathaniel clarified.

Margaret felt someone come up behind her. "A word, Miss Margaret, if I may?" The stench of alcohol on Blair's breath was overpowering, so much so Margaret was forced to turn her nose away, hiding her discomfort behind a bashful smile. She excused herself from Nathaniel and Priscilla's company and followed Blair to a corner of the room.

She couldn't help but notice Blair's agitation. He seemed so much more in control of himself the other day it hardly seemed like him at all. He avoided her gaze while he composed himself. Margaret waited, twisting her fingers nervously, wondering what he could possibly have to say to her. A confession, perhaps? Admission to Ainsley's charge?

"Who is Dr. Davies to you?" he asked bluntly, running his hand over his mouth.

"I beg your pardon?" Margaret was so taken aback by his line of questioning she wasn't quite sure she had heard him correctly.

"I noticed how you looked at him across the dinner table," Blair said, leaning his arm on the mantel. "We've known each other long enough there should be no need to act coy. The other day—"

"The other day you were sober," Margaret said, angered by his forthright questioning. A true gentleman would never put a lady on the spot in such a way. "I liked you far better then." She moved as if to walk away but Blair pulled her back, tugging on her elbow. Margaret could have slapped him, and certainly wouldn't have felt sorry for it, but decorum demanded that she be discreet.

"He's a tradesman, you know," Blair said, slurring slightly. "He'll be unable to provide for you the way you deserve."

Margaret snatched her arm away but kept her gaze on him. "He's a hundred times the man you pretend to be," she said. She took a breath to relax her shoulders before returning to the card table where only Priscilla and Nathaniel remained in conversation. She felt Blair's gaze on her as she went and found it difficult to calm her thundering heart even after she took a seat.

She hadn't expected such behaviour from so dear a friend. Perhaps her brother had been right. People grow up. They change, sometimes never again resembling the people they were as children. She wanted so much to believe that Blair and Brandon were good people, that they were incapable of what Ainsley accused them of. So many times before had she believed someone innocent only to be proven wrong. The fact that they were childhood friends should not have affected her skepticism and yet she allowed their history to cloud her judgement. Perhaps they were involved in Mr. Owen's death. Could Blair be the father of Ivy's baby?

"Cousin Margaret?"

Margaret was snapped from her thoughts to find she was

alone at the table with Nathaniel.

"Are you well?"

Nodding feebly, she glanced over her shoulder to find Blair had gone. "Where is Miss Priscilla?" she asked in an attempt to change the subject.

"Her mother called her away," Nathaniel explained. "Do you think it may have had something to do with me?"

Margaret shook her head and reached over the table to touch Nathaniel's arm. "If you expect to fit in with society, you need to develop a thicker skin." Nathaniel nodded but she knew it would be a while before he'd be able to shed his insecurities. Margaret herself could relate and knew it was only through the passing of time that she had grown used to the scrutiny and judgements.

"You do realize Priscilla is promised to Brandon Thornton?" Margaret asked, taking care to keep her voice low.

"Yes, indeed, but she seems so forlorn with no one to speak with. The nerve of that man, leaving her here all by her lonesome." Nathaniel appeared particularly agitated that Brandon still had not arrived. "If I had someone as sweet as that waiting on me…well, she wouldn't be waiting on me. That's for sure."

Margaret smiled at her cousin's remarks. "I doubt you would be speaking so if your mother was here."

At the mention of his mother, Nathaniel's expression fell. "Probably not."

"I do not understand why she declined such a lovely invitation," Margaret said. "Even I can handle a simple dinner party."

Nathaniel squared his shoulders as Margaret spoke and she could see his relaxed hand on the table curl into a slight fist. He averted his gaze and licked his lips.

"What did I say?" Margaret leaned in closer. "Tell me, Nathaniel."

Reluctantly, Nathaniel spoke, scanning the room to make sure no one else was in earshot. "I'm afraid Mother won't be up to these gatherings for some time, not after what Father did to her."

"What do you mean?"

Nathaniel took a breath before he began. "Father was never kind to Mother. I used to hear them fighting almost every night from my room. The walls in those houses are so paper thin, you see. They'd disagree about money or discipline for the boys but mostly it was about Mother's homesickness. She never did feel at home in India." He looked to his hands. "They never fought about his mistresses, though."

"Mistresses?" Margaret felt her voice rise but caught herself in time before she drew attention from the room. "He entertained more than one?"

Nathaniel nodded. Margaret could see his eyes welling up before he blinked it away. "Mother told me she didn't care. She said as long as he came home to her each night and provided us with a home, it didn't matter. I could see it hurt her though, inside." He pointed to his chest. "Everyone's husband took a mistress there but no one ever spoke about it openly. But then Father made a mess of things."

Margaret swallowed. She was unsure she wanted to hear anymore. What was relayed to her already seemed more than a woman could bear.

"There was a dinner party. Mother and Father were both invited as were nearly every other aristocratic family of English origin. It was quite special, you see. On the day of the event Mother fell ill with a headache. The humidity always seemed to cause her suffering. She couldn't go and Father decided to go without her. He decided to bring his mistress instead."

Margaret raised a hand to her mouth and bowed her head. "Oh, Aunt Louisa."

"That is not the worst of it," Nathaniel said. "An hour later Mother said she felt better and decided to go. I wasn't there," he said, suffering genuine regret at not being present to support his mother. "But to hear tell of it things did not go well. Mother was embarrassed, in front of all English-Indian society, no less. I don't believe she is over the shock, really. All those people you believed were your friends. It's unimaginable." Nathaniel shifted in his seat and sniffled. "She confessed to me on the ship heading back to England that she was glad of it. That she could consider herself free to do as she pleased now. But I'm not so sure."

"Does she plan to seek a divorce?" Margaret was careful to whisper though she needn't have worried. Everyone else in the room was enjoying their drink and laughing at each other's jokes without a care in the world.

"I don't know," Nathaniel answered truthfully. "I do know that she is grateful to you and Peter for allowing us a place to stay. Mother has been in much higher spirits since we arrived at your doorstep. I don't know how we would have survived these last few weeks without you." Nathaniel reached over the table and squeezed Margaret's hand, blinking back tears as she looked at him.

Margaret placed her other hand on top of his and returned his squeeze. "All of you may stay as long as you like."

Chapter 31

And for my freedom's sake
With such I'll pattern take,

The rain pounded on the roof of the carriage as it left the shelter of the trees in front of Breaside. The noise grew like a thousand beating hearts thumping and pulsing as they drove on. Ainsley found himself becoming uneasy and tried to steady his breathing but found it difficult against the bouncing of the carriage on the uneven roads.

"Peter, are you well?" Jonas asked.

"Yes," Ainsley said quickly, readjusting in his seat and pulling at his collar. "Quite well."

Margaret eyed him suspiciously but said nothing, which was a relief to Ainsley, who was in no mood to discuss his rapidly changing state of mind.

The carriage continued on, cutting its way through the torrential rain. Halfway through their journey Ainsley slipped forward in his seat and craned his neck so he could see out the window, hoping the fresh air would help him. The carriage moved quickly, periodically bouncing its occupants this way and that as it maneuvered the ruts in the road.

"Goodness!" Margaret threw out her arms to steady herself in her seat.

"I will be happy to get out of this rain," Nathaniel said in an attempt to lighten the foreboding mood in the carriage.

Ainsley looked intently out the window, seeking any sign that they were close to home, and that is when he saw her, a girl, standing at the side of the road, soaking wet and bleeding from an injury to the head.

"Stop the carriage!" Ainsley yelled. He banged on the ceiling of the coach and unlatched the door while it still moved. "Stop the carriage!" Without waiting for the carriage to stop he jumped down and ran back to where he had seen the girl.

The rain pelted his face and his feet slid on the muddy road as he ran. Unable to see where he was and not knowing where exactly she had been standing when they passed, he ran as far as he could along the roadside. After a time, he stopped. "Where are you?" he yelled into the rain. "I can help you!" He turned in place, retracing his steps before turning back to the road they had just driven down. It made no sense. He had seen her, as clear as he saw anything, but now the blackness of night had swallowed her.

"Peter, what is it?" Jonas ran toward him.

When Ainsley looked back to the carriage he saw Margaret pulling one of the lanterns from the side of the carriage. "I saw a girl," Ainsley said to Jonas, ignoring the torrents of rain that ran down his face. "She was standing right here."

"In this rain?"

"She was bleeding from her head, I think. The blood ran down her neck and arms." Ainsley gestured with his hands as he spoke.

"Peter, stop this!" Margaret barked as she neared them.

The rain overtook them, seeping into their clothes and soaking their many layers in seconds. Margaret's hair clung to the sides of her face as she lifted the lantern to see Ainsley.

"There's no girl," Jonas said, examining the side of the road.

"What girl?" Margaret asked.

"I saw her!" Ainsley yelled against the noise of the rain. "She needed help. She was hit by the carriage or something." He turned from them and ran farther into the darkness, farther back along the road. "Hey! Hey!" he called into the storm. "We can help you!"

Jonas and Margaret caught up to him just as he was contemplating entering the woods that flanked the road.

"There's no one here!" Jonas yelled. He tried to grab hold of Ainsley but he shook him off and stepped toward the trees.

"Peter, that's enough!" Margaret stepped in front of him, her face lighted by the dim glow of the lantern.

Ainsley looked back to the carriage and saw how far away from it he had run. The girl had not been half so far back and still there was no sign of her. No footprints in the mud or evidence of anyone else but them walking the road. He ran his hands through his hair as he thought over all possible scenarios but nothing made any sense.

"You are not well."

Ainsley exhaled as he felt Margaret's hands touch him. Her face had gone from stern to compassionate in a single heartbeat. Her touch brought him to his knees, collapsing under the weight of his overburdened heart.

He had taken his sanity for granted for so long and now, with all these sightings and sounds, he knew what was happening to him. He knew that there was only a shred of his former self that remained.

"I killed him," he said suddenly. He closed his eyes, the weight of the world easing slightly.

"Peter, stop." Jonas caught hold of him.

"What did he say?" Margaret came in front of him.

"I killed him, Margaret." The tears streamed down Ainsley's face, mixing with the rain that drowned out the world beyond, cocooning them in their misery.

"Who?"

"The man who killed those children. I killed him and I shouldn't feel sorry for it. He would have killed more and I saved them, didn't I?" Ainsley grabbed hold of her, searching her eyes for the kindness that he knew abounded in her.

"The man in the papers?" Margaret choked out the words. "The man who..." her voice trailed off as she swallowed back her words.

"I didn't mean to," Ainsley said. "I was going to hand him over to the inspector, I swear. I just wanted to rough him up a bit. Teach him a lesson."

"Peter, it's not your fault." Jonas knelt beside him. "He had no choice, Margaret."

Margaret shook her head but she didn't appear angry. "What about this girl? Who did you see?" She reached for him and held his shoulders.

"I don't know," Ainsley said defeated. "They follow me everywhere. They haunt my dreams. I can't escape them. I'm losing my mind." He fell into her arms and cried.

"We need to get you both out of this rain," Ainsley heard Jonas say. "You'll catch your death."

Steps approached them and when Ainsley looked up he saw

Walter and Nathaniel with the other lantern moving gingerly through the unstable mud. "Is everything all right?" Walter asked.

"We need to get home as quickly as we can," Margaret said, still holding tight to her brother. "My brother is not well."

Chapter 32

And rove and revel on.
Your gall shall never make

When they first arrived home, Maxwell and Jamieson helped Ainsley into dry bedclothes and built a fire in the fireplace. Then Margaret sat with him in his bed, whispering funny stories to him of their childhood at The Briar and avoiding all topics of murder and death that would be sure to unsettle him further. Satisfied that he was sound asleep, Margaret left him and exited his room, mindful of her footfalls and the silence in the rest of the house.

"Is he feeling restored?"

Margaret nearly jumped when she heard Jonas's voice in the darkness of the hall beyond her bedroom door. He stepped from the shadows. "I'm sorry," he said quietly. "I didn't mean to startle you."

She waved off his concern. "He is better," she said, stopping short of entering her room. She turned her attention to him. "It took a while to get him relaxed enough to sleep but I think he should be good until morning."

Margaret could feel an uneasiness between them, a wall that had not been there earlier. "I don't blame you for keeping his secret from me," she said, "if that is what worries you." She could just make out his form, recognizing the angle of his jaw and the point of his nose in the darkness. She could not tell if he was relieved by her acceptance. Truth be told, the facts revealed to her hadn't quite set in. She could scarcely believe her brother had been the one responsible for dispatching the man who maimed her.

"Or is it Blair Thornton that worries you?" The realization hit her instantly. Jonas had been witness to a great deal of flirting that evening, nothing that she instigated, but still it must have been unnerving all the same. "I care nothing for him, you must know that."

"I was wondering if perhaps you had changed your mind," Jonas said.

"Certainly not." She stepped toward him, her lips stopping inches from his. "I'm only playing a part until I am able to set Ivy free." Reaching up, she pulled at a tuft of his hair, smiling at how soft it felt in her fingers. "Send me word and I will follow you to the ends of the earth, Jonas Davies."

His expression remained serious despite Margaret's touch. "I fear I will be a disappointment to you. I cannot promise lavish dinners or crystal goblets. I am a surgeon, nothing more."

Her hand slipped from his hair to the back of his neck, holding him to her. "A greater fool there never was than he who believes I want any of that." She kissed him expressly, savouring the feeling of his lips touching hers. She allowed him to gather her in his arms, wishing to meld into him further than their clothed bodies could allow. He pulled away, leaving his hands on her waist as he kissed the side of her neck gently. With her right hand Margaret reached behind her and turned the iron knob of her door.

Jonas stepped back but she did not release his hand. She pulled him in as she stepped back, smiling, knowing he wanted her as much as she wanted him. "Don't be afraid," she said softly. "I'm not."

Chapter 33

Me honied paths forsake;
So prythee get thee gone.

The morning brought a thin mist that draped the landscape in a fabric veil that softened the light of the sun. Ainsley had lost all enthusiasm for the hunt and would have rather stayed home than venture out into the damp woods but he had no choice. Aunt Louisa insisted he and Margaret go as they said they would.

Not wanting to be left out, Margaret intended to ride as well and appeared at the front door wearing the traditional navy jacket, breeches, and top boots. Seeing her made Ainsley anxious. He worried that he would not be able to keep his composure. His mind had been made too fragile and he worried he wouldn't be able to steady himself. He must have borne his worry on his face because Margaret came directly to him.

"You don't have to go," she said. "I don't care what Aunt Louisa says."

Ainsley smiled at her concern. "I want to go. I need a good dash through the woods to take my mind off things. It clears my head."

Margaret nodded but he could tell she was doubtful.

"Where's Jonas?" Ainsley asked, glancing into the library.

"He's gone," Margaret said sharply. "I asked Walter to see him to the train station a few moments ago." She paused, studying Ainsley's face for a moment before licking her lips. "He wanted to say goodbye but we didn't wish to wake you."

Ainsley would have liked to offer a proper farewell but he knew he'd be seeing him in London within the next few days. His old friend had been right. He couldn't avoid the city for long. He'd have to face the evils, both real and imaginary, if he had any hope of regaining control of himself.

Nathaniel nearly skipped down the stairs to meet them at the front door. Donning a broad smile it was quite evident he was eager to be on their way.

"Shall we go?" Margaret tapped her whip on the side of her boot and turned for the door. They let Nathaniel pass them on the front steps as they walked toward the barn.

"I've made a decision about Ivy," Ainsley said before they got too far. "I believe you and I should pay a visit to St. Andrew's house and order her release."

"When?" Margaret asked eagerly.

"This afternoon."

She nodded. "Yes, absolutely."

"I'm sorry I didn't tell you," he said cautiously. "I swear to you I told them to keep her away from there."

Margaret studied him for a time before speaking. "I believe you," she said softly, "about everything."

The sky had grown pink by the time they entered The Briar's stable. Maxwell and the stable boy had already prepared their horses and had them waiting in the centre of the barn. "I fear the fog is not letting up," Maxwell warned as they mounted their horses. "I daresay your quarry will outsmart you."

"I doubt we will be catching many foxes," Ainsley said truthfully, "we go for the hunt not the prize."

Maxwell tipped his cap as Ainsley, Margaret, and Nathaniel set off for Breaside.

They were to meet at the meadow farther down the road from the house. The trio said nothing as they led their horses past the spot where Ainsley insisted he had seen something in the woods. They passed the estate and weaved their way along the path next to the stables before spying the hunting party along the fence line of one of the fields.

A pair of dog handlers, each with half a dozen eager hounds, held fast to the tethers of the dogs as the animals struggled against their restraints. Intermittent barks broke the silence of the dawn, sending the pack into a chorus of yelps before finally settling down. They could smell the excitement and wanted to be set free to chase down their quarry.

"Miss Priscilla looks lovely this morning, does she not?" Nathaniel said as they gingerly led their horses through the tall grass.

Margaret was quick to give their cousin a disparaging look.

"I strongly caution you, cousin," she said, adjusting her grip on her reins. "Not many English gentlemen would look kindly on such attention being given to their fiancée."

Nathaniel pressed his lips together as he looked toward the girl who was quickly becoming an infatuation. "If that were true then why hasn't Mr. Thornton made a point to claim her as his wife?" He gave Margaret and Ainsley a mirthful smile before leading his horse in Priscilla's direction.

Margaret drew in a long breath as she watched him leave. "How do you suppose Brandon will react to Nathaniel's attentions toward his bride?"

Ainsley gave a quick laugh. "You assume he will even grace us with his presence today."

They led their horses deeper into the meadow, beyond the dozen or so hounds that periodically pulled at their tethers, to the gathering of the hunters—Lord Thornton, Sir John, and Blair, who stood near a weathered fence.

Blair smiled when he saw Margaret and reached for her horse's bridle when she neared. "Good morning," he said.

Ainsley brought his horse alongside Margaret's. "Feeling well?" Ainsley asked, remembering the number of drinks Blair had consumed the night before. He hadn't meant it as an insult but Blair indeed took offence.

"Well enough to ride, if that's what you mean," he replied bitterly. Blair returned his attention to Margaret. "I hope you are not offended by my behaviour last evening," he said. "It was the drink, you realize."

Margaret offered a forced smile. "Of course."

Ainsley slipped from his horse's saddle and pulled the reins over the mare's head. When he rounded the front of his horse he looked to Margaret again and noticed Blair had gone to speak with his father and Sir John. "That was a fine morning greeting," Ainsley said, amused by Blair's disdain toward him.

"He was acting rather strangely last evening," Margaret said after dismounting. Together they led their horses to the fence to tie them. "It seemed out of character for him."

"So many years have passed, Margaret. We can scarcely say we know their character at all," Ainsley answered honestly.

Another horse had been led to the fence and when Ainsley

and Margaret turned, they saw Brandon, haggard and looking poorly. Ainsley recognized the look well enough, having suffered his own ill effects the morning after heavy drinking. When Brandon pulled out a flask from his inside pocket Ainsley realized the drinking hadn't yet ended.

Brandon turned as if never noticing them standing at the fence and began walking toward his father. "Let's get this hunt underway!" he yelled to those gathered. "I have an insatiable desire to kill something."

Ainsley watched as he took a long drink from his flask. If Ainsley had ever behaved such as that in public, or at the very least in his father's presence, he'd be whisked away and threatened with the strap. Lord Thornton, however, paid no attention to his son's drunken shouts.

They watched as Priscilla approached Brandon on foot, the reins of her horse held loosely in her grasp. Appearing distracted, Brandon nodded at some unheard words she spoke and then as quickly as he had turned to her, he left, stumbling awkwardly.

"I wonder what he is escaping," Ainsley said quietly so only Margaret could hear.

"How do you mean?"

"A man who imbibes that much is trying to drown out something," Ainsley explained.

"As you have done?"

"Yes." Ainsley no longer bothered to hide his fondness for his own flask. He'd only recently become aware of his dependence for it, though he wasn't sure exactly how to deal with it.

Margaret seemed to ponder his words for a moment before speaking. "The clerk at the asylum said something that's been bothering me since yesterday."

"Yes?"

"She said Ivy had already received two visitors that day. She almost didn't let me see her." Margaret placed her hands on her hips and continued to watch Brandon make his way to the other side of the encampment. "He seemed very concerned for Ivy's welfare following the fire. Do you think Brandon may have gone to visit her?"

The realization overtook Ainsley like a sudden breeze rushing over their skin. "He's the father of Ivy's baby."

He heard Margaret gasp before turning from the group and placing her hand over her face. "Oh Ivy," she whispered. "Why didn't she tell me?"

"Let us away!" Lord Thornton's thunderous voice hushed the gathering quickly. As the handlers released the tethers of the dogs everyone looked on in rapt anticipation. Ainsley had suddenly lost interest in the hunt, caring nothing for the outcome. The party mobilized and everyone headed for their mounts. Lord Thornton and Sir John secured their rifles, and threw themselves up into their saddles.

"Brandon was her second visitor yesterday," Ainsley said as they pulled their horses from the fence.

"And now he's drinking away the memory of it," Margaret added as horse after horse was led by them, trotting single file through the gate, headed for the woods. "Do you think he knows she was pregnant?"

Ainsley watched as the party rode past them. Brandon's engagement to Priscilla would have prevented him from claiming the child as his. Other nobles often paid for the education of their illegitimate children, even if the relationship with the child's mother had met an end. Others still abandoned their bastard children altogether, knowing a fallen woman of lower birth wouldn't dare come forward claiming any relationship took place. Often, such acts created worse situations for the mothers than they did for the nobles. The fact that Brandon risked discovery by visiting St. Andrew's House meant he still had feelings for the girl and most likely had not known that, until recently, she was carrying his child.

"Come, Margaret," Ainsley said, readying to mount his horse, "or we shall never catch up to them."

The party spread out through the woods, slowly following the hounds that sniffed, noses pressed to the underbrush, searching for any hint of their desired quarry. Within minutes, a sharp bark echoed through the woods, inciting raucous yelps from the others, who were excited to be on the hunt. Ainsley tightened his grip on his reins, in anticipation of a speedy jaunt through the woods. He glanced to his left and saw Margaret do the same.

The entire pack of dogs began a chorus of yips and yelps, and then took off deeper into the woods as a collective. The hunters kicked their horses in pursuit and began bounding through the woods.

"Stay close, Margaret," Ainsley instructed as they guided their horses toward the direction the other hunters headed.

The hunt started slow until the dogs found a stronger scent and charged through the woods, causing the hunters to barrel after them. Ainsley fell into the chase, darting between tree trunks and jumping creek beds, all the while keeping an eye on Brandon, who kept pace near the front of the party. Ainsley could feel the beat of his heart, pounding the confinement of his ribcage. He needed to speak to Brandon, if only to find out what he suspected was true.

"Over there!" Ainsley saw Blair just ahead, pointing to the right and redirecting his horse to follow. A quick glance over his shoulder told him Margaret was close enough to follow so he led the way, converging with the group as the trees gave way to a stream, with steep banks leading down and then up again. The group slowed to a trot as they approached. Nathaniel brought his horse alongside Ainsley. "Jolly good fun, isn't it?"

Ainsley wasn't sure exactly what to say. The sport of it had left him the minute he realized Brandon had taken advantage of a young girl and, perhaps, had caused the girl's admittance to the asylum.

"Peter, take Priscilla and Margaret that way," Blair said, pointing to the section of water with a gentler bank on the opposite side. "We'll follow the dogs this way and we can meet up on the other side of that ridge."

Ainsley nodded and moved the reins to bring his horse around. The horses scaled the hill and crested the top easily. He paused to allow Priscilla the chance to catch up and noticed Nathaniel following him as well. Slightly out of breath, Margaret appeared at his side.

"They said they'd meet us over there," Ainsley said, pointing so Priscilla could understand. She gave a quick nod but said nothing.

They came out of the woods at the opposite side of the clearing but saw no sign of the other hunters. Ainsley stopped his horse as they reached the trees to listen.

"Where could they—?" Priscilla began to speak but Ainsley hushed her.

Ainsley placed a finger over his mouth and inched his horse closer to the line of trees.

Just to the left Ainsley heard a horse exhaling and when he scanned the tress he saw a shadow gliding through the mist between the trees.

Margaret brought her horse alongside Ainsley's. "What is it?"

"I thought I saw something." Whether what he saw was rooted in reality remained to be seen. His heart quickened at the thought of it, realizing this was his worst fear realized. What was real and what was imagined, even Ainsley could not rightly say.

A faint series of barks could be heard down the hill in front of them but any visual evidence of their partners was marred by a thick stand of trees.

"This way." Ainsley kicked his horse and urged it forward, away from the shadow that unnerved him. They took the downhill slowly, inching toward the thick mist that hugged the low-lying areas of the woods. The dogs grew silent and Ainsley struggled to find his bearings.

"We're losing the hunt," Priscilla said from behind Margaret.

"We'll stick to the path," Ainsley said decisively. He picked up his pace slightly, urging his horse through the dim woods, zigzagging between tree trunks that popped out suddenly from the fog. As they went, Ainsley could hear a horse keeping pace alongside them, farther into the trees at their right and away from the path.

"Margaret, are Miss Priscilla and Nathaniel with you?" Ainsley stopped and the horse to his right stopped as well.

"We're here, behind you," Margaret said.

Turning slightly in his saddle, he noticed they were directly behind him, looking at him curiously. It was clear to him then that they were being shadowed. Whoever followed them remained hidden in the fog.

Margaret's face fell as she looked at him. "Peter, what's wrong?"

He saw her glance apprehensively into the mist around them. Whatever it was, she felt its presence too and he wasn't imagining things.

A hound let out a throaty howl not too far ahead of them and the unknown horse crashed through the trees, charging them before veering right and galloping ahead on the path. Ainsley only caught a glimpse of the rider but it was enough for him to see who it was who had been following them.

Margaret must have recognized him as well. "Was that Garret?" she asked.

A chorus of howls erupted just ahead of them, followed by shouts from the other hunters.

"Let's go," Ainsley said. Kicking his heels, he urged his horse forward and hoped Margaret was able to keep pace with him.

The red coat of another horseman came into view as the fog thinned slightly and Ainsley realized it was Blair, stopped and surveying his surroundings. Brandon was two paces from him, replacing a silver flask to his breast coat pocket. Ainsley brought his horse alongside them and stopped. "I think we should call off the hunt," Ainsley said, out of breath.

"Don't be ridiculous," Blair scoffed.

"We're being—"

A single gunshot, within ten feet of the gathering, rang out, silencing everyone instantly, except Priscilla, who screamed. Garret appeared briefly through the fog before kicking the sides of his horse and taking off through the trees.

Blood trickled from Brandon's mouth as he jerked slightly in his saddle. A second later, he slumped over and then fell from his horse, crashing into the undergrowth, blood and alcohol seeping into the fabric of his jacket.

Within seconds, Ainsley was at his side. "Stay with us," Ainsley said. "Keep breathing."

Blair collapsed into the ground beside his brother. The shock was evident on the man's face as he cradled Brandon's head in his arms. "Brandon?" Blair struggled to find any words as he cried.

Margaret appeared and knelt down beside Brandon as Ainsley pulled apart Brandon's red jacket and shirt to look at the wound. The single shot had penetrated his left abdomen, just below the rib, and exited out his back.

Ainsley pulled at his jacket, preparing to use it to stop the bleeding before Margaret presented him with a wad of linen. Without thought, he bunched it and pressed it into the wound tightly. A yelp escaped Brandon, who until then hadn't made any sound.

As Ainsley held the fabric in place he realized it had been Margaret's scarf, religiously worn to hide her wound. He looked to her and finally saw the long, bubbled scar at her collarbone. Although healed, the injury remained purple in colour and rose where the stitches had pinched her flesh.

Brandon's hand snatched Margaret's wrist and he pulled her in closer to him. "Help Ivy," he sputtered, sending beads of blood into the air. "Get her out of that place."

Margaret nodded furiously. "Yes," she said, "yes."

"What do we do?" Blair yelled. "Help! Help!"

"Peter?" Margaret looked to Ainsley imploringly.

Struggling for his own breath, Ainsley had nothing with him that could help. Even if by some miracle he could stop the bleeding, there was no telling how he bled on the inside. He lowered his ear to Brandon's mouth and listened. "His lung is punctured," he said. "He'll die before we get him back to the house."

"We have to get him home," Blair demanded between tears.

Brandon raised a bloody hand toward his brother and clasped onto the sleeve of his jacket. He gestured for his horse, who during the entire ordeal remained close by. Margaret stood and drew in the reins. She brought the horse closer still and watched as Brandon ran his hand over the mare's nose.

Brandon smiled as the horse exhaled in his face. A single tear trailed down the side of his face to the ground. And then a fit of coughing began, sending spatters of blood into the air all around them. Ainsley rolled him to the side in an effort to keep him from drowning in his own blood, but it was clear the lungs were already flooded. Brandon drew in one final breath before his body stopped all movement. A stream of blood slid down from his mouth and pooled on the ground, and that is when Ainsley knew Brandon was dead.

"Brandon?" Priscilla inched forward and stopped herself. She had been hanging back the entire time and even now she hesitated to come close. Nathaniel looked on uneasily, unsure what to say or who to comfort.

A throaty wail escaped Blair, who still held his brother's head in his hands. "Whoever did this is a dead man!" he growled. He looked over the body of his brother. "I'll track him down, and do him in myself."

Blair stood and went for his horse. Seconds later, he kicked his horse into a gallop, retracing Garret's escape through the woods.

"Peter?"

"I'm going after him," Ainsley said, marching for his horse. "You, Priscilla, and Nathaniel go back to Breaside!" Ainsley hoisted himself into the saddle.

Ainsley found it difficult to catch up to Blair, who rode with abandon through the shrouded woods. At one point, Blair looked back and saw Ainsley following him. But he rode on, slowing periodically to inspect the ground for evidence of Garret's direction. They changed direction frequently but only caught sight of him once the woods gave way to meadow, an overgrown pasture that had fallen into disuse in recent years. A fast-flowing river, swollen by weeks of rain, circled the meadow on the far side while a steep escarpment of sand eroded away on the other side.

They had been there before.

Blair charged ahead, driving his horse straight for his brother's murderer, who skirted the edge of the meadow near the river. Ainsley could just see a weathered footbridge traversing the water where the cliff wasn't nearly so steep on the opposite side. Garret looked back once, no doubt hearing the pounding of Blair's horse behind him. Ainsley struggled to keep up but knew he must get to them before Blair was able to extract his revenge.

Chapter 34

And when my toil is blest

Priscilla's lips trembled as she knelt down at Brandon's side. "He can't be dead," she said, looking to Margaret.

Margaret felt the forest spin around them as the realization of what happened hit her. Garret had killed Brandon. In retribution, she thought, for disgracing Ivy and giving her a child. Had Garret known the entire time? Margaret pushed a tear from her cheek and tried to steady her breathing as her heart thundered in her chest. Garret believed he had avenged his sister, and now he would assuredly get himself killed.

"What do we do?" Priscilla's tiny voice penetrated Margaret's thoughts, bringing the spinning world to a dead stop.

"I must get Samuel," she said. She turned to her horse and gathered the reins. "He can help Peter." Margaret hoisted herself into the saddle and looked down at Priscilla, who resembled a lost kitten, delicate and tiny. Nathaniel swallowed nervously as he stood over her. "Stay here with her," Margaret told him. "Tell the others where I have gone if they come back."

"And Lord Thornton?" Nathaniel asked.

Margaret scanned the woods around them but saw no reason to avoid it. "Tell him the truth."

Her horse sped on with little coaxing. As if sensing the urgency of their task, the gelding took off through the trees, scrambled up each hill and volleyed over fallen logs and dips in the terrain. They had been closer to Summer Hill Farm than she originally thought and was thankful to see the pasture fence and side of the house though the trees.

No one loitered in the nearby fields, and there was no sign of life by the shed. She didn't even attempt to knock. "Samuel!" She first found the parlour, a sad excuse for a room, empty of anything save a threadbare sofa and two thoroughly stained arms chairs. "Samuel! It's Garret. He needs our help!" She zigzagged the hallway, going room to room, while shouting for Ivy's brother.

If Margaret hadn't seen the bustling activity in the fields the week prior, she'd have thought the farmhouse had been abandoned years prior. The kitchen turned up empty. She stood at the bottom of the stairs, leaning on the bannister for strength and looked up, eyeing the darkness.

"Samuel, please help me." Her throat was dry and she couldn't yell so her words came out as a whimper. She was about to leave when she spied a door she hadn't noticed before on the other side of the parlour.

The glow of the mist-veiled sun cast a grey aura on the floorboards beneath the door. As she looked at it she saw a shadow, a brief movement that temporarily blocked the line of sunshine.

"Samuel?"

She went for the door and knocked daintily. "Samuel, it's me, Margaret. Please, come help. Your brother has done something awful but something worse is going to happen." She spoke to the door, directing her mouth to the crack. "Samuel?"

Trying the knob, Margaret was surprised when she found the door locked. She looked down at the knob and spied a slender, iron key. Without any thought to what she might find she turned the key in place and pushed forward.

A cloud of flies erupted from the room, rushing toward Margaret, who screeched while covering her face. Once certain the throng had clear, Margaret lowered her arms and found a long dining room table centred in the room with ten chairs and a dark, leathery corpse positioned in each. Three chairs, however, sat empty.

She fought to keep the bile in her stomach as she took in the tableau, which had clearly been there for a long while. There were three women and four men, including the newly added Mr. Owen, propped up with a large aluminum bucket beneath his chair, collecting the liquid that seeped from his decaying mass. Next to him a petite female was placed, nearly all bone with patches of skin and hair clinging helplessly to what remained. Ivy's mother.

The body of one man sat the head of the table, a bony arm positioned on the edge of the table, a fork in its grasp. His spectacles gave the illusion of life, while the sun reflected off the glass, forcing Margaret to look, even though all parts of her begged her to flee. Ivy's grandfather.

Her fear gave way to confusion as Margaret's mind scrambled to put the pieces together.

My friends won't visit me here, Ivy had said.

We are a very close family, aren't we Ivy? Garret had said during their first meal together.

Gasping for air, Margaret turned on her heels, covering her convulsing stomach with her hand. She needed out. The smell permeated and the sight sickened her.

At the door she collided with Samuel, his ax balanced on his shoulder while a hand held the long, wooden handle. "You shouldn't have come, Lady Margaret," he said, grabbing her upper arms and forcing her to look at him. "Grandfather doesn't like unannounced guests."

Chapter 35

And I find a maid possest

Fifty yards behind, Ainsley watched as Blair brought his racehorse alongside Garret's. The men kept a reckless pace across the meadow, no longer seated in their saddles. "Come on. Come on." Ainsley gritted his teeth as he pushed his horse faster. There was no way the two men could tackle the narrow bridge riding abreast. One would have to give way to the other or risk falling into the swift current. Before they got so far, however, Blair left his saddle and sprung at Garret, pushing him from the saddle and clinging to him as they both fell from their horses.

Any pain from the impact was ignored as they wrestled on the ground. Ainsley saw Blair give two hard blows to Garret's face before Garret was able to land a punch of his own.

Ainsley jumped from his horse before the animal had time to stop and ran for the brawling men, caught in an equal exchange of wallops. Growls escaped them as they punched and kicked, rolling in the tall grass. A swift kick sent Blair groaning in agony. Seeing his chance, Garret began to crawl away.

"You killed my brother," Blair snarled as he pulled himself to stand. "Stop and face me like a man!"

Garret did not stop. He slinked through the grass, giving terrified glances over his shoulder as he went.

Ainsley went to Blair to look over his injuries but Blair acted as if Ainsley weren't there. He kept his gaze trained on Garret, who continued to crawl away like an injured animal. Blair followed along behind, a scowl hardening on his features as he trailed his prey.

Garret began to cough, and spat out a considerable amount of blood onto the grass in front of him. He looked back over his shoulder, revealing a wide, slather of blood dripping over his chin.

No further fighting was necessary. Garret could barely crawl, let alone walk, and his horse had abandoned him by running from the scene. Ainsley saw that he held his arm over his chest as another fit of coughing ensued. With this knowledge, Ainsley wondered if Garret had broken a rib or two when he fell from his horse. The pain would have been immense and he wouldn't get far. Given proper medical attention, he might live, though this far out in the woods, Ainsley highly doubted it.

Blair understood none of this. He could not read the signs of a broken man as Ainsley could. He followed closely, keeping pace slightly behind Garret as if teasing his prey, playing with it, and enjoying the view of his suffering. He gave a kick to Garret's backside, pushing him into the ground.

"Blair, stop," Ainsley commanded. He held a hand to Blair's chest but Blair slapped it away.

Garret collapsed, rolling onto his back and lowering his head to the swath of grass beside him. Any terror had disappeared as he accepted his lot. Spitting out another mouthful of blood, Garret smiled. "I told him to leave her be, you know," he said struggling for breath. "I warned him."

"You killed him because of the baby," Ainsley said.

Garret lowered his eyes. "No." Garret spat into the grass. "I killed him because he defied me, and our grandfather. He believed himself to be better than us and refused to leave my sister alone. The baby was her punishment for not listening to her family."

"What baby?" Blair snarled, dividing his gaze between Ainsley and Garret.

Garret nearly smiled as he rose up slightly in the grass. "The one I had the good doctor rip out of her!"

Blair swung widely and landed a solid punch to Garret's jaw. He grabbed Garret by the collar and readied his fist for another blow.

"Wait, wait!" Ainsley slid himself between Garret and Blair and held up his hands to halt the beating. "Stop!" Ainsley yelled. "You must stop."

"He killed my brother and my brother's child! He deserves no less than death." Blair pushed against Ainsley's body to get to his victim.

Ainsley grabbed Blair's wrist. "Killing him will not ease that pain!"

Blair's struggle lessened as he looked Ainsley in the eyes.

"It doesn't help," Ainsley said, nearly crying. "You wish it would but it doesn't. That battle is in here." Ainsley pointed to his chest with his free hand. "It cannot be won with force. It only subsides with time."

Blair remained stone-faced for some time, staring at Ainsley and breathing heavily. Ainsley felt Blair's need to strike diminish and the strength in his arm weakened. A second later, Blair shook off Ainsley's grasp and turned. He ran a hand through his hair as he walked some paces away before collapsing in the grass to cry.

A laugh came from behind him. When Ainsley turned he saw Garret gathering himself to stand. "I was right about you," Garret said with a chuckle as he wiped his bloodied chin with his forearm. "You're too good." He smiled as he came to his knees, keeping one arm cradled at his side. "You wouldn't know the power that can be felt when you take another man's life."

Ainsley took one step toward him and swung hard. The impact sent Garret off his knees and back into the grass, a new gush of blood spraying from his mouth. "It's not power," he said, as he stood over Garret, "its fear."

"Peter."

Ainsley turned to Blair and then followed his gaze to the cliffs where two figures stood at the edge of the trees.

"It's Samuel," Blair said somberly. "He has Margaret."

Chapter 36

Of truth that's not in thee,
Like bird that finds its nest

Twice Margaret tried to run and twice she was caught by Samuel's long, unforgiving grasp. The second time he held fast to her arm, digging his fingers in the soft flesh of her arm when her steps took her too far from him. With the ax balanced on his shoulder, he led her down the path through the fields, along the same route Ivy had taken her upon her first visit. His limp prevented him from walking fast but his grip was determined. Margaret knew what he meant to do.

"Matthew, was that his name?" Margaret spoke, knowing he heard her. "He saw your family, didn't he?"

She felt his grip tighten and yelped as he pulled her even closer. The heaviness of his boots hit the back of her legs as she walked. The pain at her heels propelled her forward but the pain in her arm kept her back.

"He didn't fall," she yelled, her voice growling. She pulled her arm free, ignoring the rush of warmth radiating from her arm, and turned to look Samuel in the eye. "You pushed him."

Samuel towered over her, long and lean, with vise-grip hands and a farmworker's muscles. "I didn't have any other choice. But dead men can be controlled."

Margaret struggled for air as her heart beat in her throat. "And your father, was killing him a choice?"

Samuel forced her to turn and pushed her along the path. "That was unfortunate," he said, in a tone that could have almost been mistaken for regret. "He beat the wrong horse."

"You killed your own father because he beat a horse?"

From the corner of her eye she could see Samuel smiling.

"He's my favourite horse."

Margaret's legs gave out from under her as the shock took hold. She slumped to the ground beneath her feet. Samuel found it easy to kill. He held no reverence for life, no kinship with his fellow man. The bodies positioned around the family table were proof that the Owens family could not delineate between this world and the next.

All this time she had thought Ivy peculiar and perhaps even responsible for Mr. Owen's end. She could not believe Ivy did it for any other reason than duress. Now everything was made clear. Their drunken father was another victim, probably amongst countless victims, who died at the hands of the men he raised.

"Get up and walk!" Samuel grabbed her hair, digging his thick fingers between her curls and yanking her to her feet. Margaret squealed against the pain and stumbled as he pushed her forward. She cried silent tears as he marched the last two hundred yards to where the earth fell into the river.

She turned to look at him, perhaps hoping to distract him so she could run away. "What story will you tell my family? What lie will you concoct?" she asked defiantly, hoping he could not hear her distress.

He kept walking, pushing her backward, his face inches from her own. "I will tell them you were leading me back to the woods to help find Garret. Given your frantic state, you slipped."

"I do not subscribe to panic."

"So I see." Samuel raised his eyebrows. "Perhaps this will change your mind." He turned her away from him and held her at the very edge of the cliff with a hand on each of her arms.

Below her feet the eroding soil shifted. Her legs wanted to give way, to crumple at the sight, but she held fast, closing her eyes briefly to the view of the rushing river below and the meadow on the other side.

"It's too bad, Lady Margaret," Samuel said. "My sister was rather fond of you."

Shouts in the valley below forced her eyes open and she saw Ainsley, Blair, and Garret below them. Blair and Ainsley spoke rapidly to each other, though she could not hear what they said over the rush of the water.

"It's them," she said suddenly, savouring the draw of breath she was able to finally take.

Samuel inched closer to the edge and peered over.

"You can't kill all of us."

They watched as Ainsley grabbed Garret by the back of the collar and dragged him to where Samuel could see him better. "Give us Margaret!" he boomed. Blair went to the other side of the kneeling Garret and together he and Ainsley pulled him to the water's edge, threatening to throw him in.

From the corner of her eye, Margaret could see Samuel panting slightly. His brow perspired and his jaw clenched. He could not throw her now, not with so many witnesses.

"Let me go back to my horse," she said. "I can ride down to them in a few minutes."

"No." Samuel let go of her and she stumbled forward slightly. She saw Ainsley flinch, moving as if to try his best to catch her. If she fell there would nothing he could do on the opposite side of the river. She would most assuredly bash her head on a rock, break a limb or two before being deposited in the water and carried away.

"Don't you dare hurt her!" Blair yelled.

Samuel grabbed her by the arm and pulled her to the side. A very narrow path was etched into the side of the drop-off. The soil, more sand than clay, clung to the hairlike roots that protruded outward. The stability of the route was questionable as rocks and deposits of sand broke free under the weight of Margaret's feet. Samuel let her go first and released her arm only after she had committed to the path.

Scarcely able to breathe, Margaret gingerly made her way down, calculating each step, all the while knowing the faster she went the further distance she put between herself and Samuel. She was aware of Ainsley and Blair making their way across the footbridge, waiting for her at the bottom.

Suddenly a rock broke free, which set her off balance. She grabbed the slim trunk of sapling and prayed it had a better hold of the ground than she did.

"It's all right, Margaret," she heard Ainsley say. "A bit more."

After twenty baby steps she could go no farther. Each step, left or right, resulted in crumbling ground and an avalanche of debris beneath her feet. She halted on a tuft of grass, which seemed to be the only thing keeping the dirt under her. Samuel paused just behind her, proving even more unsteady on the near-vertical descent.

She noticed a tree root jutting out beside her and a sizeable rock not much farther. Calculatedly, Margaret anchored herself by clinging to the tree root and snatching the fist-sized rock in her hands. She felt Samuel's hand scratching at her arm, trying to pull her back toward him and that's when she swung. The rock landed with a crunch to his cheekbone and set him off balance. Blood running down his cheek, he grabbed Margaret's boot as his body slid down toward the water.

The root Margaret held to snapped under the weight of both of them. Samuel rolled down the rocks while Margaret slid, clawing at everything and anything that she could to slow her descent. She felt the rocks scraping her arms and face as she slid and then the water, cold and turbulent, hit her like a slap to the face.

Churning in the current, she fumbled to find air. Her navy jacket billowed and ripped against the rocks before she was able to get hold of something downstream. Samuel floated past, blood oozing from a second gash to his head, heavily tainting the water around him red.

Margaret gasped when she felt her hands slipping from the boulder, the current rushing over her as she watched Samuel's body taken downstream.

"Margaret!"

Blair appeared beside her, struggling against the same current. "Take my hand!"

She did as he ordered and he turned to give the signal to Ainsley. Using all her remaining strength, Margaret clung to the side of Blair as Ainsley pulled them to shore. Blair passed Margaret's hand to Ainsley before pulling himself onto the rocks.

The cold overtook her then, sending her into convulsions, shaking uncontrollably against the chill of the air and the temperature of the water that soaked her. Ainsley helped her remove her coat, while Blair discreetly looked away.

"We need to get you to the house," Ainsley said, giving her his own coat. Margaret nodded feebly as she curled her near-frozen fingers around the lapel of his coat.

On the opposite bank they could see Garret looking downstream, wailing as his brother's body was carried by the river farther and farther downstream. As the seconds passed, Margaret felt her body grow weaker and weaker. A fatigue overtook her as Ainsley held her, trying to get her warm.

"I'm sorry," she said against chattering teeth. "I thought he could help us track Garret. I never meant for any of this to happen."

Ainsley shook his head. "Your apology means nothing," he said, "because you have nothing to apologize for."

When Margaret opened her eyes next she discovered she was seated on Ainsley's horse, her brother holding her in front of him as he guided the mare through the woods at a swift pace.

"I'm taking you home," he said just as her eyes slid back into darkness.

Awareness nipping at her consciousness, Margaret snapped her eyes open and realized she was warm in bed at The Briar. A fire crackled raucously in the hearth. A copper bath filled with water sat nearby. Julia was plucking her wet clothes from the floor when she looked over and saw Margaret was awake.

"Oh thank heavens!" Aunt Louisa called out from the opposite side of the bed. "Peter! Peter! She's awake!" Margaret watched as Aunt Louisa circled the bed and made for the door, a joyous expression plastered on her features.

When Margaret turned her head to follow the movement of her aunt she saw Ainsley at the door, speaking with Maxwell in the hall. Margaret could not help but smile when she saw the relief on his face. "You gave us quite a scare, Miss Margaret," he said as he neared the bed. He placed an overturned hand on her cheek to check her temperature.

She swatted his hand away and moved to position herself higher on her pillow. "Don't fuss so," she said.

"You two are quite the pair, you know," Aunt Louisa said, clicking her tongue to show her disapproval. "I've never witnessed such excitement as I have while living here."

Ainsley looked to Margaret and raised an eyebrow. Neither of them could disagree.

"Mother! Mother!" George and Hubert rushed into the room and stopped suddenly in front of Aunt Louisa. "Is Cousin Margaret going to die?"

Aunt Louisa's shoulders sank. "Certainly not! Not for a good long while. Now out you go. She's had quite enough excitement for one day." Aunt Louisa ushered her boys out of the room, including Nathaniel, who hovered at the door.

When Julia closed the door after everyone's exit the room fell quiet, leaving only Margaret and Ainsley alone. Margaret reached over and placed her hand on top of his. "How is Blair?" she asked. "And Lady Thornton?"

Ainsley took a deep breath. "As well as can be expected. Priscilla is beside herself. I've sent Dr. Hollingsworth word that he should check in on her while the family remains in Tunbridge Wells."

"I don't know what is more tragic, the loss of her intended husband or the knowledge that he loved someone else," Margaret confessed.

Ainsley nodded. His face turned solemn as he sat on the edge of the bed. "How come you never showed me?" he asked as he reached over and ran his finger over the bubbled scar at her throat.

"It's hideous," she said, fighting back tears that stung her eyes. "And it reminds me of the hideous person who gave it to me."

"That's interesting," he said, smiling. "It reminds me how strong you are."

Chapter 37

I'll stop and take my rest;
And love as she loves me.

Margaret was unusually quiet the next day as she and Ainsley rode in the carriage toward St. Andrew's House. Ainsley shifted uncomfortably as he took in his sister's somber expression.

"You are not still vexed with me, are you?" he asked cautiously.

Margaret looked to him as if taken by surprised. "No."

Ainsley could tell she was still grappling with the events of the previous day, turning them around in her head, as he had been doing, and trying to put the pieces in a logical order.

"Aunt Louisa told me Samuel's body was found this morning ten miles downriver," he explained, hoping the news would bring about a sense of closure.

Margaret gave a nod but her eyes remained vacant.

"She didn't want to tell you directly," he said, "for fear you were too *delicate*."

That brought about a chuckle from Margaret, who finally looked up at him. "Does she know me at all?" Margaret asked.

"Apparently not. I imagine she will be quite shocked once she finds out your aspirations to study medicine."

Margaret's face turned solemn then. "Don't tease."

"I don't. A friend of mine, who's been travelling extensively in North America, wrote to me a few weeks ago about a women's medical school that has formed in Philadelphia. "

"Jonas told me he's going to propose a class for females at Edinburgh," she said.

"Did he?" Ainsley smiled. "Edinburgh is a great distance away," he said airily.

"Not too great a distance," Margaret corrected. Ainsley watched as she nervously pressed out the folds of her skirt and readjusted her gloves. She cleared her throat and proceeded to change the subject. "Peter, I know about you and Julia."

Every cell in Ainsley's body froze. He was not ready for such a conversation. She refused to make eye contact with him and instead she appeared to be studying the passing landscape outside her carriage window. "Your need for a new conquest astounds me."

"She is not my new conquest," he answered, angered that Julia was referred to in such a way.

"What would you call it then?"

"Two people in need of each other," he said, "for one reason or another. She's one of the only good things in my life. Don't take her away from me." Ainsley realized he was pleading then, unsure how his sister wished to proceed. By rights she could have Julia sent from the house, stripped of her employment, and their father would probably order him to never have contact with her, not that Ainsley planned to obey any such order. It would surely complicate things and Ainsley was in no great need for further complications. "I haven't said a word about you and Jonas to anyone," he continued. "And if you need to go to him I understand."

Margaret's eyes shot up. "Who said I will go to him?"

Ainsley needn't answer. The circumstances were plain enough to see. He reached over then, took a firm grasp of Margaret's hand, which lay on her skirt, and looked her firmly in the eyes. "Let us keep each other's secrets for a little while longer," he said.

"A lady's maid is a close relationship," Margaret said. "I need to trust her in all things."

"I promise she has not said a word to me," Ainsley reassured her.

Margaret's shoulders sank as her gaze flittered about the carriage in thought. Finally, she looked at him and gave a nod of agreement. "All right," she said, "your secret is safe with me. I will not tell a soul"— Margaret gave him a pointed finger— "unless circumstances force me," she clarified.

He nodded, agreeing to her caveat. "Thank you." He kissed her gloved hand and released it before settling back into the opposite bench. He could see Margaret chuckle to herself. "Dear brother," she said teasingly, "whatever shall I do with you?"

Ivy kept close to Margaret's side as they exited the asylum's front door and only paused once when she lifted her face to the warm midday sun. Ainsley, who was waiting at the carriage, smiled at the sight and tried to suppress the shame he felt for having been a part of her short imprisonment. Ivy, however, seemed to direct no blame at him and smiled warmly as she and Margaret approached. She bobbed a curtsey. "Good day, Mr. Marshall."

"Miss Owen."

Margaret gestured to the open carriage door when Ivy looked at her unsure. Margaret smiled at her brother as Ivy climbed inside. "She is as a child," she said.

"Have you told her about Brandon?"

Margaret nodded. "Yes, though I don't believe the truth of it has been impressed upon her."

"While you were collecting our new charge we had a visitor," Ainsley explained.

"Oh really?"

Ainsley gestured to inside the carriage, where a young, well-dressed man sat opposite Ivy. "Allow me to introduce Dr. Jeremiah Hertz."

Dr. Hertz looked quite uncomfortable as he sat in the Marshall carriage. He tried to stand as tall as the low ceiling would allow and offered a hand to assist Margaret as she climbed into the carriage. Ainsley sat alongside the doctor.

"For what do we owe this pleasure?" Margaret asked, settling in beside Ivy.

Before the doctor could speak, Ainsley cut in. "The good doctor is on his way to the train station and I offered him a ride in our conveyance."

Margaret smiled dryly. "How kind, brother."

Dr. Hertz licked his lips and glanced between Ainsley and Margaret.

"Dr. Hertz is an alienist, are you not?" Ainsley asked, as the carriage rolled into motion.

"Yes," he stammered, "I work, that is to say, I *run* a small asylum of my own, if you could call it that."

Margaret raised an eyebrow and clung closer to Ivy, who slipped easily into Margaret's grasp. "Imagine that." It was clear

Margaret was not in mood. Ainsley's little jest was wearing her thin and so he decided to be out with it.

"Dr. Hertz specializes in afflictions such as Ivy's," Ainsley explained. "He came down here from the city just to see her."

Dr. Hertz moved forward on the bench, eager to share his enthusiasm for his practice. "I have heard much regarding Miss Owen and I am certain she will find a place with us."

"You have not spent enough time with her to make that sort of claim," Margaret said dismissively. Her distrust was grossly evident.

"I have read her files, which include the statements from her brothers—"

"Which were highly falsified!"

"True. But Mr. Marshall here and others at St. Andrew's have given me much to go on and I believe Miss Owen suffers from a disassociation disorder. Her panics, as they are described, point to trauma."

Margaret snorted.

Dr. Hertz licked his lips nervously and glanced to Ainsley, who only indicated that he should go on. "This trauma has caused her consciousness to disconnect, in a way, leading her behaviour and then no recollection of having done anything amiss. Cases abound of such things, though I agree with Mr. Marshall here that Ivy's symptoms are far less severe."

As the alienist spoke, Ivy grew tired and lowered her head onto Margaret's shoulder. She seemed perfectly content to have Margaret speak for her and never raised a peep of protest.

"What do you suggest?" Margaret pressed.

"I run a small, private asylum, housing no more than a hundred souls, all who suffer from milder forms of lunacy and who we believe to be curable." The doctor spoke with a growing smile. "If we can study them there is much we can learn."

"Study them how?"

"Well, asking questions, observing their actions. I understand your trepidation, Lady Margaret. I have no desire to send Miss Owen anywhere that resembles St. Andrew's House. I'm sure it's a fine institution—"

"It's hell on earth, Dr. Hertz. I wouldn't darken its doors no matter the sum offered to me."

"Fair enough. An institution such as that will only worsen Miss Owen's condition. We must offer her space for calm, so that she may be calm up here as well." He pointed to the side of his head.

"His research facility is in London, Margaret," Ainsley said.

"Yes, you may visit her any time you like," Dr. Hertz offered.

Soon Ivy laid her head down to rest on Margaret's lap while Margaret cradled her and petted her like a mother with a child. Ainsley could tell she was contemplating the doctor's words, weighing his claims carefully before finally asking a question. "You say you are from London. How did you come to know about us, and our need for such a place?"

"Dr. Davies came to visit my facility just last evening. He said it was a matter of dire emergency. I came as soon as I was able."

Margaret smiled at the mention of their family friend. Her apprehension disappeared almost instantly. "Why didn't you say as much in the first place?"

Epilogue

Ainsley's dreams about his father, bound to a chair and unable to speak, haunted him for many days, appearing almost nightly even after the family made the strategic decision to return to Marshall House in Belgravia so that renovations could be completed at The Briar. He told no one of the growing sense of foreboding that rose up in him, causing him a great deal of anxiety as he went about his daily tasks. The dreams stopped abruptly, however, on the day when Aunt Louisa came to Ainsley's room, an unfolded letter in her grasp.

"What is it?" Ainsley asked, seeing how his aunt's hand trembled.

"Lord Benedict writes to say your father has suffered some sort of medical attack." Aunt Louisa paused and placed a hand over her mouth in a feeble effort to stifle the tears.

"Does he live?" Ainsley asked, ignoring the heavy feeling that bombarded his head. The thought of both his parents gone within the span of a year was too difficult to comprehend.

Aunt Louisa nodded but then proceeded to thrust the paper at him, unable to form the words to relay the rest of the missive. His father's business partner offered no explanation for what exactly had transpired while abroad but said they would be making their way home and would telegraph their expected arrival by train once they reached a British port.

The four-day wait was excruciating, with Margaret, Nathanial, and Aunt Louisa speculating widely. Their theories ranged in intensity from a slight bump to the head to complete cardiac failure. Ainsley remained silent. His vivid, medically trained imagination would not help the family find calm. Eventually, the telegraph did arrive and they readied themselves to head to Charing Cross for the three o'clock train.

Train after train arrived and departed, blowing smoke and steam into the air around the Marshall family as they waited. With each train, the platforms became bloated with travellers, returning or departing, though none took any special notice of the apprehensive family that waited on platform four.

When Lord Marshall's train arrived, Aunt Louisa recognized it instinctively and tapped Ainsley's arm. "This is it," she said. She looked at him with a downtrodden exhale, which made him place a reassuring hand on her back.

Passengers disembarked and scurried along, leaving the family to wonder if they understood the date of the arrival wrong. "Perhaps Lord Benedict meant tomorrow's train," Margaret suggested glumly. She turned to Ainsley but as she did so, a final compartment door at the far end was opened and two porters rushed to aid the passengers inside. Benedict appeared first, waving his hat toward the family, but lingering as a third porter clamoured up into the compartment.

Aunt Louisa stepped forward first, inching along the platform with trepidation. Margaret took Ainsley's hand and together they walked. By the time they reached Lord Benedict's side Lord Marshall appeared, carried by the two porters, one on each side, a third holding a wheeled chair.

At first, Lord Marshall looked as if he were speaking. Over the chug of the nearby engine, Ainsley imagined him barking orders to the men helping him. But the movement of his father's lips did not cease. The chair had been facing away from the family, who now walked slower, confused and unsure. It was only when the chair was turned did Ainsley, Margaret, and Aunt Louisa see the true extent of Lord Marshall's condition.

Seeing his father's head slightly slouched to the side, his mouth downturned at the corner, and a recognizable tremble to his right hand, Ainsley knew right away what it was that had befallen his father, even before Lord Benedict said the word.

Apoplexy.

The porters rolled the chair along, but Margaret rushed them, throwing herself at her father's feet and crying into his lap. Lord Marshall placed his left hand on Margaret's head while his lips moved but no words came out.

Ainsley saw Aunt Louisa swallow back accumulating tears before tapping her niece on the shoulder. "Now child, let's not make a fuss." She glanced around them, scanning for onlookers, known or unknown to the family.

Lord Benedict spoke quietly, offering quick details of the

calamity, but Ainsley heard none of it. He watched his sister cry at his father's feet and studied the features, once proud and angular, that had become slack and withered. He hardly looked like their father at all.

It was only when Lord Marshall's blue eyes lifted, catching Ainsley's stare, that the son recognized the man behind the body ravaged by stroke. His father lived, inside that malfunctioning body, trapped by circumstance and silenced by immobility.

In that instant, all the worry and fear erupted, cascading down Ainsley's face and crashing into the cement beneath them. He wept openly, not for the father gone but for the man constrained by a malady that came without warning. They may have never seen eye to eye, or agreed on much of anything, but for all their chest puffing, curt phrases, and spiteful remarks there could be no denying how much Ainsley had grown to love this man.

Approaching Night

By John Clare (1793-1864)

O take this world away from me;
Its strife I cannot bear to see,
Its very praises hurt me more
Than een its coldness did before,
Its hollow ways torment me now
And start a cold sweat on my brow,
Its noise I cannot bear to hear,
Its joy is trouble to my ear,
Its ways I cannot bear to see,
Its crowds are solitudes to me.

O, how I long to be agen
That poor and independent man,
With labour's lot from morn to night
And books to read at candle light;
That followed labour in the field
From light to dark when toil could yield
Real happiness with little gain,
Rich thoughtless health unknown to pain:
Though, leaning on my spade to rest,
I've thought how richer folks were blest
And knew not quiet was the best.

Go with your tauntings, go;
Neer think to hurt me so;
I'll scoff at your disdain.
Cold though the winter blow,
When hills are free from snow

It will be spring again.

So go, and fare thee well,
Nor think ye'll have to tell
Of wounded hearts from me,
Locked up in your hearts cell.
Mine still at home doth dwell
In its first liberty.

Bees sip not at one flower,
Spring comes not with one shower,
Nor shines the sun alone
Upon one favoured hour,
But with unstinted power
Makes every day his own.

And for my freedom's sake
With such I'll pattern take,
And rove and revel on.
Your gall shall never make
Me honied paths forsake;
So prythee get thee gone.

And when my toil is blest
And I find a maid possest
Of truth that's not in thee,
Like bird that finds its nest
I'll stop and take my rest;
And love as she loves me.

The Marshall House Mystery Series

CHORUS OF THE DEAD
DEAD SILENT
THE DEAD AMONG US
SWEET ASYLUM
PRAYERS FOR THE DYING
SHADOWS OF MADNESS

About the Author

A former journalist and graduate from Humber College's School for Writers, Tracy L. Ward has been hard at work developing her favourite protagonist, Peter Ainsley, and chronicling his adventures as a young surgeon in Victorian England. She lives north of Toronto, Ontario, with her husband, two kids, and an intellectually-challenged cocker-spaniel named Watson.

For all the latest updates her website can be found at www.gothicmysterywriter.blogspot.com. Find her on Facebook at www.facebook.com/TracyWardAuthor

Made in the USA
Charleston, SC
23 November 2016